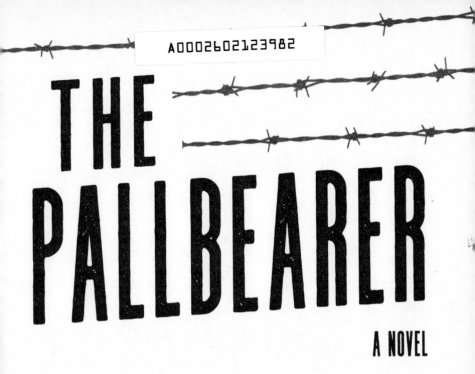

THE PALLBEARER

A NOVEL

JORDAN FARMER

Skyhorse Publishing

Skyhorse Publishing books may be purchased in bulk at special discounts for sales promotion, corporate gifts, fund-raising, or educational purposes. Special editions can also be created to specifications. For details, contact the Special Sales Department, Skyhorse Publishing, 307 West 36th Street, 11th Floor, New York, NY 10018 or info@skyhorsepublishing.com.

Skyhorse® and Skyhorse Publishing® are registered trademarks of Skyhorse Publishing, Inc.®, a Delaware corporation.

Visit our website at www.skyhorsepublishing.com.

10 9 8 7 6 5 4 3 2 1

Library of Congress Cataloging-in-Publication Data is available on file.

Cover design by Erin Seaward-Hiatt
Cover photo by iStockphoto

ISBN: 978-1-5107-3650-4
Ebook ISBN: 978-1-5107-3651-1

Printed in the United States of America

For my family,
whose support and sacrifice made these pages possible

PROLOGUE

THEY TOOK THE Dairy Road toward Huntington with a sawed-off twelve gauge, two Glocks, and some premium hydro that Shane had been skunking the Chevy with since Lynch, its smooth haze leaving Huddles with raw retinas. Rain cascaded down the windshield and drenched the road until their headlights reflected off the drowning yellow lines. This glare helped Huddles fight sleep while Shane, fortified by his daily cocktail of meth and steroids, rested like a stump in the passenger seat. The big man's deltoids bulged with strips of chemical muscle, his shoulders great hunks of chiseled flesh that made Huddles feel scrawny beside him.

Late runs rarely bothered Huddles. He preferred traveling at night, the last driver on the road with only the occasional yattering from coyotes on the hillside. It was the departures at dusk, times when the sun had just begun its descent behind the mountains, that let his lethargy take over. Often, he could avoid those trips. He would complain about a lack of sleep and beg his brother for a few hours to nap on the couch. Better at night anyway, he'd say. Less traffic, only the few state troopers roving to bust drunk kids, but standing on the steps of The Cat's Den earlier that evening, his nostrils filled with the scent of some distant neighbor's burning trash, he knew Ferris would send him anyway.

The Dairy Road began to straighten. The narrow margins were marked for two lanes of traffic, but really only wide enough to safely accommodate one. In the days of the real coal boom, when the road was the only way to Huntington from Lynch, coal trucks constantly moved from the mine at the crest of the mountain. Now, it was mostly for the people who still lived in the backwoods that diverged from the route or night runners, like Huddles and Shane. With the mines closing, Huddles figured in ten more years there would be no cars left on the road at all. The woods would reclaim things by growing over the asphalt.

In the distance, Huddles made out the black humps of cattle. There weren't many farms in West Virginia, just strip mines that killed the fish in the creek. Before he dropped out of high school, his teacher referred to this sort of mentality as a product of Appalachian fatalism, but that always sounded like shit to Huddles. No one in Vermont, the Yankee state Mr. Walker hailed from, ever paid the teacher's great granddaddy in scrip. Maybe that's why Huddles loved taking the college kids' money. There was real satisfaction in wadding crisp denominations up with rough hands and shoving the cash inside his pocket.

Shane packed another bowl. "Your brother should have let us sleep," he said.

Things would have been easier if Huddles could've avoided Shane's death metal. When his partner finally tired of the thrash guitars and relinquished control of the radio, Huddles left it on the classic country station where the spectral voices of dead crooners seeped from the speakers. All the twang and outlaw fiddle helped him focus.

Ahead loomed a barn with all the windows busted out, its rotting wood eaten away by termites and years of elemental erosion. Behind the barn, a giant oak grew alone in the field, its crooked branches like the broken necks of young turkeys still alive enough to stretch skyward. Huddles watched the building so intensely that the Chevy hydroplaned across a deep puddle, but he regained control without colliding into the guardrail. He checked the speedometer. They'd been pushing nearly seventy, so he slowed down.

"Careful," Shane took a long hit off the pipe and hacked into his elbow.

From behind them came the whimper of something in the distance. At first, Huddles thought it might be a catbird that had yet to roost, but then a blue glow filled the rearview and Huddles' mind immediately jumped to his brother. He thought about the older man's scarred knuckles covered with faded ink and how those knuckles would feel knocking against his bare teeth, loosening them from the root.

Shane hacked again, fanned the smoke in the car and said, "You'd better pull over." He cracked the window and pitched the pipe out into the night. It sailed a moment in the weak lights before the darkness swallowed it.

The Chevy didn't slow. It was as if the motor had become sentient and wanted to keep moving. The Dairy Road hugged close enough to the mountain for Huddles to pretend he was searching for a wide spot to pull over. He used this time to consider the lies he'd spout to the officer. Their stash was hidden in the trunk, but Huddles knew Shane's pistol was under the passenger seat. The gun worried him. Shane seemed frantic, almost shaking as he lit a Marlboro and sucked deep to fill the car with some scent that might mask the weed.

"Be cool when you pull off," Shane said. "Just let me talk."

Huddles looked over Shane's face, the hard jaw and bruises around his dark eyes from barroom brawls. No cop would believe any story from them. An ex-con and a sixteen-year-old traveling a useless road together was too suspicious. Ahead on the left sat a Marathon station that was robbed every other month, the last stop for gas for anyone headed towards Lynch, the first sign of civilization for travelers headed toward Huntington. Huddles knew he should pull off among the deserted pumps and let Shane try his luck, but something in him went rabbit and he pushed the throttle down.

"Fuck," Shane said. Huddles buckled his seatbelt while his friend's fingers splayed on the dash. The knuckles bulged from multiple breaks and poor splints.

The radio changed over from a Hank Williams tune to Merle Haggard's lonesome intro on "Mama Tried." Huddles felt the Chevy's grip on the road loosen again. The car skidded into the guardrail, bounced off, and Huddles kept driving while the Crown Vic grew in the rearview. The siren became a wildcat scream behind them as the blue lights flashed inside the car. Ten feet separated their bumpers.

Huddles' brother kept invading his thoughts. He imagined the first few days after Ferris finished his prison stint. It was the same year their father died, and Ferris attended the wake swollen from all the time inside with nothing to do but build his body into some kind of flesh machine, proof he'd refused to yield to the diet of Wonder Bread and bologna. Something about him seemed invincible, unwilling to acquiesce to the inevitable mortality they'd recently witnessed.

Shane pulled the Glock. The strip of duct tape used to secure it beneath his seat still hung from the slide. Huddles watched it flutter near the AC vent like a flag. "I'm lighting his ass up," Shane said.

The cruiser connected with the Chevy's back bumper. Shane dropped the pistol onto the floorboards. He scrambled to pick it up, but it slipped too far under the seat for him to get a grip. Huddles put the pedal down harder.

Another connection and they spun a half turn, their headlights shining through the cruiser's windshield. The Chevy's hood crunched into the guardrail and they stalled. Huddles tried to throw it into reverse, but the car's engine simply gurgled. The brown sugar sweetness of coolant evaporating on the radiator filled his nostrils.

The trooper exited the car with his gun and flashlight raised. Huddles squinted against the beam while Shane still tried to get a handle on his piece.

"Leave it," Huddles said.

The trooper stood at the window screaming for them to place their palms on the dash and not move a fucking muscle. Huddles looked at Shane and tried to let his eyes say what his mouth couldn't. When the officer opened the door, Huddles got a better look at him. A big young trooper, Smokey the Bear lid concealing light eyes full of fear. He seemed to vibrate as he stood with his feet spread and the gun trained on Huddles in that perfect stance that was still academy fresh. Huddles put his feet on the ground and the trooper threw him around into the car door, yanked his arms back and cuffed them while screaming for Shane to lie on his belly. After the bracelets were biting his wrists, Huddles sat on the wet ground and watched as the trooper tossed the car. He considered hitting the hills while the cop was busy in the back seat, but the idea of stumbling through the woods with the cuffs on didn't make much sense. The trooper mumbled into his radio and threw fast food wrappers out of the Chevy's floorboards as he searched.

It didn't take long to find the guns. The trooper pulled them from under the back seat, cleared the chambers on the pistols, ejected the clips and laid them on the hood. He came out of the trunk holding one of the Ziploc bags of pills in front of him, his Maglite shining on the assorted capsules as he shook it like a man calling chickens to feed.

"I guess you boys had good cause to run," he said.

The trooper read their rights. Huddles tuned it out, his mind lost on the woods and the way his brother used to run through them, bare chested and dirty in the early fall when the mountain leaves changed into a multitude of colors. He recalled the animal scent of Ferris when he came home, the way the mud would be caked on his shins, clinging in the coarse hair of his legs. Huddles was never able to keep up with his brother's long strides whenever he tagged along.

Huddles and Shane were both loaded into the back seat of the cruiser, and then they were moving again, the country ghosts' singing replaced by the static from the cop's radio as he called in the arrest.

"You boys got anything to say?" the trooper asked as they drove back towards Lynch.

"Lawyer," Huddles said and laid his head back, eyes closed until the only thing left was the sound of tires on asphalt, the occasional random piece of coal lost from a truck pinging as it was tossed up into the wheel well.

PART I
THE CHILDREN

CHAPTER ONE

AN EARLY SUMMER storm had killed the power on Fuller Street, casting the turn of the century coal company duplexes into darkness. The high winds tore branches from trees rooted low on the mountains and collapsed a sizable oak onto a generator. The live wire lay convulsing in the road beside a church that had been converted from the old company store, the pulpit now sitting where the cash register once resided. Repair men stood around the downed line, its wiring hanging out of the black casing like the exposed guts of a slain beast. They removed their hard hats, wiped perspiring brows and debated who would go tell the neighborhood it might be days before the lights were back on.

Fuller Street had never been a place of wealth, but it contained a sense of economic diversity rare in America as suburbia continued its sprawl. The two rows of houses were bisected by derelict railroad tracks and status. The poorest on the left, slightly better off on the right. The few families not destitute often bulldozed the old company houses, building more modern homes with central heat and bay windows. These renovations sat near houses ready to fall in on themselves, the porches rotten with splintered planks bowed up like malformed spines, the yards constantly filled with cinder blocks and scavenged lumber as the owners tried to get a tourniquet on the slow decay.

Henry Felts' place was the worst on the street. For many years it was the local drug den, a nuisance due to the migration of addicts who flocked there for week-long binges. Fuller Street was too far from town for anyone to give a damn until someone in the house was shot with a squirrel rifle. After the incident, the police raided the hovel and the county auctioned it cheap.

Terry Blankenship had been helping Felts with the repairs. Even at sixteen, Terry was no stranger to labor and didn't mind the work, but the place felt like a lost cause to him. There were holes in the roof, like God routinely put his fist through the ceiling in a rage, and the front of the house remained bare to the lumber, the patchwork of half-aluminum and half-wooden siding either gone completely or hanging from the frame like skin flayed from bone. The entire structure seemed as if it were staggering before it fell over. Worse still, old man Felts preferred to bend his elbow and supervise. Terry's young back did most of the work. Considering Felts' penchant for injuries, it may have been the better system. Terry had worked alongside his father on unlicensed contracting since he was twelve, had witnessed all manner of workplace mishaps, including a man shooting himself through the calf with a nail gun, but he'd never seen someone as accident prone as Felts. Three consecutive days of minor electrical shocks, multiple fingers crushed by hammers, and trips over extension cords kept Felts hobbled while Terry took over whatever half-finished duty felled the boss.

They worked at night to avoid the heat and since the sun would be rising soon, Terry decided to finish prying up the kitchen floor around the sink. He felt bad every time he drove his pry bar into the pulp that had once been blond hardwood before the water damage. It was too hurtful to consider what the place had been in the past, so Terry just focused on work until the dirt underneath the house was exposed. He was looking at the nests of torn cloth brought under the foundations by creek rats when Felts shambled into the room and handed him a chilled Old Milwaukee.

"Let's call it a day," Felts said. "My nephew's coming up to look at the place."

"You want him to see it like this?" Terry asked. The cold can felt good in his blistered hand. Terry placed it against his warm neck.

"He's seen worse."

They sat on the porch steps and looked out across the overgrown yard. A pile of aluminum siding lay near the gravel driveway. Another stack of vinyl beside it. Eventually, all this mismatched shit would be stripped from the house, and Terry would be responsible for replacing it with something new. He was thankful for the weeks of work. The money was better than any other opportunity in town, and Terry needed all he could get his hands on. Boys in Lynch grew up aware of what other young Americans were just beginning to understand. This generation would have to work three times as hard as their parents or starve.

A battered Ford truck pulled off the highway. When the engine died, Terry watched a small man jump down from the high cab. He might have stood five feet tall, the overgrown grass brushing against his shirttail. As he approached, Terry noticed the man's stunted legs were the only strange appendage on him, the torso and arms proportional to a slightly larger body. His face was startling once close enough for Terry to make out his features in the darkness. A heavy brow with green eyes, cheekbones so high and sharp they might chisel through his tight skin. His nose ran a tad long, the end pointed downward like the blade on a hawkbill knife.

The man grinned at them on the porch, only the left side of his mouth rising into a smirk, and Terry felt a stirring he hadn't believed such a small man could create. He was certainly handsome in an unconventional sort of way. Terry thought he might have been truly beautiful if those femurs were only afforded a limp pecker's worth of added inches. The tragedy was this missing stature would keep the man invisible to so many. Terry knew what it meant to be different in a nowhere town. Strange is hard enough anywhere, but small towns hammer down on the unusual. Any absence of conformity and you find yourself marked. Terry knew people talked about him, aired their private suspicions in small congregations, but he could hide if necessary. Staying closeted created a certain pain, but it was still an option in a place where being yourself meant risking your life. He felt sorry for the little man. It must've been scary being branded with difference for all to see.

"You have bought yourself one serious mess," the small man said. His voice sounded like dry reeds rubbing together.

Felts smiled. "Wait until the bats come."

"Bats?"

"Living inside my eaves." Felts pointed to a small opening in the shingles. "They'll fly home soon, but I'm ready." His finger traced down to the corner of the porch where a Remington pump sat against the railing.

"You'll never hit one," Terry said.

"Gonna try," Felts replied. He looked at the house, perhaps speculating where the first bat might enter before turning back to the small man. "Terry, this is my nephew, Jason Felts. Jason, this is Terry Blankenship. He's helping me out around here."

Earlier, Terry had wrapped a bit of black electrician tape around his index finger to staunch a cut. This made their handshake awkward.

Even standing from the lowest step, Terry noticed he was twice Jason's size, chest high over this elder.

"Jason here used to help out at the funeral home when he was your age," Felts said. "He works up at The Shell now. I'm gonna get him to come over Thursday when we tear that carpet out."

"That's the first I've heard about it," Jason said.

The Shell was the local nickname for The Shelby Youth Correctional Facility. The place swallowed up more Bradshaw Hollow boys than overdoses or the mines. Terry had been lucky enough to avoid it, but still found it hard to imagine Jason walking the halls, telling adolescents twice his size to lock down. The guards would be even worse. A child-sized man forced to operate in a land of hard-asses who only respected brawn and cynicism. He wasn't sure whether to pity or respect Jason.

Terry turned his attention to Felts to avoid the subject. "I got most of them holes in the hallway patched. That kitchen's gonna take longer."

"Sure," Felts said. He dug a fifty-dollar bill from his wallet and passed it to Terry. "You need a ride home?"

"I'll walk after my beer."

Terry couldn't tell them that he wasn't going home. His father had kicked him out over a week ago, but he'd managed to keep the eviction, and the reason for it, a secret. Felts might be prejudice if he had all the details.

"You think this dumpster fire can be saved?" Jason asked Terry.

"What else was I gonna do?" Felts interrupted. "Without something to fiddle with, I'll just lay drunk. Only a few years of that before a man's liver explodes."

"What about finding a wife?" Jason said.

"That worked real well the last three times. No, this is it. You're the one who needs a woman."

Jason looked embarrassed. Terry guessed he was the sort often told by relatives of his handsome attributes, reminded how bright and charming he was to the point of exhaustion because others thought he needed to hear it. Probably set up on blind dates, encouraged to flirt at any public event as if it were practice. The curly dark hair atop his head was no doubt mussed by a thousand older women who found the act safe on such a tiny man. If Jason stayed lonely, it was likely more the ignorance of his environment. Another thing Terry understood.

"Never believe who they arrested tonight," Jason said. "Ferris Gilbert's brother."

The name tied a knot inside Terry's stomach, but he hoped the shadows hid any visible reaction. The men didn't seem to have noticed. Still, the next sip of his beer tasted like ashes.

"The sheriff will be by to lean on him," Felts said. "When I bought this house at auction, the whole courthouse was going on about the task force."

The group looked towards the mountainside where the woods hulked over them like a testament to the weakness of brick and mortar.

"When my father still ran the funeral home, I rode the bus to school with the other kids," Felts said. "Dad didn't want money to make me feel entitled. So, on my first day of high school, I get on and Francis Gilbert, that's the Gilbert I grew up with raising Hell, is sitting in the back. He's sipping from a pint stowed in his lunch sack. After he finishes the bottle and we round the turn at Porter's Hardware, he chucks it out the window and puts it through the windshield of a Cadillac in the oncoming lane."

"Jesus," Terry said.

"When we get to school, Officer Millhouse is waiting. Sitting on the front of his cruiser and saying, 'Come on out and have a word with us, Francis.' Well, Francis comes out, spits on the man's shoes, and tells him 'Just take me to jail, faggot.'"

The word made Terry shudder. He hoped his employer hadn't seen the reaction, but Felts just set his empty beer aside and let the story hang a moment.

"Some men are always walking about with a hard-on for trouble. Francis Gilbert was one of them, and his boys ain't different. You'd best remember that."

Terry was surprised to hear fear in the voice of a man with such a hard reputation. After Henry Felts lost the funeral parlor, he used to haunt bars with a Saturday night special stuck inside his boot, his Harley making the climb up Mount Gay so he could imbibe in the worst watering holes. There was something wild in his blood, something that in his youth led him out to the honky-tonks at night, slinking home against dawn like a vampire.

The conversation stalled as lightning bugs illuminated the brush with an on and off glow. Terry had heard enough stories. He didn't want to think any more about the outlaw family, just to watch the fireflies communicate in their mute language of light.

"I've gotta get home," Terry said. "Nice to meet you, Jason."

Terry shook Jason's hand a final time as Henry Felts produced a hairnet from his jean pocket and pulled it over his graying mane. He loaded the breech of the shotgun and took aim just as the first bats flew toward the eaves. Buckshot belched from the barrel, but none plummeted like furry fruit.

*   *   *

Terry didn't want to break into another house. It wasn't a moral dilemma—circumstances had pushed him beyond that. Working late had just left him tired. There was nothing more he wanted to do than finish the long hike back to his cabin, settle in with Davey, and crush up a few pills. He always arrived at the improvised home with the need to have hands laid on him.

Terry removed the fifty-dollar bill from his pocket and examined the wrinkled visage of President Grant. The amount of work he'd poured into that place warranted at least a hundred every few days. He rubbed the fifty between his fingers, reminded himself that money was the only salvation from his predicament and moved on.

The few homes at the end of Fuller looked worse in the darkness. Without porch lights to cast a glow on the well-manicured lawns and overflowing flowerbeds, every stitch of poverty stood out. The fresh wax jobs on the cars and trucks couldn't be seen, only their age and the Bondo that held them together. Peeling paint flecked off walls and loose shingles flapped in the wind like tongues taken over by the presence of the Holy Spirit. Terry wondered if any of these places were worth the risk. The residents would be on high alert with the power off, and Felt's shotgun might as well have been an air raid signal. Desperation kept him going, but Terry promised himself he'd retreat at the first sign of trouble.

He slipped down from the tracks, crossed the road, and hopped the chain-link fence that surrounded Mrs. Frasier's property. A giant chestnut tree sat in the center of the yard. It dropped burrs in its blooming months, leaving the grass a minefield for anyone foolish enough to stroll barefoot. Terry worried the softening soles of his Chuck Taylors might be penetrated by the quills, but no car sat parked in the driveway, and the house looked empty. This was his best option.

He climbed the steps to the back porch. The door was locked, so he put his shoulder into it.

The small kitchen stank of urine and garbage. The sink still held dirty dishes. Cups with the dregs of coffee and spoiled cream, a saucer with a dab of blackberry jelly on the edge. The space was cramped, the cheap tile backsplash ready to clatter atop a stove several decades old. Terry could almost feel the lingering presence of the miners' wives who'd hovered over the appliance. Two families once shared the space in the coal camp days. Two families trying to cook in the same kitchen, two wives trying to wrangle each other's kids while their husbands were away underground. It seemed a barbaric way to live, but it had happened here. Terry could feel the ripples of it.

Terry opened the kitchen cabinets and read the labels of several pill bottles. Plenty of blood pressure medication, but he didn't see anything for pain. Sometimes the old women had diet pills that really kept you moving if you popped enough. A sudden hunger pain came upon him, so he pocketed a can of salmon from the pantry.

Inside the bathroom medicine cabinet, Terry found a bottle of Bactrim and some Augmentin on the lower shelf. He took both. Further inspection revealed a half a prescription of Lortab and a whole bottle of Xanax. He'd hoped for some Oxycodone, but the Xanax was still a treat. Terry took a moment to inspect his face in the mirror. It was still bruised, so he gently fingered his purple jaw before going upstairs.

The master bedroom was a testament to a time past. The closet held nothing of interest aside from a Vietnam era Army uniform. The fatigue green of the dress jacket had faded, and the airborne patch hung from the shoulder by threads. Terry put his nose to the sleeve. The smells of foreign shores remained trapped in the fibers. In a shoebox, Terry found two hundred dollars in small bills that he placed in his pocket. There was more to search, but he was anxious to leave the house.

Once outside, he could see a light at the end of the street provided by a resident's generator. The machine powered a single bulb inside the home, and if Terry had to guess, probably a refrigerator. Still, it was enough activity to make him retreat. Davey would probably be wondering where he was. He stepped up onto the tracks, selected a large chunk of slate that filled his palm in case he was jumped in the woods or chased by stray dogs, and set off on the three-mile walk back to his shack. The Gilberts stayed fresh in his mind from Felts' stories. His footsteps made little noise on the wood of the rails. The only cadence came from the pills in his pockets, a slight rattle only he could hear.

CANDLES BURNED THROUGH the broken windows of the shack. Terry watched the flames flicker as the wind spun the carpet of last fall's leaves under his feet. Most men he knew found something peaceful in the woods, but Terry never shared that. The only thing more ominous than the eternal green stillness was the occasional cracking branch. He didn't trust nature. Some days, he dug up handfuls of dirt in the shade and found just a few inches of topsoil before hitting rock. It surprised Terry anything could take root in this earth, especially the tall trees growing around the cabin.

The building had been the hunting lodge of a man named Randall Kittredge who owned a convenience store at the mouth of Bradshaw Hollow. He retired there each summer to hunt turkey until a worker coming in to stock shelfs found him dead beside the deli counter, the hunk of bologna above him not yet sliced. Afterward, the cabin set unused for years until Davey and Terry began to spend nights inside.

Terry knew the penalty if his father caught him with another boy. The old man never asked the question aloud. He didn't need to. Terry's father identified certain qualities in him from birth and decided if his son had to be what he suspected, absolute certainty must remain a secret. He vented scorn to make sure Terry would never tell him, did his best to show disdain, and growled insults at the men from town he thought queer. Anyone who showed the slightest weakness could be a suspect. Eventually, the pair decided the cabin was the safest way to sneak around.

The four rooms stayed drafty and the roof leaked in certain corners, but aside from a raccoon that briefly took up residence in the hallway, the boys had no other domestic worries. They used the stove for heat and candles for light. The nearby creek served for bathing, the woods for an outhouse.

When Terry entered, he found Davey squatted in front of the pot-bellied stove. His palms lingered near the fire as if trying to capture the heat inside cupped hands like a squirming insect. The summer air carried only the hint of a chill, but Davey stayed constantly cold. He would seek out excess sources of warmth the way a reptile might sun itself on a slab of sandstone. The stove's light cast shadows on Davey's cheeks, illuminating the long scar that crossed the bridge of his nose. Terry never asked where the scar came from, but it appeared too purposeful a brand on the flesh to be any accident. Someone must have given it to him. Terry found himself strangely thankful to the unknown assailant.

"What took so long?" Davey asked.

Terry sank down and began to drop the pills onto the floor. It surprised him how badly he need one. He never allowed himself to show up high when assisting in the renovations. Felts pounded beer all day and might not have noticed, but Terry knew addicts didn't like a reminder of their own condition. Anyway, he might be out of a job if Felts caught him patching drywall stoned. He couldn't risk that.

Davey squinted to read the fine print on the labels. He needed glasses, but Terry doubted he would have worn them. Despite the dirt they'd accumulated living in the cabin, Davey remained vain, always combing the matted hair that fell on his shoulders, always biting his nails to avoid letting them grow long.

"Damned Lortab," Davey said. "This shit makes me itch."

"I thought that was the Percocet."

"Percocet gives me bad dreams, but other than that, it's cool."

"Bad dreams how?" Terry asked as he wrapped an arm around Davey's waist.

"Once, back when I was still at home, I was on Percocet and fell asleep in my brother's room. Well, he had all these army men . . ."

"The kind from a bucket?"

"Not those plastic cheap shits. These were like a Ken doll, but with uniforms and everything. He kept them set up around the room, fighting on dressers. I fell asleep and dreamed those sons of bitches sprang an ambush. All creeping forward at the foot of the bed."

Terry popped open the Lortab bottle and dry swallowed a pill. "That's pretty rough."

"Scared me till I was hiding under the covers." Davey extended his hand. Terry shook two pills into his palm. "Any cash?"

"A bit."

"Enough for Gilbert?"

"Not nearly." Terry went to work on the salmon with a can opener. The wheel refused to turn no matter how hard he strained, so Davey took it from him.

"Should take two of those," Davey said, gesturing towards the Lortab. "It would help your chin."

Terry received his wounded jaw the previous night at the Bradshaw pit fights. He and Davey had brought his dog Roscoe to scrape up some cash. The dog had never been violent aside from a quick tussle with a neighbor's Bluetick, but it tore that hound's throat out and Davey believed Roscoe could earn. After Terry's father passed out on the couch with the evening's last High Life balanced on his knee, Terry snuck Roscoe into his father's truck.

Terry had never been to the pits, but Davey was a regular since he'd turned eighteen. The brawls were held in an abandoned barn, first the chickens tossed into the ring and later the dogs. Watching the chickens spar made Terry sick. He disliked the quick movement of the birds as they lunged for one another, tearing out feathers when their spurs connected. The losers tried to revive their fowl by giving them an injection or, as one desperate man had done, blowing in the animal's ass in hopes of bringing it around. Terry could still see the old redneck's lips on the limp rooster, blowing hard as if he were playing a trumpet made of ruined flesh.

Roscoe held his own in the first round. He ducked in low, seizing the other mutt on the forepaw, but by the second his ear was chewed to mince and he bled hard from deep marks in his muzzle, Davey threw in the towel. At the end of the night, they'd lost over fifteen hundred dollars. Ferris Gilbert came over with his dog muzzled at the end of a steel chain and placed a tattooed hand on Terry's shoulder.

"Mutt fought hard," he said. "I know you don't have it all, but I expect to be paid in five days."

Terry and Davey fought over the loss out in the parking lot. Terry told Davey he called the fight too early and swung a poor John Wayne haymaker. When he missed, Davey hit him in the jaw with a quick jab. Davey had spent the next morning apologizing to Terry, telling him he shouldn't have hit him, but Terry let him suffer by pouting. Even if he'd thrown the first punch, he wanted to punish Davey for the stupid idea of fighting Roscoe.

Once the salmon was open, they passed it back and forth, digging the fish out of the water with their fingertips. Numbness began to ebb its way into Terry's extremities. Outside, the moon moved behind a heavy blanket of clouds. The sky looked ready to break a sweat and drop rain on them. Terry hoped the roof would hold, hoped that the water wouldn't find new holes to drip through, and that if they did end up sleeping soaked that at least the water might be warm. He found the Bactrim and the Augmentin in the pile of meds. He wasn't sure on doses, but figured the combination of both should keep Roscoe's tattered ear and muzzle from festering.

"Gotta go see Ferris Gilbert tomorrow," Terry said, but Davey was already curled upon himself, arms tucked over his knees as he slept.

CHAPTER TWO

AFTER THEIR FATHER died, Ferris never let Huddles operate under any illusions. Days after the funeral, just around the time Huddles turned ten years old, Ferris took his brother up on the flat roof of The Cat's Den that was packed with December snow and poured them both a few fingers of whiskey while he laid it all out. He explained their way of life was just a law of averages. Enough times running product or enough times with a loaded pistol in your pocket, eventually you'll get caught. With that truth in mind, he told Huddles about his own time inside, about the guards and the gangs, the regulations and the wolves. Ferris said the hardest night was the first. The rest of the time he was free to stroll about in the corridors of his own memory. It wasn't any known meditative technique he used, just some exercise Ferris' created out of necessity. After some instruction, Huddles learned to slip outside his mind into a self-made void. There was nothing in this darkness but a comforting vibration, something to reassure him he was safe.

Huddles tried to remember these things on the night of his arrest, but regardless of the control over his breathing, he couldn't escape reality with The Shell producing a cacophony of machine sounds. Rather than be taken to the courthouse or held at the police barracks until the magistrate could be woken from sleep and court could begin,

Huddles went straight into the seclusion of a holding cell. He lay on a mattress covered in thick plastic that clung to his skin. This was odd. Juveniles were supposed to have a hearing right away before they could be incarcerated, but the guards informed him that there was nowhere else to house him until court convened. Huddles thought there was likely an ulterior motive. No one in Lynch would be in a hurry to arraign the brother of Ferris Gilbert. They'd sweat him for as long as possible, probably drag their feet informing Ferris that he'd been picked up at all.

All he really wanted was a book. One of the officers had mentioned that Education kept a small library of paperbacks, but he'd made a silent vow to himself in the back of the cruiser to only accept what was necessary. Any additional comfort would make it easier for them to break him down.

Huddles expected panic to seize him when the door's heavy bolt slid home. Instead, he was filled with a manic energy, but knew circling the room like a trapped animal would only display another sort of weakness. The guards would read it as anxiety and the other boys would think him soft. Best to just lay down, let the mattress suck at his sweating skin and ignore the desire to pace that made him roll in bed, fighting the thin blanket he'd been provided.

A moth circled in the room. It fluttered from one cinder block wall to another, the brown speckled wings powdering the air. Huddles tried to catch it, but the insect evaded him until he closed his eyes. Eventually, as his mind glazed over into practiced calm, he felt the moth's wing kiss his bottom lip. Huddles crushed it with his palm, smearing its body across his chin.

*　*　*

AFTER MAYBE AN hour, an officer named Hendricks fetched him. Hendricks was tall, well over six feet with a slight frame rendered more athletic by a shaved head. Everything about the man looked agitated. His pursed lips seemed ready to spill obscenities. Even his hairless forearms were bisected with scars, the flesh puckered like a distended worm surfacing through the skin. Huddles had overheard the other officers call him Sir Hendricks in the hall. He didn't understand the nickname, but it felt proper. Hendricks acted as if noble authority were another item issued along with his uniform.

"Where's my brother and my lawyer?" Huddles asked.

"On their way. You come with me."

The control room buzzed them onto the main floor where they passed several octagon shaped tables. Long bench seats connected to each one by tentacles of pipe. They reminded Huddles of stainless steel krakens. He could imagine boys crowded together here, heads down over their chow as some guard paced the periphery. Already he felt the constant observation. The knowledge that every movement was being watched by men or the mechanical eyes recording from the black orbs on the ceiling. This smothering feeling persisted as they exited the dining hall. Since it was almost daylight, Huddles assumed it was time for court, but Sir Hendricks led him down a long corridor toward Recreation.

While the rest of The Shell felt sterile, the Rec area smelled of sweat. A full-length basketball court stretched out across the gymnasium where the B-Unit boys lined the far wall. Half stood stripped to bare torsos, bodies covered in wounds from flagrant fouls. The paint on the court was the same vibrant blue as their bruises, but the wood had fared better than any exposed flesh. The only blemish Huddles could see on the hardwood was the foul line dulled by years of sneakers shifting in free-throw preparation. He inhaled the stale locker room scent in the air. There was life here. Not just the paltry life of insects encountered in his cell, but the real energy of brief enjoyment.

"The wood was donated from Mercer High when they tore the school down," Sir Hendricks said as if reading Huddles' mind. "Some state worker wanted you boys to have something special. Probably saved a buck, too."

The B-Unit boys exercised using a deck of playing cards. Each suit assigned a different task. A ten of spades required ten push-ups. A queen of diamonds twelve crunches. When the pack ended, the boys broke up into shirts and skins.

"Why don't you shoot some hoops while you wait?" Hendricks said.

Huddles pulled on a pair of old Converse that Hendricks offered and went to shoot alone at the opposite rim. The others kept their distance. No one even bothered to shout an insult when he bricked a three-pointer off the backboard.

Sheriff Thompson entered just as Huddles missed another shot. The low-heeled maroon boots he wore, strange and useless in mountain country, clicked on the hardwood. His hat traveled in his left hand as if delivering bad news to a freshly made widow, his right fingers absently rubbing the empty holster where he'd checked his sidearm. Huddles was surprised he gave the weapon up, but Thompson had always been a man of manners. He referred to Ferris as Mr. Gilbert when they spoke even if the name seemed to sour in his mouth.

"Morning, Huddles." Thompson's voice bounced off the cinder block walls. The balls stopped dribbling.

"I got nothing to say." Every young ear was tuned to their conversation. Thompson placed a hand on his shoulder. Huddles tried to shrug it off, but Thompson clamped down hard.

"Let's have a talk anyway," he said.

Sir Hendricks unlocked the side door on the far end of the court. Thompson led Huddles out into a fenced-in section of yard. Huddle should've felt some joy at being outside. Even if he'd only spent a few hours in The Shell, it was still time without freedom, locked into a room with the knowledge he couldn't open the door if he wished. It would be best to soak up the brief amber rays of dawn, but Thompson's presence seemed to eclipse the sun. Huddles told himself it didn't matter. The view behind The Shell was the same tired mountains. The only thing worthy of note was a stream than ran at the base of the hill where a few ducks swam circles. One of the mallards dipped its emerald green head underwater to snatch minnows.

Thompson stepped across the tall grass and kicked his boots through the weeds.

"You ever see such a place for snakes?" he asked. A jaw packed full of tobacco distorted his speech. "I wanted a word with you before court."

For the better part of a year, Sheriff Thompson had sat outside The Cat's Den in the same blue Chevy Cavalier with deep rust stains eating away the passenger door. A plain clothes deputy usually rode shotgun. Huddles knew it was the same man since the deputy was foolish enough to hang his tattooed arm out the window most mornings, a Celtic cross always visible against sunburnt skin.

"You ain't been subtle about things," Huddles said. "Sending undercovers in like they were looking for lap dances."

Thompson took off his hat and wiped away sweat with the back of his sleeve. He wasn't looking at Huddles, just staring off into the morning fog that blanketed the distant valley.

"What I have is you," Thompson said. "Your brother's either smarter or just don't give a shit about anyone else. So, if you aren't prepared to tell me what you know, then I'm gonna see to it that Judge Wallace makes life as hard as possible. You'll be detained until trial, then I'll see to it your ass is shipped on up to Tiger Morton where that last name loses clout."

A breeze blew through carrying scents from the surrounding mountains. Huddles closed his eyes and tried to separate animal musk from new saplings, spoiled acorns from plain wet dirt, but time refused to cease. The world would not bend to his will and allow him to escape into one of his brother's trances. Ferris must have possessed some magic he didn't.

"You know how hard Tiger is, Huddles? Just tell me who supplies the pharmaceuticals. Does Ferris have an arrangement further south? Maybe one of those pain clinic doctors gets a cut? You give me something solid and you go home. No wires or any of that shit."

"I've got nothing to say."

Thompson spit a stream of tobacco and shook his head. "Your friend Shane is a little less willing to fall on his sword."

Huddles tried to see if this was a bluff, but the sheriff seemed too steady. It didn't sound like posturing, just fact.

"Why tell me?" Huddles asked.

"I thought you should know before you're boxed out. You'd make the better informant."

"What makes you think I won't tell Ferris as soon as I see him?" Huddles asked. He couldn't look up at Thompson. Instead, Huddles watched some of the ducks take wing and circle low over the horizon.

"You're smart, Huddles. You'll think on it awhile before you make a call."

Thompson wiped his lower lip with his thumb, examined the dab of juice on the digit and cleaned it on his pant leg.

"Just don't wait too long," he said. "Court's in two hours. I told the judge to really drag his feet."

Thompson kicked the door with the toe of his boot. Back inside, a stampede of boys sprinted the length of the court. Their soles slapping the hardwood drowned out all other sound, but Huddles could see mouths contorting into smiles, eyes bright in the red faces until they could almost be mistaken for normal kids at play.

"Think about it," Thompson said.

Huddles braced his back against the cold wall, slid down to the floor feeling as if his lungs were deflating as the sheriff left the court. One of the B-Unit boys came toward him dribbling a basketball. He stood loose and cocky, body swaying as the ball moved from left to right and then through the columns of his spread legs.

"What'd you have to say to the lawman?" the boy asked.

"I didn't have nothing to say." Huddles prepared to stand. Already his voice had developed an edge.

The ball kept pounding against the wood. Left, right, through the legs and back out. Huddles wanted to kick it away.

"Little snitching bitch," the boy said.

Huddles sprang up and gave the boy a hard push that sent the basketball rolling across the court. The kid stumbled, but Huddles grabbed a handful of his shirt while he was falling. The guards were already coming, so Huddles spun the boy, administered two hard jabs to his face and an elbow so deep in the stomach that it felt like he connected with backbone. Huddles hit him a final time as foamy white vomit leaked from the corner of the boy's mouth, then let the officers grab his arms, pull him down, and shackle his wrists. The others were watching, so Huddles yelled insults all the way to isolation.

WHEN THEY'D FIRST brought him inside, Huddles tried to memorize as much of the layout as possible, but entering through Intake was confusing. It involved a series of labyrinthine corridors meant to leave him uncertain of exactly how deep he was inside the facility. The institutional white walls blended together after so many turns and all the steel doors were painted the same gray. The only splashes of color were the walls in the main dining hall painted light pastels, pinks like raw meat and purples the shade of swelling lips. Soft Easter egg colors as if the boys were inside a maximum-security day care.

After another hour, Sir Hendricks led him from Holding into an area Huddles hadn't seen before. A group of officers stood chatting outside an open door. From beyond them came the sounds of lockers slamming, the hum of a loud refrigerator as someone opened its sealed door and forks scrapping plates. The door at the end of the hall had no window, but Huddles guessed that the other side would lead into a seating area where men would clock-in and chat. Beyond that would likely lead outside into the parking lot. They didn't travel close enough to confirm this. Sir Hendricks turned him by the shoulder and they went left down another hall.

When Officer Hendricks opened the door to Visitation, Ferris looked too large for the chair he squatted in. His hands lay folded on the tabletop until the blue and black ink on each finger created a web of playing card symbols and letters too scarred over to read. The beard he wore days before was gone. Graying stubble splotched the deep craters of his cheeks and tried to sprout between the sun cracked lines.

Floyd Mitchum, the arthritic lawyer Ferris kept on the payroll, sat next to him clad in rumpled houndstooth. A polka-dotted bowtie constricted his wrinkled neck.

Floyd rubbed his rheumy eyes. "As your legal counsel, I'm gonna tell you that you fucked up real good. How's it gonna look you beat on somebody before seeing the goddamned judge?"

"I didn't have a choice," Huddles said.

Ferris waved his hand to silence them both. He sat a bottle of Dr. Pepper on the table. "They told me you can have it if I buy it during a visit."

The plastic was still cold from the vending machine. Huddles twisted the cap off and took a sip. The carbonation burned like whiskey and his chapped lips tingled with the fizz.

"Thompson sent two deputies by the club early this morning," Ferris said. "They distracted me with some bullshit while he slipped up here to see you."

Huddles hadn't realized that Ferris already knew about Thompson's visit, but he wasn't surprised. His brother possessed an almost uncanny way of inferring a man's next move. Huddles wondered what else he knew. He'd spent all morning debating whether to tell Ferris what Thompson said about Shane. If it was true, Ferris should be warned, but it might only be Thompson feeding him lies, misinformation to divide them before court. Shane had gone away without complaint before, but a man could only stand so many years in lockup. He might talk, only Huddles couldn't see his friend killed over maybes.

"Thompson said I could go home if I told him what I knew. Otherwise, the judge will keep me here, then I'm going to Tiger."

Mitchum shook his head. "You were never going home. Not with that last name, and certainly not after assaulting that boy."

"Why haven't I been to court yet?" Huddles asked. "I was arrested last night."

"Thompson needed to get a crack at you first," Mitchum said. "This is Lynch, son. Normal rules don't apply here. We'll be on the way soon now that he had his moment alone."

"What about Shane?" Huddles asked.

"We'll see," Mitchum said. "Boys got a lot of paper."

"Thompson will be back to see you again," Ferris said. "You call over at Megan's when he comes, understand?"

Megan had danced at The Cat's Den since Huddles was eight years old. She was the first woman he'd ever seen naked, sliding down the tarnished metal pole onto the rickety stage constructed out of particle board and plywood, the cheap materials reinforced with bricks underneath to support the weight of the dancers tromping along in their stilettos. She'd caught him sneaking downstairs for a look at her and, after a few beers, still liked to remind Huddles of the expression on his face until he could feel the same heat on his neck as that distant night. Occasionally, Ferris crashed at her place. Since they assumed the club's phone to be tapped, she handled all his calls.

Ferris watched him with eyes gray as boiled meat. Huddles wanted to let his brother know he was strong, but the officer's close presence reduced them to silent gestures. He tried to read his brother's body language, to discern if his approval could be found in the hard set of his shoulders. Huddles became more conscious of his own body, tried to look as if he were calm and comfortable.

"You're gonna make it in here," Ferris said.

They sat with it a moment to let it become truth.

CHAPTER THREE

THE SHINGLES BLOWN from the roof of The Cat's Den bobbed in the deep puddles around Terry's feet like fish killed by dynamite. Cherry Tree hadn't resembled anything decent in years, but the consecutive nights of harsh storms had left the community in a fresh state of ruin. Trash from the vacant lots lay strewn down the alleys and the large storefront windows of the pawnshop next door to the club were shattered. Shards littered the asphalt, reflecting dingy rainbows against the brick walls. In the old days, Cherry Tree was a more prosperous part of town the elderly called Black Bottom, a section of Lynch where African American merchants had set up shop in the thirties. It had been a vibrant street until the original residents moved out, headed to Charleston or further north, and Black Bottom became inhabited by white addicts who occupied the rented rooms over the closed shops. Within a generation, all the stores converted to bars or strip clubs, creating a sort of red-light district that the state hadn't seen since the days of Cinder Bottom. A good deal of Lynch's crime that didn't take place on the hillside occurred here.

The Cat's Den was the first of the all nude joints. That alone would have given it an air of infamy, but the Gilbert's ownership increased the frequency of tall tales. Old men repeated the stories until Freddy Monroe being shot-gunned in the parking lot became apocryphal myth. Each retelling muddied the truth. The only story Terry knew to be without embellishment involved an unnamed out-of-towner beaten nearly to death in one of the back rooms for pulling his dick out during a lap dance. His father told him that one, and despite the fact his old man was a world-class liar, Terry recognized authentic fear each time his father recited the event.

The bar became something of an icon. The sort of place where high school boys dared each other to spend a Saturday night. The club had weathered worse than the week's storms over the years and its lack of damage seemed to speak to some indestructible nature. The wood paneling around the doors and windows lost none of its dark paint and the glass itself, blacked out and baking in a haze of summer heat, bore only a single long fissure that didn't even bisect Terry's reflection. There were no mirrors in his shack on the mountain. Aside from Davey's comments, the only recent indication Terry had of his appearance was a moment staring into the brown waters of Cow Creek. The mustache he'd tried for years to cultivate had thickened and his chin finally sprouted more than a few whiskers. Still, looking at his reflection in the onyx pool of the bar's windows, none of these changes helped him feel more like a man.

Inside, a blue hued lamp cast its light on the narrow stage where a woman strutted down the runway in a pair of stilettos. She wore a tight clenched satin cover over her waist that Terry had seen noble-women wearing in old movies, but he couldn't recall its name. The blue fabric matched her panties and laced up the back. Two men sat in swivel chairs next to the stage. Their coal blackened hands were filled with bills while beer mugs sweated wet rings in front of them. Both tried to converse with the woman in quiet tones, but she only leaned against the brass pole and scratched an itch in her blonde curls.

On the other side of the room, two men stood behind the bar surrounded by an array of half-empty bottles. The bearded of the pair read a newspaper, his lips mouthing words as his eyes scanned the page. The other, a heavy man with skin so white it looked as if he'd never seen daylight, stared at Terry. When he was ten years old, Terry and his father had found the body of a drowned man in the Guyandotte River. Days submerged had left the floater's skin thin as wax paper. The swelled body split open when they drug him ashore, allowing Terry to see insides that were no longer composed of normal tissue, but almost a jelly that seeped out. The sallow man reminded Terry of that corpse.

"What the fuck are you doing in here?" the pale man asked.

The woman on the stage stopped her dancing, and for a moment, Terry believed she might cover her bare legs, but she just waited as grinding blues wailed from the speakers.

"I came to see Mr. Gilbert," Terry said.

The words came as involuntarily as vomit, but they stopped the pale man coming towards him. The bearded man placed a finger between the pages of his newspaper to mark his place.

"Go get him, Jeff," the man with the newspaper said.

The pale man seemed ready to protest, but turned and opened a door behind the stage.

"What's that thing called?" Terry asked the dancing woman.

"What thing?" she asked. Her voice sounded soft against the music.

"That thing 'round your stomach. Ladies in old movies wear them."

"A corset," she said. "It makes your waist smaller."

"Does it hurt?"

"Not too bad." She seemed to weight her answer.

Terry was about to ask more when the man called him over. Inside the back room, Ferris Gilbert sat behind a desk covered in newspapers. Several craters filled the wall behind him where someone had ripped free hunks of plaster trying to extract some nails. A single bare bulb lit the room and cast long shadows that made Gilbert look different in the low light. His previous beard, long and coarse like porcupine quills, had been trimmed down. His fingertips, smeared with ink that converged with his tattoos, struggled with the knot in his red necktie.

"I'll give you a minute to get yourself together," Ferris said. "But I've gotta be at court soon. You can't just sit there and shake all morning."

Terry sat in front of Ferris' desk and smoothed the wrinkles of his dirty shirt. He could smell himself in the small room, a reek hidden under the baby powder he doused his body with before going to work. Aside from applying a wet washcloth to his armpits and genitals, he hadn't washed in three days. Ferris didn't seem to notice. He barely breathed as he waited on Terry to stop fidgeting in the uncomfortable wooden chair. Something about his patience implied time only affected others.

"I can tell you don't have it," Ferris said. "But I also know you've been trying to get it. That right?"

"Yes."

"What were you doing for it?"

"Some construction."

"And what else?" Ferris asked.

"I robbed a house over on Fuller Street."

Ferris nodded. "Make out okay?" It was the first time he didn't seem bored.

"Not enough."

"Might have, though. Might have gotten close anyway, but something sidetracked you."

Heat flushed Terry's chest and the skin at the nap of his neck tightened. Rumors hadn't prepared him for this. Sitting alone in the back room, it occurred to Terry how calm Ferris seemed, as if Ferris could throttle him as easy as wringing a chicken's neck and just get back to whatever business had stained his hands.

"I guess so," Terry said.

"Ain't nothing to guess," Ferris said. "Them pills got the better of you."

Even without meth teeth and the scratching of B-movie junkies, Terry was embarrassed that Ferris could look at him and know how weak he was against the ache to use.

"I've got two hundred on me." Terry said. "It's every cent I can manage now. You give me some time to get back to hitting the houses, and I'll have more."

"More that you'll spend," Ferris said. "You can't walk on two hundred."

Ferris retrieved a small revolver from the top drawer and placed it on the desk. Terry's father owned countless guns over the years. As a boy, Terry had carried, cleaned, and shot most of them, but the gun in front of him seemed different from the rest. Firearms in his father's house were always preserved behind the locked glass of their cabinet and unloaded. He could see the dull brass of bullets filling the cylinder of this weapon. No doubt its barrel had been stuck to at least one man's cheek. Terry imagined feeling it's barrel pressed against his lips like a silencing finger.

"Are you seventeen yet?" Ferris asked.

"Not till December."

"I know a bit about your situation," Ferris said. "Your dad kicked you out, and now you're living up in the hills. Personally, I think it's a shame, but that doesn't mean I'm not about to use it to my advantage."

Terry didn't reply. He wasn't surprised Ferris knew as much as he did, but waited to see if Davey or his father would be brought into their negotiations. With Gilbert, nothing would be off limits.

"What I mean is, you and I are about to enter into an agreement. No, that's not the word I'm looking for." Ferris chewed his lower lip as he searched his vocabulary. "An obligation." He tapped the gun with a tattooed finger. "You do this one thing, and all debts are forgiven. I give you a bag of pills and Willis out there drives you to Pittsburgh, Lexington, Knoxville. Hell, anywhere within three hundred miles where you can have pavement underfoot and plenty of lights at night."

"What do I have to do?" Terry asked.

Ferris slid the gun forward. "I want you to kill Sheriff Thompson."

Just that easy. A man asking him to murder as simply as asking to borrow something from a toolshed.

Terry shook his head. "I'd be better off letting you shoot me."

"I know it ain't much of a choice, but you'll do it. You've got no other options except a certainty you don't wanna meet. Afterwards, we're square. Nothing more owed. By you or any of your kin."

Gilbert pushed the gun closer. Two of his fingers lingered on the handle and traced slow circles in the wood grain until Terry picked it up. The grip felt warm and solid in his hand.

"Anywhere I wanna go afterward?" he asked.

"Anywhere within three hundred miles."

Terry closed his eyes and pictured the sort of tall buildings he'd seen on television, tried to conjure the sound of a city, the constant nature of something that sustained such a mass of life. He'd never been fifteen miles outside of Lynch and couldn't comprehend what it would be like to look up at a building the size of one of his mountains. Not something solid and from the earth, but crafted by men and populated by more than deer and raccoons. Perhaps he could send word to Davey and they could have a real place together, the sort of home that didn't have to be hidden. Terry rested the gun against his knee, then stood and left without Gilbert dismissing him.

He crossed the floor of the club aware of eyes on him, but refused to turn and look despite the urge to see the woman in her corset one last time, perhaps a quick glimpse of her popping the front snaps open to reveal the way its snug grip left deep imprints on her flesh, marking her the way bootheels mark the soil.

CHAPTER FOUR

BEFORE LEAVING FOR court, Huddles tried to fortify his mind. In the old days, the meditation techniques were only a way to connect with his brother. They lost so much time to Ferris' incarceration that Huddles enjoyed just sitting quietly with him, synchronizing their breathing and clearing his mind until only the precision of the two bodies in unison mattered. The times he experienced anything remotely close to transcendence were seldom, and his memory of those occasions were indescribable. Huddles always opened his eyes knowing something had transpired, but it would be gone seconds later, leaving him thinking it was more Ferris' influence than any real epiphany. Still, he hoped to find the displacement Ferris always mentioned, a sort of psychological sweet spot where all fears might expire.

Ferris told him when trying to overcome panic that it was important to visualize the worst possible scenario and let it become reality for a moment. Huddles closed his eyes and considered constant confinement in one of the cells. Rather than hold on to the things he loved, he wiped his memory of everything from home. He felled the trees on the mountains before they changed colors in the fall, removed the buzz in his head always left by good herb and the lingering warmth of another's touch on his skin. Everything had to be exorcised. If Huddles were to ever endure lifelong incarceration, even Ferris would need to be lost.

After he erased the outside world, Huddles checked his pale reflection in the glass of the holding cell. Even if nothing else were tangible, if these cement walls were the only things left, Huddles knew he could survive. The knowledge gave him solace as he waited.

SIR HENDRICKS MADE Huddles change into an orange jumpsuit before shackling him. The handcuffs attached to a chain that squeezed across his belly, then trailed down and connected to similar bracelets secured on his ankles. Walking was difficult, reduced to more of an unsteady shuffle as the terrain underfoot changed from The Shell's smooth linoleum to the parking lot's gravel. Huddles couldn't step up into the transport van, so Sir Hendricks helped him with a push. Already, another's touch seemed foreign. Everything normal had begun to change. They were only in the morning light for a moment, but the sun burned Huddles' eyes and the air felt too full in his lungs after days of the recycled breath in his cell. He wondered if freedom would ever feel normal again.

Officer Fitzgerald, a giant black man with arms like country hams, locked him in behind the steel screen that separated prisoners from the van's cab and they rode down the hill, merging onto the interstate towards Lynch. The highway unwound around mountains that had been blasted back to make room for the road. Their jagged rock faces carved away in levels that resembled great stone staircases. Higher up on the rolling peaks, Huddles could see the trees had been cut back. The mining companies were supposed to reclaim the land by planting saplings and grass, but he couldn't see any sign of renewal. The Eco boys from the university would come soon to take pictures for their pamphlets and blogs.

They took the Lynch exit and came down off the incline of the highway, speeding past the larger homes built on the outskirts, the little bit of money in the county trying to move as far from town as possible. Huddles looked at the mock plantation houses with gazebos in their manicured yards, big wooden front porches with pergolas behind wrought iron gates. He didn't envy them their counterfeit southern charm. It made him proud that he and Ferris lived above the trashiest club in town even though they'd squirreled away more cash than anyone in this hick suburbia. Out the window, wealth petered away as they approached downtown.

The Lynch County court house looked as if it were hued out of granite. The steps polished stone and the front archway adorned with beautiful sculptures of pioneer men dipping their hands into wild streams, women by log cabins and animals peering through a deep thicket of trees. Huddles didn't get the chance to observe them closely. The van drove past, pulled down an alley and they took him inside through a basement that smelled of old floodwaters. They rode the rickety elevator to the fifth floor where a bailiff waited. He was an old man, the corners of his mouth covered by an overgrown mustache. A long-barreled revolver rode high on his left hip as he ran a handheld metal detector over Huddles despite the chains.

"That necessary?" Huddles asked.

The bailiff just stared. Huddles looked past him and saw Mitchum. He'd changed even though his visit was only hours ago. A fresh charcoal suit, his shirt a bright white with a bowtie that hadn't wilted against his collar despite the humidity. A briefcase rested between his oxblood wingtips.

"Just like we discussed," Mitchum whispered to him.

The courtroom was nearly empty inside. Just rows of bare benches, two tables up front with only the prosecutor sitting as he flipped through a pad of notes. Ferris sat hidden in the far corner of the final row, his arms hung over the back of the bench in front of him and his chin resting on the wood. Sheriff Thompson sat up front in his uniform, hat on his knee as if he were in church.

Mitchum left Huddles alone at the table while he spoke to the prosecutor. The old man gripped the other lawyer's padded shoulder, and leaned in close to make sure no one else heard their conversation. Huddles glanced behind him to where Sheriff Thompson sat fiddling with his hat. Once he was caught looking, the sheriff offered a wink that made Huddles avert his eyes.

Mitchum jabbed Huddles hard in his ribs. "Fuck him. I want you to focus."

"What did the prosecutor say?" Huddles asked.

"That you wouldn't be going home. Not even with a bracelet."

The bailiff made the introduction for Judge Wallace and everyone stood as he entered the court. Huddle expected robes, but the judge wore only a blue blazer and a striped tie. His hair was an elaborate comb-over, the thinning wave matted down with hair spray until it resembled a collapsed orca fin. Mitchum started in on the judge before he could take his seat.

"Your Honor, I request these shackles be removed from my client. No reason he should be treated like a criminal at this proceeding."

"It's just me, Counselor," Judge Wallace said. "There isn't any jury to influence."

Huddles imagined a smirk must be growing across Thompson's face.

"Your client has been charged with possession of a controlled substance with intent to deliver, resisting arrest, and carrying an unlicensed concealed weapon. How does the defendant plead?"

"Not guilty, your Honor."

Judge Wallace rubbed his temples. "Very well."

"Your Honor, we request that my client be remanded to the custody of his brother until the time of the trial. He has no prior criminal record and is not a flight risk."

The prosecutor stood, hands smoothing his pinstripe slacks as he began to speak. Each word came out succinct and clear in a way Huddles rarely heard from a mountain vernacular. The man probably won most arguments solely with elocution.

"I have to object, Judge Wallace. These are very serious charges, and I think we are all aware of the reputation of the accused's brother in our community. The man is a known felon and is suspected in several unsolved cases. Sending this boy home with him is a true disservice. Both to the community and the boy himself."

Mitchum started to speak, but Judge Wallace pronounced over him. "The accused will be remanded to the custody of The Shelby Youth Correctional Facility until the time of trial. He will be safe in state custody, but accessible to both family and council. We're dismissed."

No gavel cracked. Judge Wallace just walked out as Sir Hendricks took Huddles by the arm.

"What's that mean?" Huddles asked.

"It means '*stay hard.*'"

WHEN THEY RETURNED to the alley, Sir Hendricks loaded Huddles into the back of the van and checked his chains. That morning,

Hendricks carried a book under his arm titled *The Art of Medieval Combat*. The book, along with the scars, were enough to finally pin down where the name came from. Huddles imagined Sir Hendricks clad in chain mail, a helm with an open visor under his arm as he stepped onto some renaissance fairground, ready to duel with other men still wallowing in the past. It even made sense why Hendricks allowed the nickname. He didn't understand they were mocking him.

Hendricks loosened the chains a bit until they jostled. The double doors were just closing as a voice rang out.

"Wait a minute," Sheriff Thompson said. Sir Hendricks stepped aside as Thompson filled the van's opening with his girth. This close, he smelled of damp polyester and oiled patented leather.

"I told you how this would go," Sheriff Thompson said. He reached inside the van and rubbed his palms over the steel cage. "I'd like to think this would be an eye opener."

"I told you I haven't got anything to say," Huddles said.

Thompson raised his hand in a gesture of dismissal. "That brother of yours must be pretty goddamned scary. Keep in mind, Shane will have more to say every day."

HUDDLES MADE IT back to The Shell in time to attend Counselor Beverly's group. Woods, a redneck boy from Pocahontas County, was discussing his recent breakup. It seemed like boring stuff to Huddles, but a smaller black boy resting against a pair of crutches assured him it was better than the typical stuff on the dangers of cigarettes and childcare. Huddles almost thought he must be joking about these therapeutic topics. He counted at least three junkies in the circle.

Aside from his brief freedom during Recreation, Huddles hadn't spent any time with the B-Unit boys. They all knew him by reputation, but his isolation had kept him from any interactions. They weren't what he expected. Aside from OUTLAUW tattooed across the side of Woods' neck, the boys were clean cut. Most were scrawny, baby-faced with ears not yet grown into, shaved heads or frizzy cowlicks. A few had high voices as if their balls were still dropping. The only common factor Huddles noticed were their eyes. Every set whether green, brown, blue or hazel had the same rheumy vacancy only interrupted by each blink. A bloodshot stare as if their brains had atrophied and only the reptilian portions remained. It was the defeated look common to boys raised in the system.

Group therapy didn't seem to be working, but Counselor Beverly looked the part. Middle aged and attractive. The only soft-hearted woman in the place. It was the other counselor Huddles couldn't figure. Counselor Felts was a shrunken dwarf in a black cashmere overcoat that looked a hundred years old. According to the rumors Huddles heard, Counselor Felts was never without the coat, its double-breasted front usually buttoned to the neck like a priest's cassock. Such a holy role would have been a better fit for Counselor Felts. He looked out of place surrounded by taller men in uniforms, their arms ropes of muscle used to intimidate the delinquents. Counselor Felts looked too delicate, his long pianist's fingers often shaped like a steeple as he sat and listened, brow furrowed while Woods continued with his romantic woes.

"I just can't figure what it could've been," Woods said. He scratched the beard that spotted his neck the way moss grows on a tree. "I thought we got along fine."

"What about the rumors?" Beverly asked. Despite attempts to hide herself in a baggy windbreaker and mom jeans, Huddles couldn't help but trace his eyes over the counselor's thighs, consider what she looked like off duty, the baggy clothes replaced with tight denim and her plum lips coated in red gloss. Even in B-Unit, with only a dab of concealer to hide the dark circles under her eyes, she carried a sort of beauty that must have been maddening to boys locked inside so long.

"They were all bragging about her," Woods said as he sat forward in his chair.

"Think about the things you told the other boys," Beverly said. "Think how it must have made her feel."

"I thought she'd be real proud of that."

"Maybe they made her feel objectified." Beverly scratched at her scalp as if her nails could dig away whatever was vexing her. "Did you ever consider that it was something just for the two of you? I understand that you didn't mean to embarrass her. It's just that you're not adults yet."

"Shit," said another of the other inmates. "I've got a son, and I'm locked up. Feels pretty well adult enough to me."

Counselor Felts gave a little smile at this. Huddles doubted anyone else saw it.

The door buzzed open. Sir Hendricks came onto the floor leading a young boy whose state-issued clothing hung off him. The shirt ran at least two sizes too large, the hem ending below his knee like an elderly woman's nightdress and the pants wide enough to fit his whole body inside one leg. His face still carried traces of baby fat, cheeks dimpled and powdered in freckles. Hair shorn off until his scalp was covered in the white blond down of a gosling. The boy walked beside Hendricks, not in front like the rest in the facility, and his hands hung loose at his side instead of creating the regulation diamond shape on the small of his back.

"Officer Fitzgerald thought Malcolm should be here for group," Hendricks said to Beverly. Huddles sensed something well up inside her as she looked the boy over. The kid's size kept her from seeing that he was not the least bothered by all the eyes watching or the electronic steel doors. Huddles understood immediately. From the way his brow furrowed, Counselor Felts must have too.

"Come on and sit down," Beverly said, voice high as if she were speaking to a kitten.

Woods and a few others hid bucked teeth behind their palms as they snorted. The boy beside Huddles jabbed him with an elbow and leaned on his crutch.

"Shit's so hard out there that they're snatching fuckers up off Sesame Street," he said. The table erupted in laughter. The whole group rolling and smacking their knees. Beverly waved her arms in an attempt to cool things while Sir Hendricks hid a grin.

"What'd you do, man?" the boy on crutches continued. "You cut Big Bird? Steal that monster's cookies?"

Officer Hendricks was too busy stifling his laughter to react when Malcolm stepped forward, snatched a crutch from where it rested against the side of the table, and swung. The aluminum bars sliced the air as the rubber end meant to cradle an armpit connected with the boy's upper back. The shock of the blow knocked the child forward and his face smacked the tabletop as the crutch came down again, crushing the fingers of his right hand. The boy tried to scream, but what emitted from his mouth was hollow, more sputter than shriek. Malcolm raised the crutch again, but Hendricks was on him before he could strike a final blow, wrenching the crutch away and pulling

Malcolm to the floor, the boy's small legs kicking at Hendricks' crotch and the little mouth all obscenity and gnashing teeth. Beverly circled the table, telling everyone to stay seated. Counselor Felts knelt with the injured boy who held aloft the crooked digits on his mashed hand. His ring finger pointed upwards in an angle it was never intended to create.

"Medical to B-Unit," Beverly said on her radio. "Officer assistance and Medical to B-Unit."

The door buzzed open and two officers ran in to help Hendricks. They tried to get Malcolm to stand on his feet, but he was still slinging kicks at Hendricks' nose. They loaded him up, hands under Malcolm's arms and around his tensing knees as they carried him off the floor towards Holding.

THAT EVENING AS they housed Huddles on B-Unit, he began to discover the bodies of long dead insects scattered across the floor. The corpses clung together in the tight corners, swept aside by housekeeping staff that hadn't bothered to pick them up. Their dry, broken bodies only husks, exoskeletons with their legs or wings absent. Evening on B-Unit was a time of quiet tension that left the boys restless, but it gave Huddles time to contemplate how the flies and moths came to be inside. He wondered if they traveled in on a guard's clothes, or if a lone pair had found each other years ago and generations of their offspring were forced to live a perpetual cycle of birth, incest and death inside the walls.

He wondered where the maggots hatched, where new larvae would incubate and, in the case of the moth he'd killed the first night, where a caterpillar might secretly cocoon itself to undergo metamorphosis.

It seemed a miracle in this place where all evening Officer Hendricks sat in B-Unit and listened to the boys play spades, their conversation droning on about the beating they'd witnessed.

Woods shuffled an ancient pack of cards and dealt them out. Robison, an obese black boy whose blubber shuddered with each breath as if he were in perpetual motion, collected them while a ginger haired loud mouth named Callan fanned his hand.

"Got the good shit right here," Callan said. "Crown me king of B-Unit." He arranged his cards by suite and looked to the top tier of the section where cells six through ten were located.

"We really had one today," Callan said. "Best ass beating in months."

"Ain't no kid could do that to me," Woods said. "I'd stomp his brain out his ears if he tried."

"Malcolm ain't no kid," Callan said. "Fucker was raised by wolves. Probably chewed his own momma's tit off."

Huddles watched the way Officer Hendricks observed the group. It was unnerving to know that even when he slept someone would be posted in the spherical room of Control, keeping an eye on the monitors to see if anyone tried to jimmy a door.

For a brief moment in court, Huddles had almost confessed everything to Judge Wallace. The Shell hadn't broken him, but his mind wouldn't stop the loop of Malcolm beating that boy with a crutch. The sound of the rubber cracking bone, the smell of violence as they drug Malcolm away. Regardless of how strong he was, eventually this place would hollow him out. Ferris knew that and so did Thompson. He was going to call his brother about Shane, tell him everything about Thompson's claim that he was an informant. The idea had moved past consideration, and there was a comfort in knowing.

Once the card game slowed, Huddles went into his cell to lie down. He sat on the bed, his back against the cold stone of the cinder block wall. His legs were long enough for him to stretch out his toe and touch the doorframe. He sat still like that until Sir Hendricks came by, called for lights out, and locked him inside.

CHAPTER FIVE

FOR TWO DAYS, Terry and Davey sat in front of the dying embers of the potbelly stove and drifted on one pill after another. Terry needed some escape from the task Ferris had given him, a chemical slip that would allow him to sink below reality, but even finding this time released euphoria could only offer partial relief. Each high always ended with him thinking about the gun, hidden outside in the hollow of a nearby tree, no doubt accruing rust that might make the weapon a useless prop. With the gun came guilt. Guilt that he'd omitted the encounter when talking with Davey, guilt that he'd yet to brave town to help mend Roscoe's wounds. Still, guilt was preferable to fear. Terry could close his eyes, push the guilt down the well of his stomach and go back to searching the multicolored pills for some solace.

Terry wasn't certain what Davey was chasing with their binge. He watched as his man swallowed whichever pill he picked up regardless of the effect it might have on his current high. Some moments he seemed in love with the very oxygen pulled into his lungs and seduced by the warmth of the fire he insisted on building. Other times he raged, loathed the particles of wood that made up the cabin and looked ready to grab hot coals from the smoldering oven to singe the floor. By the end, Davey must have felt every emotion.

They made love once in that state, an encounter that began when Davey seized Terry from behind and the two stripped soiled garments off each other. Their sex was always sloppy and inept, both wanting, but unsure of themselves in their attempts to act on the desire. Afterward, they lay wrapped together. Davey smoked a joint while Terry stared at the ceiling, his eyes watching a water stain that expanded across the roof a bit more each day. It dripped steady warmth the color of rust onto Terry's outstretched foot.

"You're doing it again," Davey said as he puffed on the joint. "Here, but gone at the same time."

"I get that way."

"Doesn't make it easy."

Sometimes, when the two of them were still feeling each other's sweat drying, Terry couldn't figure out what he was doing with Davey. Occasionally, when he was privy to intense clarity through the usual inebriation, it all felt like nothing more than lust and familiarity. Maybe they were only together to avoid being alone. Sometimes, this made Terry want to leave. Other times, he told himself this was simply the truth about love. That the real thing was just two broken people trying to stand together despite the world's constant barrage. All he knew for certain was he didn't want Davey's unconditional love. Both members needed to earn it or else devotion was simply a curse. Thinking of his secrets that night, Terry felt as if he'd hexed the man.

Eventually, Terry slipped from Davey's grasp and walked to the window. The night was too dark to see far, the trees and leaves at a distance nothing more than shadows. When Terry was eleven, he and his father went up the hill to shoot squirrels with the shotgun he received that Christmas from his grandfather. When Terry shot the first one from the high branches, he aimed at the fluffy tail. His father was forced to finish the animal off by grabbing it up by the wounded appendage and swinging it at the nearest tree trunk like a living club. Afterwards, his father cut off the tiny hands and made a slit in the squirrel's back, slid his fingers under the fur and pulled the skin over the animal's head as if he were taking off a child's shirt. The smell of half-digested acorns made Terry gag until he cried quiet tears. After that trip, Terry knew he couldn't kill even when it meant filling an empty stomach. There was little chance he could pull the trigger on Thompson. Pills hadn't made him forget any of this.

Terry stepped away from the window and rested his hand on Davey's flank. Even with the drugs' effect on his appetite, Davey carried a thickness in the hips that made him seem much older, a paunch most men would have been self-conscious over, but Davey never hid when nude. He lay on the floor propped up on an elbow, his fat stomach divided into rolls. Terry took the joint from him, hit it deep and looked at the burning tip.

"You gotta trust that I wanna be here," Terry said.

The pair went quiet the rest of the night. They sat in the flicker of the candle flame and smoked the joint down to ash.

THE NEXT MORNING, Terry arrived early to help Henry Felts rip up the carpet. His head pounded a dull ache along with his heartbeat and the sunlight fried his eyes after such a late night, but Terry felt in decent spirits, pleased to expend his anxiety on something productive. The only reminder of the Gilberts was the revolver stuffed into the pocket of his jean jacket. Terry couldn't leave it in the tree any longer. Even if the gun could endure a century inside the rotting wood, he didn't trust Davey not to discover it. He recognized this as paranoia. Still, he'd brought the gun.

The smell of wet mold met him inside. Henry Felts didn't bother to formally greet him, just removed his work gloves to wipe at his greasy forehead. Things had deteriorated since Terry's last visit. The yard had accumulated more trash, and the taped cardboard on the broken windows in the front room had disintegrated, allowing the previous night's rain inside. Bits of glass from the long ago shattered panes lay hidden in the waterlogged carpet. Henry provided Terry with gloves to keep him from cutting himself.

"Better use them," he said and offered a look at his own lacerated palm to illustrate the point.

Terry grabbed the carpet, adopted a wide stance and jerked to get a corner section free. The bit tugged loose, but wouldn't tear. He kneeled down and began to work at the fibers with his box cutter, slicing angry as if butchering an animal that had tasked him for days.

He became so intent in mangling the carpet, Terry didn't hear Jason Felts enter.

Henry stood in the doorway winded, his gut trembling as he wheezed in the heat of the house.

"Goddamned place is gonna end me," Henry said to Jason.

"How long you boys been at it?" Jason asked.

"Just got going thirty minutes ago," Henry said.

"Tired already?" Jason asked and gave his uncle a weak shot in the shoulder. Henry swatted back with his hat.

There were ten rooms in all. Four of them outfitted in the same beige carpet sullied with a variety of undefinable stains. Sometimes Terry imagined these abstract patterns were messages left behind by the ghosts of the derelicts. Their markings were all over. Black dirt ground into the carpet in the shape of a steel-toed motorcycle boot, and a series of fist sized holes in the walls of the hallway. When Terry started, Henry told him that the wiring under the house was a mess. Lines had been cut almost at random after the group ran out of cash and decided to sell the copper to keep their high going.

Terry sawed at the floor again. Despite his cuts, the carpet still wouldn't come free.

Jason tried to shoo him away, but Terry stopped his slashing and cut more deliberate. The new incisions made it easier to rip the mess from the floor and expose the hardwood underneath. It had been quality flooring once, but no amount of buffing or refinishing seemed like it would restore its previous luster.

"Careful," Terry told Jason. "There's glass in some of this."

"Cut my fingers," Henry said, raising his hand again.

Henry used these wounds as an excuse to relegate tasks to the younger men. Terry did most of the work, jerking strips of carpet up with such speed he knew he must look frantic to the others. It embarrassed him, but Terry couldn't help it. He'd been working this way his entire life and knew the toil would never be behind him. All this work to furnish another man's home when Terry didn't have one of his own. It made him envious of the hand dealt the elder Felts. The privilege of a solid family business squandered on drink. Of course, maybe he was thinking of his own weakness for pills. Whatever it was, the reminders of his station were constant.

Henry turned the portable radio to a station that was in the middle of an hour-long block of rockabilly and the men fell into the rhythm of the music. After they finished two rooms, Jason and Terry went out on the front porch to smoke. Watching the small man puff on the cigarette was surreal. Aside from the scruff of new beard, he looked like a weary child hunched on the porch, the smoldering butt inching towards his flawless knuckles. Halfway through their second cigarette, Henry came outside.

"Why don't you and Terry go grab us some lunch?" He handed Jason a few bills.

"What do you say, Terry?" Jason asked. "Wanna ride along?"

Terry lay flat on his back, the Marlboro wagging in the corner of his mouth. He felt too tired to rise, but something about being alone with the man intrigued him. Jason's silence seemed to promise something. As if an absolute truth might escape his lips if one were only present at the right moment.

"Can I smoke in the car?" he asked.

THEY DROVE ALONG a road flanked by gnarled oaks toward the Mega Drive-Inn. The asphalt lay broken beneath them, the years of neglect making it seem left over from a previous civilization. Everything was dead here. Trees blighted until their branches were left bald. The final leaves fell seasons ago, and even though it was early summer, their tires crunched the dry remnants that blew into the road. Terry cranked the air-conditioner to full blast and sat back to peel dead skin from his knuckles.

"You like working for my uncle?" Jason asked.

"He's all right," Terry said.

"You can speak your mind in this truck," Jason said.

Terry brushed the flaked skin from his pant leg. "He's cool, but he works me hard."

"He used to make me do twice as much work as anybody else at the funeral home," Jason said.

"Did it scare you?" Terry asked. "Being around all those dead people?"

It was hard for Terry to imagine living among the dead. A family sitting around a kitchen table while below their upstairs apartment neighbors lay in the morgue, their bodies purged of fluids and pre-pared for the grave. The corpses arranged like cut flowers for the mourners to pass by. It was even harder to imagine this little man ushering widows to their seat beside the casket.

"Didn't see too many really. Just carried a lot of caskets for folks didn't have anybody else to tote them. I sort of liked the funerals."

Terry twirled an unlit cigarette to keep his hands busy.

"I thought they were kind of beautiful. Sad, but it's something to see everyone come together to send a fella off." Jason licked his lower lip, cast a solemn eye to the rearview as if imagining his own burial and taking attendance. "Maybe that's why I still rent that apartment over the mortuary," Jason said. "It still feels like home."

Home never made that deep an impression on Terry. When his father sent him packing, he told himself the cursed ground was some-thing he'd always wanted to escape anyway. How could a place leave so strong an imprint that Jason didn't mind seeing the family business in the hands of strangers?

"All I know is Henry didn't do much work today," Terry said. He grinned, but was careful to keep his lips tight over his crooked teeth. They hadn't been brushed in days. Thick plague stained his incisors.

"You know why he drinks?" Jason asked.

"Didn't notice really," Terry said.

"Yeah, you did," Jason said. "The man smells like a brewery. You know why?"

Terry shook his head, wondered why the little man wanted to tell him this story.

"His son Ben was murdered over in Huntington years ago. He'd been selling dope in an abandoned apartment. Whoever killed him dismembered his body in an old claw-foot tub, rolled the pieces up in a rug and tried to burn them that night in a dumpster. Neighbors called the law over the smell."

"Why are you telling me this?" Terry asked.

Jason gave a shrug. "People see him drunk at noon and think he's just an old fool. I guess I wanted you to know so you wouldn't be too hard on him. I mean, Uncle Henry identified Ben by the Doc Martens still on his feet and a charred tattoo."

The lot of the Mega Drive-Inn was empty aside from a purple Geo Metro that resembled a dented egg. The car's owners, a man with gray hair pulled into a ponytail and a woman in a pair of white jean shorts, sat at one of the picnic tables beneath the billboard that served as the drive-inn's menu. The rest of the tables were empty, their sun umbrellas hanging at crooked angles while pigeons paced for dropped french fries. Cigarettes littered the lot, but the lack of customers left Terry wondering who'd smoked them all. This hadn't always been a mystery. The Mega Drive-Inn had stayed packed when Terry's father was still in school. Carloads of teenagers stopped to eat burgers before driving to where the blacktop ended.

"I'd rather go in than make these ladies run back and forth from the car," Jason said.

Terry shrugged and followed Jason past an old tin sign advertising Coca-Cola. The building itself didn't look large enough to contain even a kitchen but was spacious inside with a Formica lunch counter and a row of booths. Two waitresses sat smoking and sipping coffee while off in the opposite corner a few men circled a pool table outfitted in torn felt. They chalked the end of their cues, leaned on the poles in a way that made Jason think of bored soldiers with their rifles. A jukebox played country low enough for the sizzle and popping of grease in the kitchen to be heard along with the conversation of the fry cooks. When an old woman came to the counter with a notepad, Jason ordered three deluxe burger baskets to go. Terry removed some money from his pocket, but Jason shook his head.

"I got it," he said.

Terry watched the men play pool while they waited on the food. A shooter with skinny, scarecrow legs moved from shot to shot knocking all the solids in. Each time, he whispered the future before sending the cue ball rolling. "Three in the corner. Six in the side."

Money began to be displayed. Some of the onlookers tossed bills down on the rail and called out bets on the chances of this streak continuing. Terry watched their freedom with cash in a state of avarice. He couldn't fathom having enough money to risk some on chance. This went on until the waitress behind the counter called Jason's name, and he picked up the white paper bags gone nearly translucent with grease.

"This game legal?" Terry heard a voice ask as the front door swung wide. The men looked up from their game as Sheriff Thompson came in. Thompson turned toward one of the waitresses in her stained apron.

"We turn this place into a gambling den, Tilly?" he asked with a wide grin. "Cause if so, I want my cut." He let out a chuckle and bent at the force of his own joke. The men shooting pool smiled half-heartedly as he waved a hand their way.

"Go on with your game, boys," he said.

"Ready?" Jason asked, but Terry couldn't respond. He could feel his breath tighten, the pistol a sudden heavy secret warming his pocket. He slipped his hand inside, touched the handle and wasn't the least surprised that the wood felt alive. It could happen here. He could just pull it and kill Thompson in front of these hicks, slurping up the dregs of their milkshakes through straws. Better to let them all see and not live with the secret. It would alleviate the constant threat of being found out regardless of how far Gilbert took him from the hills.

Terry approached the table with a hundred-dollar bill. He held it up for the men, particularly Thompson, to see and laid it on the corner of the table.

"I got a hundred says he scratches before the eight ball," Terry said.

The men looked to one another to see if the intrusion could be tolerated.

"Coming over here just to bet against my friend?" said a man picking at his fried chicken basket. His pool cue lay forgotten across two chairs, a drumstick waving in his hand as he gestured. "Ain't polite to wanna see a man lose."

"I just wanna win some money," Terry said. "Everyone's been betting."

"Everybody over here are already friends," the man countered. He tugged on the corners of a long mustache and picked up his cue.

"Let him alone," Thompson said. "Boy's made things interesting."

The shooter rubbed chalk on the end of his cue. Up close, Terry saw a large black mole grew under his left eye. Once noticed, Terry found it hard to focus on anything else.

"Anybody wanna take the bet?" The shooter asked.

No takers. The man with the mole went back to prowling around the table, bent over at the far end and whispered, "Six ball, corner."

He sunk the six, dropped another in as well and lined up behind a peach shot where he could put either the ten or the two in the side pocket. The man took a deep breath and tapped the cue easy. It spun hard right, inched forward and sank the ten. He did the same with the two, moved to the end of the table and knocked the eight ball into the far corner pocket.

The shooter pocketed the money and took a seat while another player moved to replace him. Thompson let out a wolf whistle and patted Terry's shoulder.

"Better luck next time, son," he said.

TERRY SCARFED THE fries from the bag in his lap, shoveling each one into his mouth before he finished chewing the first. Seeing Thompson had left him feeling ravenous as soon as the initial fear subsided. He finished all the fries and had started on his burger before they were back on the road towards Fuller Street. Eating so quickly in front of a stranger was an embarrassment. Jason looked at his hollow cheeks and Terry could feel his pity over his malnourishment. If he wasn't careful, they'd begin to understand there was something more to his appearance than mere poverty.

"An entire day's pay just pissed away," Jason said. "Stupid thing to do."

Terry shrugged. "Wasn't enough anyway. I might as well have tried to make it more."

Jason let the truck drift to the side of the road. He lifted himself from the seat, retrieved his wallet from his back pocket, pulled out five twenties and tossed them at Terry. "Can't let you go home with no cash at all."

"You already bought lunch," Terry said.

"A man shouldn't have to work just for food."

Terry considered the money for a moment, then placed it in his pocket. "I just needed more," he said.

"For what?" Jason asked.

"Gotta take my dog to the vet." Terry pointed ahead to a wide spot beside the road. "You mind if I hop out here?"

"Why?" Jason asked. Downtown Lynch was far behind them and the road they traveled was nothing but woods for miles. "At least let me drive you back home."

"I've got somewhere else to be."

The lie didn't work. Jason turned in his seat to face Terry. "Uncle Henry says you ain't accepted a ride all week. Why can't you go home?"

Jason's eyes softened into a stare that could outlast any deflection. They would sit here in silence, soaked in the man's empathy until Terry confessed something. In hindsight, Terry realized Jason had been laying the groundwork for this all morning, establishing connections ever since he discussed his uncle's drinking and past days working at the funeral home. He felt manipulated, but also a little flattered someone wanted to know more. Terry didn't confide in anyone, not even Davey, but as much as he wanted free of these secrets, he understood burdens were a way of life and no venting, whether to holy idols or equally broken men could lift them from your back. Why this universal human need for communion anyway? Seeking solace in another only created a false hope that you'd be understood. People pretended because it was too hard to admit we're each trapped in our own shell, using imprecise words to try and express something unsayable. Telling Jason everything might allow a moment of clarity, but it wouldn't absolve him of his responsibilities to Ferris. In fact, putting Jason in danger would be all he really accomplished.

"My dad drinks. So, I'm staying with some friends."

"Where are these friends?" Jason asked. "I'll drive you to their place."

Terry opened the car door and stepped out. He considered turning away and climbing the hill, but instead rested his hands in the open window.

"I don't need you looking after me. You can cut that shit, cool?"

"If that's what you want."

Jason looked ready to say something else, but Terry turned and wandered off toward Lynch.

DAYS AFTER HIS evening with Jason, Terry crossed the bridge over a low creek towards Lynch High school. It was hard coming back here. Whatever rumors already circulated about him would be bad enough without some teacher he'd disappointed witnessing his sallow skin and the unwashed tangle of his hair. Without conformation, a few faculty members might still be willing to speak up in his defense.

Terry only slowed to linger beneath the statue of The Doughboy in the center of the plaza. The soldier was decorated with faded banners and imitation VFW flowers left over from Memorial Day. Garlands of real roses wilted by its large, bronze feet. His father always got sentimental over The Doughboy. He never served himself, but imagined a certain masculine comradery with soldiers. The shell-shocked eyes always made his father weep. The only time he allowed himself this weakness was when pontificating on the selflessness of heroic acts and talking about a grandfather Terry never knew. Apparently, he'd fought the Japanese during the big one. Terry's father seemed to think this alone excused all the grandfather's other heinous acts. Drunken beatings, whoring and late-night Hell-raising filled with a solid dose of racism that passed on to his son. Perhaps, Terry's father really wept because he'd never been a war hero, and in that line of thinking could never achieve true manhood. Terry didn't feel any intense emotion looking at the strange, childlike face of The Doughboy. The statue just represented another country child who'd been duped. Another kid sent to fight a war he didn't understand because they were born with no other options.

He continued downtown, trudged past Morris Furniture where the same dusty end tables and couches occupied the display windows. The Morris' kept the store open out of some sort of spite, a refusal to admit they no longer received any customers. Clive Morris stood outside the shop every day in his suit and tie like some battle-weary holdout refusing surrender. Across the street was the movie theater where Terry had seen his first films and kissed Larisa Welch, a girl who came east with her father, a man who broke horses and rode his paint to town every Sunday wearing a pearl white Stetson. The Welch's had gone back to Wyoming when the business failed. The two-screen theater no longer showed films, but that seemed proper. Terry no longer forced himself to kiss girls.

The empty storefronts he could abide, but the worst was the charred remains of the Aracoma Hotel. In the thirties, the hotel had been a luxurious spot where the coal company bosses threw parties in the ballroom or put up wealthy travelers for a few nights. During Terry's childhood, the lower floors and basement had been renovated to hold a few businesses to counteract the vacancies. He'd taken karate lessons in the ballroom from a fat sensei and gotten his hair cut in the barber shop visitors once used. He liked the haircuts especially, sitting in the high leather chair surrounded by varnished wood and the scent of pomade while men talked or read their papers.

Now the hotel was a burnt husk, only the north wall left partially standing and ready to collapse. Even though the fire had been a year ago, the city council had yet to have the debris cleared. Terry could see men walking through the ash, work coats zipped against a cold only they felt as each one bent and turned the ruined lumber, likely looking to sell one of the missed scraps of faulty copper wiring blamed for the blaze. It had all been collected in the first few days. He'd cashed some of it in himself.

The lot behind Harris Pharmacy sat empty aside from an abandoned Impala with one headlight and a tabby cat eating from a can of tuna someone set out. The stray's muscles tensed as it prepared to duck beneath the Impala's flat tires, but it went back to eating after Terry rested against the store's brick wall. Harris Pharmacy should have been busy like most mornings. Marcus Harris had run the place for over forty years until he suffered a stroke. His son owned it now and sold prescription pills under the counter, but discretion wasn't the younger Harris' strong suit. Complaints had gotten so bad that Sheriff Thompson began to drive by during business hours. For days, Terry watched the sheriff park in the lot of the pharmacy to conduct surveillance on his lunch break. Terry had taken to stalking with ease, bumming around downtown and making mental note of the places Thompson frequented. The sheriff's routine consisted of the same lazy patrol route, his nights spent parked near The Cat's Den as if proximity alone might trouble Ferris Gilbert's sleep. Darkness would have been easier, but Terry knew it couldn't happen near Ferris. The only other time the sheriff was guaranteed to be alone was during this long lunch hour.

Terry wasn't sure how long he waited. The day grew too hot for the denim jacket, but he didn't feel comfortable taking it off and stowing the gun in the back of his jeans. The cold metal gave him chills, and he feared the weapon might blow a hole in his ass. Just when he was ready to give in, Terry heard a car approaching. He stepped behind the dumpster as Thompson's cruiser pulled into the lot. The tires crunched over random litter before resting atop a half-full Styrofoam cup. Inside the cab, the sheriff adjusted his seat until his stomach was far enough away from the wheel to eat comfortably. Thompson took a chili dog from the paper bag resting on the dash. He unwrapped the grease-stained package and stuck one of the mustard slather buns in his mouth.

In twenty paces, Terry would be next to the window. Once he began moving, he would no longer have control of the situation. His feet might carry him right past the cruiser and back up the mountain. If that happened, Terry told himself he wouldn't question it. He'd accept his body's decision as a sort of salvation and let his feet lead where they liked, but by the time he was ten steps away, Terry realized this wouldn't happen.

The sheriff wiped his mouth with a napkin and flicked away a bit of coleslaw that fell on his shirt. The dirt on Terry's skin felt like real weight, the grime in his hair itching from days without a wash. These tactile distractions didn't slow him. He paused only for a moment at the passenger door. The hammer of the revolver didn't hang on the fabric of his coat as he drew it from his pocket and the sound of the metal barrel tapping the window glass left only a faint echo in his ears.

The first shot blew the glass out. The bullet struck the sheriff just below the collar, making Thompson drop the chili dog in his lap as he fell against the door. The second bullet entered below his armpit and the third missed completely. The final shot was the only one Terry aimed. He squeezed an eye shut and looked down the barrel until the rest of his vision blurred around the gun sight. He felt the tremble up his arm as the weapon recoiled. His eyes squeezed shut at the blast, sparing him the sight of Thompson's scalp disintegrating. When he opened both eyes, the top of the man's head had simply been removed. A perfect line of erasure as if it were expunged from existence.

If the act itself was something more witnessed than experienced, the aftermath was different. After the gun's report drifted away, Terry tried to run, but his legs wouldn't obey. He stood rooted in place by the car. The broken glass glittered inside the floorboards, small fires thrown on the upholstery that would soon be snuffed out as Thompson's blood pooled. The body lay limp against the door panel, vacant eyes wide. Terry stuffed the gun into his pocket and ran across the lot. He crossed the street, cut through an alley behind the Mountaineer Diner and kept going. Terry only stopped when he reached the tracks on the outskirts of town. The rails here had not yet gone to rust like those on Fuller Street and he could see smudges of copper where some kids placed pennies on the track. He picked up a flattened coin and rubbed the smooth metal between his fingers, marveling at the sort of change pressure caused. It seemed unfair force could bend something so solid.

The run had left Terry cold with sweat and his stomach gurgled as he sat down on the rail to catch his breath. He could keep going across the tracks and head towards Cherry Tree. Ferris had promised to take him anywhere he liked, and while Terry wanted to see the lights of Knoxville or Lexington, or at least a bit of land that lay flat as the coin in his palm, he knew he couldn't go there. The deputies would be running the roads, snatching up anyone who looked suspicious. Something inside told him to just follow the tracks.

Terry walked until the rails began to run parallel with a dirt road. Ahead of him set a yellow house shaded by close growing apple trees, their branches heavy with the weight of the small green spheres. Yellow jackets swarmed the fallen fruit in the yard. The insects emerged from the rotten pulp as if just born, their wings too sticky to take flight. Trees like these grew in his yard when Terry was young. His father had strung a hammock between their twisted trunks and lay outside all spring drinking beer while Terry played in the same spot until the grass died from his constant movements. The ground was rendered to dust that filled the joints of his action figures and made their battles like that of arthritic men instead of heroes. The power company cut the trees down before they could reach into nearby telephone lines. Terry never forgave them for it, or his father for not fighting harder for their shared space.

The yellow jackets left the yard to circle around Terry. Their bodies buzzing in vibration as they came close to his ears, threatening to gouge him with venomous stingers. A single insect landed on his sleeve for a moment, then flew away. An elderly woman came out on the front porch balancing on her cane.

"Can I help you?" the woman asked.

"I was just admiring your tree, ma'am."

"Ain't good for nothing but attracting bees," she said. "I used to can the apples, but now . . ."

Terry pointed to the low hanging fruit. "May I?"

"Help yourself."

Even on tiptoes, he was unable to reach. Terry wrapped his arms around the trunk and began to hoist himself up. He couldn't remember the last time he'd climbed a tree but was still swift as he pulled himself up into the split bough. Secure in the branches, Terry plucked two apples pitted like stones. The gun rattled in his coat pocket as he climbed down, but he didn't drop it. He walked to the porch and handed one of the apples to the old woman. She took tender bites as if her teeth might break against the skin. Terry ate slowly, the tart taste filling his mouth as he rested his legs. The moment might have been perfect, but the gun in his coat spoiled it.

"Can I use your phone?" he asked.

Inside, Terry could see it was the home of a widow. Everything perfectly preserved from another life and covered in a layer of dust. She sat him down on a couch and brought him the cordless. Terry was surprised that Ferris answered on the second ring.

"I'm ready for my ride," he said.

Ferris gave him the time and place.

COW CREEK WASN'T more than a stream of piss that separated the main road from the trailers on the other side of the water. The weak tributary wouldn't have warranted a name, but the local myth was that one of the earliest residents found a heifer frozen in a deep pool one December. The story didn't seem possible by the look of the creek. The water barely gurgled along, leaving most of the rocks in the center dry and cracked as if they hadn't been submerged in a decade.

Terry rested on the bank and waited on Ferris to arrive. His jean jacket lay folded across his lap, the gun absent from the pocket. He'd buried it on the side of the hill a quarter of a mile from the old woman's home using the revolver's snub nose as a spade. His fingernails were still packed with earth from covering the hole, so Terry dipped his hands in the shallows. The water felt slimy, but it was cool and soothing. The singing of cicadas freshly emerged from the ground surrounded him, their song rose and died away like an ocean tide in the trees. Further away, a car approached. The driver didn't pull off into the grass but stopped in the middle of the road. The window rolled down and Terry saw the pale man from The Cat's Den sitting behind the wheel. He looked out of place in the sleek sedan. His movements cautious as if afraid he might break something expensive.

"Come on," he called.

Terry stood but didn't approach the car. "Where's Ferris?"

"He's busy doing shit. Told me to give you a ride."

The driver gave a tubercular hack that shook his whole body. He wiped at his mouth with his sleeve and waved at Terry.

"Come on, man. It's a long-ass ride to wherever we're going, and I ain't feeling up to it."

Wind carried the wet moss scent of Cow Creek and the tang of the pines. The man was wrong. Something told Terry he wouldn't see the first filling station, much less any flat land. He took a step back without realizing it, then he turned and began crossing the stream, his legs submerged up to his knees.

"What the fuck?" the man shouted. "You'll soak the car, dumbass."

Terry was already on his way past the first trailer and up the hillside, concealing himself in the trees as he climbed higher.

CHAPTER SIX

BY THE TIME Huddles found out about Sheriff Thompson, he'd nearly receded from reality. The cycle of Education, Rec, and lights out was so dull he found it best to simply shut down, his body only responding in miniscule ways to his surroundings. He'd made it as long as he could without taking perks from staff, but the boredom became too much, and he finally asked to borrow a book from Education. Mrs. Miller, who taught English and science, lent him a worn copy of *The Day of the Locust*. Reading helped him block out the B-Unit boys' whispering.

They were all scared of him now. Even some of the guards. Everyone remembered Sheriff Thompson dragging him off the basketball court. After the murder, the other boys kept their distance. Huddles knew his brother was responsible. It probably would have happened sooner if Thompson hadn't worn a badge. Ferris had always been fearless, but this act crossed a different line. No amount of keeping his head down or Mitchum's legal maneuvering would get him out now. He resigned himself to the idea that B-Unit was his only future. It was easier to accept than he liked. Some part of him always knew he'd spend time inside.

After lunch Officer Fitzgerald came by the cell, told Huddles he had a phone call and escorted him across the main floor to a break area near A-Unit. The room was filled with the small measurements of freedom the officers left behind. Sir Hendricks' *Guns & Ammo* magazine lay spread open to a picture of a blonde with an assault rifle. Underneath, Huddles noticed another paperback called *The Pledge: Customs and Rituals of the Knights Templar*. There was more. A hot rod magazine with greasers in leather jackets and pompadours, tattooed rockabilly girls in gingham sporting Bettie Page haircuts as they sprawled across the hood of a '52 Chevy. The place smelled of aftershave and women's jasmine lotion, coffee and stale bread.

Officer Fitzgerald sat Huddles down at a desk and pushed the telephone forward. Even before the receiver was against his ear, Huddles could hear Mitchum wheeze over the line.

"Hello," Huddles said.

There was a phlegm filled cough and spit, then Mitchum's voice came out strong.

"Calling to check in," Mitchum said. "You keeping hard?"

"Sure." Huddles wanted to say more but kept it brief. The call was likely monitored.

His court hearing was scheduled for next Friday, and Huddles had a feeling that Counselor Beverly was going to try shipping him to a more secure facility. The prosecutor couldn't lay a charge on Ferris, but his family wouldn't go unpunished. The Sheriff's promise of Tiger Harris up north made the most sense. It housed a couple hundred kids and was known to have an active gang population. Huddles knew he'd go it alone even if he didn't last long.

"I got some news," Mitchum said. "It's gonna be rough to hear." Huddles could almost see Mitchum on the other end of the line, his wrinkled fingers playing with the phone cord as he tried to find the words. "Shane died last night. Got his head caved in by a Bradshaw boy."

Huddles thought about the last time he'd seen Shane. The trooper had pulled his friend from the back seat of the cruiser with those massive arms cuffed behind his back, the bald dome of Shane's head lowered as he spoke to Huddles through the window. He'd been so strong that night, Huddles couldn't imagine anyone possibly hurting him.

"How'd it happen?" he asked. "Tell me everything."

"There was a fight in the Commons. Shane was watching TV, and the next minute two guys are breaking his head open on the floor. By the time the guards pulled them off he was just about gone."

"They didn't take him to the hospital?"

"The administrator was away on vacation and couldn't be reached. The lieutenant didn't know what to do, so he laid in medical till morning. It wouldn't have mattered much."

Huddles tried to harden his heart against Shane. If Thompson had been telling the truth, then he'd done the right thing warning Ferris. If it was a bluff to make him inform, he'd gotten Shane killed for nothing. Either way, Huddles implicated himself in the loss.

"This could work out good for us," Mitchum said. "We just put the heavy stuff on him."

"You're the fucking attorney," Huddles said.

He hung up and signaled to Officer Fitzgerald that he was finished.

Counselor Felts visited him later that evening. Huddles knew he would eventually. While most of the staff avoided contact, Jason always sat in the back row of Education during Mrs. Miller's lessons and watched the B-Unit boys. Other staff members inside The Shell let their eyes drift away when Huddles looked at them, but Jason kept his locked. In some ways, Huddles admired it. Even with all the disrespect the officers gave him, Counselor Felts wasn't just some punk college kid. He walked the halls with boys twice his size and didn't carry a radio to summon officer assistance if things went bad. He was alone and accepted it.

Huddles wanted to be left in his cell to finish his book, but after a quiet knock Counselor Felts stood in the open doorway, one uneven shoulder resting against the frame and his hands shoved into the pockets of his slacks. It was a casual Friday, the rest of the non-security staff wearing jeans with their button downs, but Jason wore his cashmere overcoat despite the heat, black slacks and a blue checkered dress shirt unbuttoned at the throat. It had been a fine coat once, but the elbows were thinning and the lapels cut too wide to be in style. A once dignified garment but worn down.

"You have a moment to talk?" Jason asked. Huddles was still surprised by the gruff quality of his voice. Raw and cracking like someone with a two pack a day habit.

"I'm reading," Huddles said. He held the book up with his finger between the pages.

Jason stepped inside the cell. It was against regulation for counselors to enter alone, but Jason didn't seem to care. He appeared unshaken by the close confines and the dead air inside.

"I always liked that one," Jason said. "Not the happiest ending."

"Haven't got that far," Huddles said.

"Well, I don't think I'm spoiling anything."

"What do you want?" Huddles asked. He sat forward on the bunk, not exactly flexing, but a posture that telegraphed his annoyance.

"I wanted to say I'm sorry about your friend. I'm here if you want to talk about it."

The counselor seemed sincere, but something still felt condescending to Huddles. What made this withered man believe he had answers? What made him think he could come into what sufficed for Huddles' home and pretend to be able to provide succor for fresh wounds? For a moment, Huddles considered grabbing him by his threadbare coat and trying to put his face through the wall.

"Shane's dead," Huddles said. "Ain't much talking is gonna do about it."

"I just wanted to offer," Jason said. He was almost gone when Huddles shouted for him to wait.

"That's a fine coat," Huddles said. "You buy that in the kids' section?"

Jason's face stayed blank while Huddles smiled at him.

"I had it tailored years ago. That offer is open, Huddles. Whenever you need it."

CHAPTER SEVEN

It was Saturday before Terry remembered to take the medicine to Roscoe. He retrieved the antibiotics from under a loose board with the other stashed pills and began to toss supplies into a satchel for the hike down the mountain. It was stupid to venture out, especially home. This is how people get caught, he told himself. They run back to familiar places, go where someone could be watching, but even if that were true, the guilt over the dog was eating at him, his mind full of images of the mutt dying slow and unattended on the back porch.

Davey stirred from his place by the stove. He rolled over and watched Terry fill a canteen from their jug of water.

"What are you doing?" he asked.

"I forgot about Roscoe," Terry said. He took a sip and submerged the canteen again until water swelled over its rim.

"I'm sure he's fine."

"You don't remember how bad it was," Terry replied. "That goddamned ear was half-off."

"Just chill out. Another hour won't make any difference."

Davey rose, stretching his body in a waking ritual that involved scratching and exaggerated yawns. Most mornings this was endearing. Terry liked to watch the way the bigger man shuffled around in nothing but underwear and socked feet. He found something sexy in the disheveled hair, morning breath and languid movements, but Terry shrugged away when Davey tried to pull him close. Terry knew it would have been better if he could linger a moment, wrap his arms around Davey and promise he'd be right back, but too many secrets lay between them. He needed to move quickly before Davey woke enough to register his fear. All it would take were soft fingers running through his hair, eyes locked with his own and the plea for an answer. After something like that, Terry knew he'd abandon all the lies.

Terry gave Davey's hand a final squeeze and slung the canteen over his shoulder as he stepped outside. A strong wind knocked acorns atop the cabin's roof with a sound like artillery fire. The barrage continued until Terry wondered if a single nut remained clinging on the trees. A few squirrels scurried across the roof to collect the fallen bounty.

Once his eyes adjusted and the light lessened from a bright orange flare, Terry started down the mountain. The grass was still damp from days of rain. The fallen leaves had soaked up the moisture, becoming soggy under his shoes instead of their usual brittle crunch. They stuck to his soles and made his feet lose traction until he clung to the nearby trees to anchor his descent. Terry cursed himself the whole way down. The dog had been too loyal for such mistreatment. He could remember the way Roscoe looked as a pup, big paws and a head too large for his body, bounding about the yard on spindly legs that might look more natural attached to a fawn. Terry couldn't even make out the color of the dog's coat when he'd left it at home, all the marbled details of red brindle obscured by the slick sheen of drying blood.

The creek had swelled. Rapids broke over the few jagged rocks that usually baked in the shallows during summer. The current wouldn't be strong enough to wash him away, but the rocks underneath his feet could only be felt, not seen. Even in the driest climate they stayed slick with moss. Any spill could cause him to lose the pills. Terry stood on the bank and mentally mapped a path that took him through the weakest of the white water. He stepped out and his feet found solid rock underneath. The current plowed into his thighs, its force making him teeter and take steps left that lengthened his advance, but he managed to stay upright until the bottom dropped out at the center and he found himself submerged to the armpits, hands held high to protect the pills in their cellophane bag. He made it to the other side and rested on a large rock to catch his breath.

His shirt had begun to dry from the sun by the time Terry reached his father's house. Only his sneakers still squished, water leaking from them with each step. A new fence sectioned off their land from the hillside and the neighbor's lot. Nothing elaborate, just simple stakes with two strands of wire running around the yard in an attempt to keep the woods from overtaking the property. The house still needed fresh paint and the front steps bowed up like fish flapping on a dry bank. Terry looked to the towering patch of sycamores by the fence. Most days their pale bark had been the only thing visible outside the kitchen window.

The stench of chicken shit filled the air. The neighbors kept nearly twenty fighting cocks in small tents built from scrap metal and mining curtain. Other fowl resided in large blue plastic barrels that had been cut vertically down the middle and laid horizontal for the birds to huddle inside. His family's chicken coop set in the corner of the yard with the roof collapsed. Inside, the few remaining feathers from their dead Rhode Island Reds littered the ground. There was something about the place, a reaction as soon as Terry bent and slid under the fence that made him feel the old familiar ache he'd been able to deny at a distance. As much as he was glad to be out from under the trees hovering like sentries and the watchful eyes of his father, he felt the tug of the old house. Something inescapable about those few cramped rooms, as if the walls knew he would never truly leave them, that each attempt to do so would only be another exodus without arrival. No other place would ever feel proper.

There were no signs of a strange car. Nothing to announce Gilbert's presence. Still, Terry moved cautiously across the patches of clover that bloomed where weeds didn't dominate. It didn't mean the man wasn't inside, a pistol pressed to his father's temple. He was already too far in to escape, standing in the weeds that sprouted especially strong around the dog house out back. Roscoe's shelter hadn't been the shapely store-bought replica of a home with a steeple roof, but a flat-topped box with no front wall. Terry could see the dog wasn't inside and the sight of it empty made him sick to his stomach. Perhaps the dog already passed, but no fresh grave mound filled the yard.

His father stood on the back porch. He wore one of his work shirts, the sleeves rolled up to bare forearms scarred from years of welding in short sleeves. A faded blue cap pulled low over his eyes, the bill twisted from all the times it had been stowed in the back pocket of his jeans. Terry watched as he removed the hat, wiped at his thinning hair and pulled it back on. His father seemed older than when he'd last seen him. The bags under his eyes dark as if filled with polluted water. Terry was surprised no beer rested between his feet.

"Did he die?" Terry asked.

"I've been seeing to him."

Terry staggered up the steps. His father seemed prepared to reach out if he fell, but no other move to embrace him was made. Inside the kitchen, a trail of ants stretched from the windowsill to the sink. The miniature army marched through the grime on the countertop toward the stagnant dish water. Terry watched as the first insect hit the suds and waited to see if the others would follow.

"In here on the couch," his father said.

Roscoe lay propped upon a mass of pillows. The dog's muzzle was crisscrossed with scabs, his jowls swelling until he couldn't properly close his mouth and a dry tongue lolled out on the pillows like some bizarre fetus. Terry could see his father had sewn the left ear back together with white dental floss. A thick yellow puss oozed out, drying in the matted fur. Roscoe didn't look up when Terry came in. Just continued to whine with his eyes closed, not even offering a twitch from the nub of his tail.

"I thought I might shoot him the first night," Terry's father said. "But the next morning he was still alive, and he ate a little."

Roscoe's head lay propped upon several feather pillows. Terry's mother bought them when he was a boy, and he could remember her pretending she liked them despite the way the feathers shifted and let her head sink whenever she slept on them. His mother was born poor, but always aspired to finer things. It surprised Terry she'd stayed with his father long enough to die broke.

"You think he'll make it?" Terry asked.

His father had gone into his shirt pocket for a pinch of Redman. "I'd give him fifty-fifty." He plugged his gum with a thick wad of the tobacco.

"I brought something for him." Terry took the pills out of his pocket and handed one to his father. "These are for the infection. Best give him two doses to really get it in his system."

His father took the pills in his palm. "These all you have?" he asked.

Roscoe kicked his back feet as he dreamed. Terry placed his fingers on the dog's muzzle and it gave another low whine. The skin felt hot under his hand.

"You fucked up proper this time," his father said. "Only a desperate man fights a dog this old."

"I ain't desperate."

"Well, you sure don't seem to be in high cotton."

His father's face softened until the wrinkled forehead and tight skin of his cheeks went slack. It was the same as when they worked the carpentry jobs or hoed the small garden they used to keep in the back-yard. His father would ride him, his comments cutting deeper and deeper with each mistake until Terry was broken down like an old rabbit-eared shotgun. Then his father would give the same tired apologies.

"I ain't outdoors," Terry said.

"I suppose that's something."

The dog began to stir. A tiny whimper emitted from its closed snout. Terry laid a hand on the cuts, felt the heat roiling off the fur and scratched gently between Rosco's eyes.

"A man came by looking for you," his father said.

"What sort of man?" Terry asked, but he already knew. The pale man Ferris had sent to pick him up. Squished face and tiny eyes glaring at him from inside the car.

"Big older guy. Gut like a fucking bear and pale as a ghost. You in trouble again?"

His father leaned forward, elbows resting on his knees. Terry knew he was trying to read his face, staring at him hard until he cracked and admitted everything as if he were still seven years old. The trick always worked, and Terry still felt the old desire to unburden himself, to just lay all the fear at his father's feet, cry and tell him how much he needed help. In that moment, there seemed to be nothing else that would offer the same feeling of salvation, but Terry wouldn't let himself. Even if his father was partly responsible for his troubles, he wouldn't bring him into it.

"No," Terry said. "If he comes back, you tell him you haven't seen me. Tell him we don't talk anymore."

"What's he want with you?" his father asked. "If he's laid a finger on you, I'll fucking kill him."

"I owe him some money. It's nothing serious."

Terry went back to petting the dog. Its whole body twitched, muzzle curling back to expose teeth as some quarry remained elusive in his dream.

"Why don't you come on home and look after him?" his father said. "I've just got the one rule."

If he stayed here, it would put his father in danger. Even if the man had never been much to him, Terry didn't think he could allow that. Besides, any real reconciliation was unlikely. Soon enough he would be back to sneaking out with Davey, back to crawling in late stoned. Any rule, especially his father's one, had always been too much for him.

"No, I'll be going," Terry said. He nodded toward the pills. "Are you sure you can get him to take them?"

"Yeah, I'll wrap them in cheese or something."

"Peanut butter," Terry said. "He likes you to roll them up in some peanut butter."

"You need anything before you go?" his father asked. "Those boots you used to wear are in my closet."

"I'm fine." Terry looked one last time on them both and knew he could walk out. "Be seeing you," he said.

His father didn't stop him as he went out the front, but Terry heard another whimper from the dog. The sound seemed to follow him until he cleared the yard, walking fast down the street back in the direction of his shack, the sun still high and hot as dust collected in his lungs.

THE GAS STATION near the mortuary was the only place that would sell cigarettes to the underage. Terry used this as an excuse to stop and buy a pack of menthols. The man who sold them to him was so elderly he seemed immortal, without beginning or end. Terry imagined he could still be manning the register with the note card stating No CREDIT, No DEBIT, JUST CASH centuries later. After paying, Terry lingered near the outdated pumps with their dial displays and smoked. Davey liked to chastise him for the habit. He claimed the menthol taste was created by fiberglass fragments cutting into the lungs, but it still felt good to inhale deeply and watch the lights go out across the street.

The funeral home's garage door began a slow descent on its mechanical track. Terry watched as the undertaker ducked underneath and came outside into the cool air. The mortician climbed into his Pontiac and sat loosening his tie, folding his blazer in the passenger seat. Apparently, the new owners didn't live above their work. The mortician looked in a hurry to get away. Terry wondered if there might be a woman at home waiting to be caressed by hands that spent all day touching dead flesh. He supposed it was no different than being a butcher. Probably less gruesome than a fisherman skewering live bait on hooks.

He'd justified the trip to the mortuary by deciding to steal some embalming fluid. Davey once told him they could remain in a state of hallucination for days by dipping cigarettes in formaldehyde. It was a poor excuse. His only experience with hallucinogens had been a bad time with a girl named Deloris who looked like she combed her mane of red hair with topsoil. Terry had still been trying to convince himself he wanted girls in those days, so they'd sat under the shade of an oak and ate a bag of mushrooms. Terry puked twice before the drugs took hold. The only pleasant memory was the racket of night birds in the trees, their immense sound stunting reality until he touched Deloris' hair and the stiff fibers brought him out of the daze, leaving him sober and lonely. She was the last woman he'd touched that way. Even if Terry had been prepared to go further, Deloris seemed to understand and told him they didn't have to continue. It had made him wonder if it was that easy for people to know.

Terry hadn't said anything about the murder, but he sensed Davey suspected something. No matter how hard Terry tried to seem normal, he worried his reactions gave him away. The previous night, he'd awakened crying and when Davey pulled him close it took everything inside not to recoil. The embrace felt suffocating, vise tight as if those arms might extract all truth. It wasn't an urge to confess necessarily, just the feeling that something was tugging him, some urge pulling him to look at the body and see just what was left after the mortician's magic. Once the Pontiac drove away, he took a final drag and pitched the cigarette.

Terry crossed the street and located a small window on the far side of the building. It was locked, but he pushed hard and the weak wooden frame splintered, allowing the glass to slide up enough for him to squeeze his head and shoulders through. He would have fallen inside on his face, but the hearse was parked close enough for him to grab the fender, his fingers slipping until he wiggled inside. Terry leaned against the hood while his eyes adjusted to the darkness. Despite his curiosity, the idea of opening the morgue made him sick. He'd only ever seen the dead prepared and looking more like wax figures of the departed than their empty vessels. It would be different on the slab. Bullets wounds alone would keep the body from appearing at rest.

The morgue was in the far corner of the room behind a steel door hung with heavy hinges. The door was thicker than Terry expected and, to his continued surprise, unlocked. Inside everything was stainless steel counters and tabletops, wooden cabinets with glass fronts holding large dark bottles. A simple cotton sheet draped over Sheriff Thompson. The shroud did nothing to camouflage the reality of what was underneath. When Terry pulled the sheet down, the face didn't resemble the one he'd seen through the windshield just days ago, burnt red by the sun's glare and moistened with sweat that trickled from the receding hairline. The only thing left to let him know it was the same man was the neat hole through the right eyebrow. Terry's fingers seemed to want to bore into that small recess, to feel the hollow space and understand what he was seeing was real. He could remember Thompson in the diner, joking with the pool players and offering belly laughs to the full room. Guilt didn't flood him. It seemed like something that had happened to a stranger.

Terry began to rummage through the cabinets for chemicals. He didn't know what he was looking for, didn't know where it was kept or what the container would look like. After peering under the sheet, the smooth glass of the bottles in his hand felt false.

Something moved on the other side of the door. Terry hunkered down below the cabinets as the sound of footsteps came closer.

"Who's in there?" a voice called. The light filtering in through the cracked door eclipsed as someone moved past it, and there came the unmistakable sound of a shotgun pumping a round into its chamber. Terry tried to silence his breath.

"I'm not asking again," a man said.

Terry swallowed to wet his voice. "I'm coming out," he called.

Terry stepped out with the bottles clutched tight to his chest like glass infants. The garage lights had been turned on, so his eyes strained a moment in the glare. Jason Felts stood wielding a shotgun almost as long as his body. Terry thought the recoil of the weapon would likely knock him down. His hair lay in a mass of dark tangles and his pale skin seemed slathered with a layer of sweat that made him almost glow in the light. The barrel stayed trained on him, but Terry could see the surprise on Jason's face.

"What the fuck are you doing here?" Jason asked. He pointed the barrel at the floor.

Terry sat down on the cold concrete. The bottles clinked together, making a musical note in the silence.

"What are you doing with those?" Jason asked.

"You can get high with them," Terry said.

Jason lowered himself down and spread the gun across his thighs. Without the barrel in his face, Terry observed Jason's torso. He was surprised again by how conventional it seemed. It was really only the man's legs that were stunted, not stopped in their growth like chopped vines, but miniature versions of what they might have been.

"How bad is it?" Jason asked.

Terry averted his eyes. "Not bad."

"Well, I wish you'd have come to me."

Terry scoffed. Why should he come to Jason for anything? Just because he said some kind words once? Such gullibility in a man who had to go around craning his neck at strangers seemed ridiculous.

"I'm sorry you had to see that," Jason said after a moment.

At first Terry wasn't sure what he meant, then realized Jason was staring into the morgue. "Do they have him all opened up?"

"No," Terry said. "It was still pretty bad."

"I can imagine. When I was little, my cousin and I came down here once and looked in on a body. They had them all cracked open. We could see inside."

Jason rubbed the gun's stock, fingers circling as if the fiddling could keep the power of his memory away.

"We knew her before. Seeing them like that, it makes you wonder." He wiped the sleep from his eyes. "Did you ever meet the sheriff?"

"No," Terry said.

Jason stood, rested the shotgun in the crook of his arm and offered Terry his hand. "Come on," he said.

Jason pulled him up. Terry left the bottles on the floor, followed him to the garage door where Jason pushed a button and the door rattled up on its track.

"Go home," Jason said. "Don't come back."

HE SHOULD HAVE followed Jason's advice and gone home, but Terry followed the tracks to Fuller Street. The electricity was back on, but at such a late hour the neighborhood had the same desolate look as weeks before. All the windows gone dark and the yards vacant. It was reckless to be here. Being released after having a shotgun aimed at him wasn't the sort of reprieve he was likely to get again, but anger made him ignore his better judgment. Just one house. Five minutes and he'd be back up the hillside.

Terry passed Mrs. Frasier's and crossed the tracks to the other side of the street where Glenn Hobart's house sat alone by the main road. He stopped beside the chain-link fence, surveying the yard to see if Hobart's little Jack Russell Terrier was outside. When he was sure there was no dog to start yipping, Terry hopped the fence. The chain link clanked together as he moved low around the house, opened the screen door, covered his fist with his sleeve and punched a portion of glass out of the back door. The shards cut into his hand as he groped for the lock. Inside, he moved through the dark corridors without bothering to staunch the flow or wipe up the dripping trail.

Terry searched the closet in the bathroom first, knocking toilet paper and folded towels onto the floor. Droplets of blood bloomed across the cloth. He went to the mirrored medicine cabinet and poured through the contents, searching the labels. Medicine for high cholesterol and pills to aid in sleep, but nothing worth the trip. Outside, he heard the sounds of a siren and tires pulling up Hobart's empty drive. Terry sat on the closed toilet seat. He could barricade the door and arm himself with a shard of the broken mirror, but he was too tired for that. Better to go out and meet them.

Two state troopers were waiting when he stepped outside onto the porch. One stood by the door with his gun drawn. The second trooper leaned against the hood of his cruiser in the driveway, arms folded over his chest and eyes obscured under the wide brim of his hat.

The first trooper holstered his gun. "You got anything in your pockets?" he asked.

"No, sir," Terry said.

The trooper took the cuffs out of a leather pouch on his belt and opened them until Terry could count the teeth on the metal sickle. "Put your hands behind your back."

The officer snapped on the bracelets and patted him down as he read his rights.

Terry made a good case for the emergency room in the back seat of the cruiser. He squeezed his fist tight to coax the flow from his wound and offered up a full palm to the officers, but they brought him inside The Shell dripping past the intake desk. An officer took down his information before they rushed him back to medical. The hand wasn't much concern to Terry. The gash was fairly shallow, already beginning to clot before the doctor made the first stitch. He'd just wanted to avoid incarceration for a few more hours.

Medical's walls were pristine white. The exam table covered with a fresh roll of paper that crinkled underneath him as he shifted. Everything smelled of antiseptic, but none of this quelled Terry's fear. Every time the doctor spoke in his quiet voice, Terry feared a confession would pour out of him. No one knew he'd been at the funeral home and even if Jason called it in, there was no reason to suspect he'd broken in for anything but the chemicals. The arrest at Hobart's house helped make him look like nothing more than another addict. All this reasoning should have calmed him, but Terry felt sure they would find out about the sheriff. His stomach felt like someone had replaced his last meal with rocks.

The doctor remained patient even though Terry squirmed each time the needle descended. He closed his eyes, opened them later to see a row of stitches bisecting his palm.

The doctor looked in his mouth with a light.

"When was the last time you ate?" he asked.

"Yesterday," Terry said.

He stripped to his underwear, embarrassed at the prominence of his thin ribs. The doctor pressed the cold metal of the stethoscope to Terry's back and told him to breathe.

"The officers told me they haven't been able to reach your father," the doctor said. "Do you know where he is?"

Terry imagined his father slumped on the couch next to Roscoe, a beer still clutched in his sleeping hand or teetering on his knee. The front door would be ajar, the phone ringing out into the night while some state trooper came up the dirt drive to tell him about his son. This was the fantasy he could allow himself. The other involved his father's brains smeared across the kitchen table, a second bullet blown through the collapsed dome of skull just to be certain.

"I don't know," Terry said.

"Would you like to talk about that?" the doctor asked.

He wanted pills. Anything the doctor might have in his cabinets. After the exam ended, they'd walk him down the hall and stick him in a little room until court. The only thing that would make that tolerable would be the right kind of high.

"I'm just not feeling well," Terry told him.

The doctor removed the stethoscope and listened while Terry lied about fabricated aches. The doctor let him lie, just nodded his head from time to time, exhaled on his wireframe glasses and cleaned them with the tail of his white coat.

"I'm going to prescribe you something to help the first few days," the doctor said as he jotted notes in a folder. "It will be very hard at first, but you'll manage."

Terry ran his fingertips over the knotted ridge of thread in his palm. It looked as if the upper portion of his hand came from another boy, a patchwork conglomerate of flesh instead of being whole. On the way to medical, Terry had watched a boy in one of the holding cell scream and throw his body into the glass wall. The noises he'd made never came close to producing words.

"What's wrong with the little boy in the holding cell?" Terry asked.

The doctor rubbed his eyes. "A lot."

"Is he always like that?" Terry asked.

"The guards have to restrain him often."

If the guards didn't reach his father, Terry would be going to court without him. His mind darkened, the scenario of a drunk dozing on the couch and crime scene replaced with an empty house where Roscoe waited on the porch, the only sign his father's truck ever existed a puddle of oil soaking into the driveway. His father might be wrapped around a tree on a back road, or asleep with a cooler of melting ice, his truck's tires bogged down in a muddy ditch. Either way, his father wouldn't bring the dog with him, and Roscoe was probably still too sick to take care of himself. He could be trapped inside the house or left outside too weak to jump the fence and search for food.

"They're not letting me out of here without my father, are they?" Terry asked.

The doctor seemed burdened by all the questions. "If you don't have anyone to be released to, then the state will keep you here."

"I need somebody to go by the house and see about my dog," Terry said.

"Not my concern," the doctor said and adjusted his stethoscope.

CHAPTER EIGHT

HUDDLE'S STOMACH SEIZED up on him after breakfast, so during Recreation he sat against the wall reading while the others played basketball. Woods and the skins were ahead since Callan joined their team. Aside from what seemed like an internal targeting system, Callan wasn't the best all-around player. He moved too slow up the court and there was no flash to his dribble, but he never missed inside the paint. A few boys tried to drag Huddles into the game, but he just waved them away. As his court date approached, he'd been waking in the middle of the night with a convulsion in his guts like some live thing wanted out. Listening to Fitzgerald and the other guards talk about the new boy's arraignment hadn't helped. Huddles overheard Hendricks saying the kid broke down when his father wasn't there, that his knees buckled, and he had to be carried from the courtroom screaming something about a dog. Huddles saw him after he returned to The Shell. The kid looked hammered flat and refused to talk to anyone during chow.

Now, the new kid paced the outskirts of the court in a lent pair of facility sneakers. A thousand boys must have stuck their feet inside those shoes. The aglets were absent from the frayed strings and the tongues hung limp, flopping against the boy's ankles with every step. His feet seemed ready to split the sides as the rubber soles squeaked on the hardwood. Eventually, the boy slid down on the floor near Huddles and began to pull the shoes off.

"Damned things are too tight," he muttered.

Huddles marked his book with a finger. "Call your people and have them send you some. You're allowed to have your own for Rec."

The boy shook his head.

"Whatever, man." Huddles opened his book. He was halfway down the page when the boy spoke again.

"They still haven't found my dad," the boy said.

Huddles wasn't sure why the boy would share this. Stoic silence in the face of any problem was an unspoken requirement of The Shell, but something about the boy's need to vent was endearing. If nothing else, Huddles realized they were on the verge of a real conversation. He hadn't had anyone say something of substance since he'd been inside where everything was threats or subterfuge. It made him miss his long talks with Shane.

"Any idea where he'd be?" Huddles asked.

"I don't know. He drinks."

Too much honesty. The kid would never survive if he remained so transparent. Still, Huddles felt a pang of empathy. In his earliest memories, he'd watched Ferris drink, smoke and snort into the wee hours and been frightened. He'd gone so far as to hide bottles when his brother passed out. It made him wonder when exactly the change occurred. When did he stop trying to lead his brother away from a destructive path and start participating? Huddles picked up one of the boy's discarded shoes. The stitching was so rotten he could have pulled them apart with his fingers.

"You can't wear this shit," Huddles said.

The boy took the shoe from him. "Nothing else to wear."

"Wait till they're cutting an ingrown toenail out. You'll wish you hadn't."

The boy chewed his lip as he slipped the shoes back on and struggled with the laces. His right hand was wrapped in a stained dressing that wouldn't allow him to get a decent grip on the strings.

"What happened?" Huddles asked.

"Cut it on some glass." The boy gave up on using both hands. He pinched the strings between his index and middle finger while trying to adjust the slack with an awkward thumb.

"Won't be able to play with that mitt anyway," Huddles said.

"I'm ambidextrous." The boy managed to form an X with the strings but couldn't thread a lace through the gap. "You ain't playing?" he asked.

"My stomach's been seizing up on me," Huddles said. Later, he'd recognize this as his first admission of weakness inside and wonder how the kid pried it from him.

"It's that meatloaf."

On the court, Robison stole the ball from Callan. He passed it to Woods who, true to form, bricked it off the backboard. One of the young scrappers from A-Unit snatched the rebound and traveled up court for an easy layup. The fight was going out of the skins, most of them bent over like saplings heavy with snow, hands resting on their knees as they sucked air.

"What are you reading?" The boy asked.

"Just something I've finished a time or two before. You going out on the court or not?"

The boy gestured to his shoes. "I can't feel my fucking toes."

Huddles unlaced the Air Jordans that one of the dancers brought him. "Take mine."

"What about you?" the boy asked.

"I'm reading."

The boy shook his head. "No thanks."

The refusal annoyed him. Huddles wanted the boy gone so he could be left alone with his book, but he also wanted to perform some act of kindness. Not only because the boy looked so pathetic. Huddles needed generosity to still exist inside a place like The Shell.

Huddles stopped untying his left shoe and held its right mate out to the boy. "You wanna play, just take the shoes."

"I appreciate it," the boy said. "It's just, I heard stories about favors here." He kicked the old shoes aside and slid the new pair on. Huddles watched him feel for his toes with a swollen thumb.

"This is kid jail," Huddles said. "You'll have to wait a few years for the blow jobs in exchange for cigarettes scene."

The boy grinned as he tugged on Huddles' shoes. "Good to know."

"Rumor is you got snatched up for breaking into houses on Fuller Street," Huddles said.

"Who says?"

"Just what I heard," Huddles took a good look at the boy. Small and skeletal, skin ashen with eyes receding back into his skull. He didn't look like a burglar, just a derelict in need of a meal. Huddles reminded himself of Malcolm screaming in the Holding Cell. All the proof he'd ever need that looks could be deceiving. "What were you doing in there?"

"I'd rather not say."

"I'd rather have shoes," Huddles said. "Least you can do is be polite and answer my question."

"I was looking for pills."

Huddles nodded. "Much dope in those old ladies' houses'?"

"Sometimes," the boy said.

The boy still struggled with the strings, so Huddles sat his book aside to help. He worked quickly, trying to keep the others from seeing. It was one thing to lend the shoes, it was too close to supplication to be seen sliding them on another boy's feet. Huddles made a sloppy job of it, the uneven bows hanging low to be trod under the soles. Still, he double knotted the strings so they wouldn't come undone. The boy stood and tried a few steps. Huddles sat the facility sneakers next to his book, its spine bent into a steeple.

"Thanks again," the boy said.

"Just don't scuff them up."

"My names Terry Blankenship," the boy said. He offered his mutilated hand before exchanging it for his left.

"Harrison Gilbert," Huddles said as he took the hand. "People call me Huddles."

A shudder traveled just underneath the surface of Terry's face. It was so faint that the moment after it was over, Huddles couldn't even be sure he'd seen it. Another one that's afraid of me, Huddles thought. It wasn't a bad thing, especially inside, but Huddles grew weary of having all relationships based on fear. Even Shane had been more subordinate than friend. Just once, he'd have liked someone to respect him for more than his name.

Terry stared at the new shoes on his feet, eyes no longer making contact with Huddles, then pulled his shirt off and ran out on the court, stopped to speak with Woods for a moment before getting into the game and covering Callan. Huddles watched Terry move fast, the pain in his stomach subsiding as the boys boxed in and the sound of the dribbling ball beat a staccato rhythmic while they hustled. Terry's lank arms reached around Callan's chest to swat the ball from his grasp. Woods goosed boys and gave little shots with his elbows. Even without being on the court, Huddles felt something peaceful in the movements, beauty in the descending arch before the ball crashed through the net. The trance only broke when Officer Fitzgerald walked over, covering him in shadow.

"Counselor Beverly wants a word," Fitzgerald said.

HE ALWAYS KNEW Counselor Beverly would come at him, but Huddles expected it to be heavy. The sort of therapist that sits behind the desk more cop than shrink, each inquiry nothing more than a spade to dig a bit deeper until they know just what to exploit. His brother warned him about such things. So, when he sat down in the interview room with Counselor Beverly, Huddles didn't let the dark eyes and ponytail soften him. It was Counselor Felts sitting beside her and cracking his knuckles that surprised him. He'd expected her to be alone.

Beverly produced a small yellow notepad and gave a tight-lipped smile. Huddles didn't return it. He knew her reputation. One of the better counselors, used to seeking out quiet ones during the slower hours.

"Would you mind if Counselor Felts sits in on your session?" Beverly asked. "You have the right to say no if you wish."

"It's fine," Huddles said.

"I'd like to start with how you've been adjusting." Beverly placed pen to paper. "Care to discuss how things have been?"

"Not too bad."

"How have you spent any free time?" she asked.

"Reading."

Huddles had developed a ritual of reciting *The Day of the Locust* aloud in the hours just before lights out. The book's passages seemed to be more effective then Ferris' techniques of thought control and regulated breathing. Whenever he recited the conclusion, the sound of his voice became soothing, yet alien. Some nights it was like another person speaking in the cell. The pages actually seemed to transport him, to allow him to slip under and come back to himself saying the words, but unaware of how long it had been. It might have been seconds or hours. The concept of time was as lost as if he'd been sedated. The practice kept his mind off Malcolm's squalling from holding.

"How has Education been?" Beverly asked. "Mrs. Miller seems to think you're bored with the work. Do you feel like the assignments aren't challenging?"

Education consisted of the B-Unit boys struggling to read *The Berenstain Bears* or being unable to concentrate long enough to solve long division. Mrs. Miller did her best with the curriculum, but she wanted to teach real literature to a bunch of kids who had no idea who Edgar Allan Poe was, much less the will to sit and listen to her long-winded discussions on symbolism in "The Raven." Huddles sat in the back and tried to look busy, but the old bitch was too crafty to believe it took him thirty minutes on basic arithmetic. She was drawn to him the way doctors are drawn to bright eyes in the triage ward. Anyone you can save helps.

"It's not too bad," he said.

Beverly tapped her pen harder at his silence, but Jason wasn't cracking. He sat waiting, hands flat on the table until his long fingers stretched like the tentacles of some squid. The clean nails almost a presentation for inspection.

"I'd like to talk about what happened to Grady," Beverly said.

"That little bitch with the crutches? What about him?"

"You were present. I'd like to hear your feelings about it."

Huddles knew she wanted a moment of hard-assed desensitization, something that showed the flaws in his wiring for her case file, or solid empathy. Neither felt like the truth. It hadn't bothered him to see Malcolm bash Grady with that crutch or to know that Grady had been admitted to the hospital in Lynch with a wired jaw, his brain swelling until the fissures in his skull were ready to crack. He'd been impressed by Malcolm. The way he could scream all night, never tiring regardless of how many times they restrained him. Huddles wanted that sort of resolve. He wanted to be beyond all the facade and street level hardness. Malcolm didn't care about the confines of incarceration, didn't care if he were born as bat-shit crazy mountain trash. Malcolm didn't care about anything. Huddles envied the freedom of that apathy.

"My feelings are don't fuck with that kid," he said. "He seems to be giving you all a run for your money."

"Does he frighten you?" Jason asked. His gravel laced baritone sounded startling from such a small body.

"I just want him to shut up at night," Huddles said. It was the first complete lie he'd told. Huddles watched Beverly write it in her pad like he'd revealed an absolute truth.

THE NEXT MORNING, Sir Hendricks found a solution regarding Malcolm. Woods saw it when he came back from a trip to the dentist, the nubs of his front teeth refurbished with porcelain veneers. The new smile made his words seem false as he reported the news to the other boys.

"They got him watching movies," Woods said as the boys lined up for Education. Each stood an arm's length from the one in front, hands shaped in the pattern of a diamond against the small of their backs as Officer Fitzgerald herded them forward.

"What do you mean?" Huddles asked. He tried to keep his voice low, but Woods was hard of hearing. All the huffed gasoline had eaten holes in his brain. Rumor was he could distinguish high test from regular unleaded just by the smell.

"They've got a TV rolled out into the hall and are playing cartoons. They said he was watching Batman."

Earlier, Malcolm had been on another rampage, tearing the pages out of his books and stuffing all the paper into the toilet, flushing until water filled his cell. The flood leaked into the hall until Control began lining their door with towels to stop the flow. The Special Response Team, or SRT, suited up to go in and restrain him. Woods said that Malcolm was laughing as he pissed out the bean hole at them, his tiny prick pinched between two fingers and sending a stream that didn't do much more than trickle down the doorframe. They breached and cracked his head like always. Malcolm fell limp with euphoria as they secured him.

Officer Fitzgerald came by and leaned in close enough for Huddles to smell the coffee on his breath.

"Huddles, shut up in line, or I'll have you in the holding cell next door," he said.

"Cool by me," Huddles said. "Shit, I like Batman."

Fitzgerald shook his head until his jowls jiggled. "I like you, Huddles. You're a funny guy, but I will fuck you up. Understand?"

The line moved across the main floor and into Education where the boys spilled into their desks while Mrs. Miller wrote on the blackboard. Terry took the seat next to Huddles. Lending the shoes was beginning to look like a mistake. As soon as he'd got back on the unit, Callan was asking why some bitch was wearing Huddles' kicks. Huddles could have broken his teeth, but Sir Hendricks got between them. Since the morning the boy came in, Huddles sensed Terry was too weak to make it alone, only now his kindness had compromised both of them. He considered making Terry find another seat, but genuinely wanted the boy close by. They wouldn't be talking or passing notes like regular schoolchildren. Still, having what sufficed for a friend nearby was worth the risk. If Callan spoke up again, Huddles would just shut him down hard.

Fitzgerald leaned against the doorframe watching them. Callan stood from his desk, went to the back of the room and pulled a copy of *The 1,001 Arabian Nights* off the shelf. Usually it took ten minutes or so of Mrs. Miller's teaching before he wandered, but he was at it early today. He flipped pages until he found an illustration of Scheherazade lying on a massive pallet. His tongue sneaked out to taste the small scar on his upper lip.

"Shit, boys," he said. "Them sultans got it all figured out." He held the book out for all to see. "Soon as I get out of here, I'm jumping on a plane and getting me some of that ass."

The room erupted in laughter. Mrs. Miller was already on him, crossing the room as quick as her arthritic bones would allow. "Give me that," she said, beckoning for the book.

"Not a chance," Callan said. "I've finally found something worth reading."

Fitzgerald came forward. "Give it over," he said.

"Fuck you, fat man," Callan said. "Come take it."

Fitzgerald squeezed into the empty desk across from Callan. He rested his head in the cradle of his fingers and massaged his temples.

"It is way too early for this shit, Callan. You can just give the book over or we can have a real situation. Understand?"

Outside the door, Sir Hendricks and another officer came forward with a handheld video camera. The officer recording stood at the window while Hendricks came inside to back Fitzgerald up. The B-Unit boys were riled. Each one leaned forward in their seats, legs shaking under the desks in anticipation of violence. Huddles watched their eyes dart to one another, searching for the next participant in the standoff.

"Go get me a TV, bitch," Callan said. "I'm harder than that little peckerwood. Time you all started fetching me shit."

"The officer has asked for the book and been refused multiple times," Fitzgerald said into his radio. He looked at the officer filming from the doorway.

"One last chance," Sir Hendricks said. He was close enough to reach out and touch the boy.

Callan opened his mouth to scream something, but Hendricks turned the desk over spilling him out on the floor. As Callan tried to scramble to his feet, Hendricks grabbed him around the wrist to pry the book from his grip. The pages flapped in the air like a frantic bird. Hendricks took his free hand and twisted Callan's fingers back until he dropped the book. Fitzgerald snatched it up from the floor, and Hendricks pulled Callan to his feet, half dragging him toward the door where the recording officer moved out of the way. His camera was pointed toward the floor.

While everyone else watched the scuffle, Huddles watched Terry. The boy sat without expression on his face, bored as a T-baller stranded deep in right field. It surprised Huddles that Terry's expression never changed. He'd underestimated the boy. There was more of a propensity for violence than he thought. Maybe he could be a real ally.

Fitzgerald seeped sweat despite his limited involvement in the scrap. He wiped his forehead with the back of his arm and looked the room over.

"Mrs. Miller, you may proceed," he said.

PART II
THE COUNSELOR

CHAPTER NINE

IN HIS EARLIEST years, Jason Felts began to believe in and wait for The Great Equalizer. The idea occurred to him when he was six years old, just after the doctors in Lexington broke and reset his pigeon-toed legs. The procedure itself had been relatively painless. A few weeks in the hospital taking the weakened painkillers prescribed to children, followed by rides around the halls in his wheelchair. He went home soon enough using a walker, but the casts were still a hindrance. They ended below his hips and the stiff plaster didn't have the range of motion his leg braces had afforded. In the braces, Jason could at least give an awkward goose-step, but the casts were like having his lower body encased in bronze. They gave off the smell of talcum and left him itching until some nights he was sure he could feel a slow liquid trickle down his thighs as if the flesh were melted candle wax and only a wick of bone remained.

After several weeks, Jason's muscle mass shrunk enough for him to reach his hand inside the casts. It was during one of these sessions of groping and scratching that he ripped out sixteen of his stitches. He held the line of thread in the palm of his hand, observing the bits of coagulated blood that clung to the fibers and resembled some sort of centipede. Even at such a young age, Jason wasn't afraid. He recognized this moment as a trial he had been given, the sort of tribulation his Sunday school preacher liked to shout about behind the pulpit. It couldn't be a random wickedness without purpose. It was a wrong done him, but one for which he would be compensated. One day something significant, the sort of event few people were blessed by, would happen and make all of this worth enduring.

Sometimes, Jason found himself drifting inside this old delusion, but the black windows in Control always brought him back to reality. Seeing the reflection of his shrunken stature sapped him of any false hopes. On the monitors, Jason and Counselor Beverly watched the Special Response Team preparing to restrain Malcolm. After so many assaults, the administrator ordered Malcolm kept in one of the holding cells where he could be constantly monitored. Jason had spent the morning stranded in Control, listening as Malcolm started squalling early, pounding with his fists until the knuckles split and left a Rorschach smear against the glass. When Officer Fitzgerald came to check on him, Malcolm stood on his tiptoes and pissed at him through the bean hole. Fitzgerald dodged most of it, only ended up with a dribble on the cuff of his slacks.

The SRT men changed in one of the private rooms for staff, strapping the black shells of body armor onto each other. SRT members were supposed to remain anonymous to prevent any future grudges with the inmates, but most of the boys knew each man. Fitzgerald was always recognizable with his dark skin and giant figure clad in armor too tight for his frame, the straps ready to pop as he lumbered inside. Sir Hendricks gave himself away with a distinct stance. The baton stayed high over his head so that he could rain down blows. Few men really hit the boys. Most just held them down long enough for the troublemaker to be confined in The Wrap, a full body blanket that resembled a sleeping bag. It cocooned too tight to allow any resistance but wiggling.

"This is exactly the wrong move," Beverly said. She had her feet up in the swivel chair, her arms locked over her knees as they watched. "He wants this confrontation."

Jason shrugged. "I don't see him being talked down."

Malcolm paced the perimeter of his cell, kicking at the metal toilet and cinder block walls every time he reached a corner, propelled as if some unseen spirit had him by the wrist and was dragging him along. Occasionally, he would stop to glare at the glass.

"Any diagnosis?" Jason asked. It hurt to watch the boy, but conversation helped.

Beverly shook her head. "He assaulted so many of the staff at Sharp's Hospital they never finished the mental hygiene."

"Pretty serious?"

"Sucker punched a doctor and hit one orderly with a bedpan. He even bit a nurse. She needed eighteen stitches in her back."

"Fuck," Jason said.

"Rumor is he swallowed a mouthful."

Even with all his anger, Malcolm looked too fragile for such a reputation, but Jason knew better. The damage his own tiny body could inflict was surprising. In his youth, Jason put holes in countless drywall and once kicked dents into the fender of a parked car at the local Kroger when some boys mocked him.

Officer Fitzgerald carried an opaque shield as he led the assault. The team traveled across the main floor beside B-Unit where the boys were lined up at the glass portion, noses and hands smudging the pane as they watched. A few cheered and offered advice on how to best wound Malcolm.

When they reached the holding cell, the SRT men stopped while Hendricks got the key ready to roll the door. Since most kept in

Holding were on suicide watch, the administration designed the doors so that manual interaction was necessary. This prevented lazy officers from lying about body checks.

"Sit on your bunk and place both hands on top of your head," Hendricks shouted. His voice was muffled by the black balaclava covering his face. Over this, he also wore a riot helmet with a visor pulled down.

"Eat my shit," Malcolm said. His voice was almost a squeak.

Hendricks rolled the door. Malcolm dove off his bunk, his elbows thrashing at Fitzgerald's neck over the shield, tiny limbs connecting with the big man's padding. Fitzgerald set the shield aside and smothered Malcolm to the ground with his weight, spreading the boy's body flat so the other SRT members could restrain his arms and legs. After he was down, the team waited while Malcolm screamed and struggled. Most of the men looked away as the boy howled and his spittle flecked their visors, unable to watch as he slurred and gnashed his teeth, but Hendricks kneeled until he was inches from the boy's ear. Jason couldn't be sure, but he thought Hendricks might be whispering.

Beverly's radio squawked to life. She spoke into the mouthpiece and turned to Jason.

"They need you in B-Unit."

JASON WATCHED AS Woods dealt blackjack, shuffling the cards in ways that let kings and queens slide from hand to hand in a muted blur. It seemed a talent inherited from old men, the sort of thing a boy takes up when he's been dragged to games in mountain shacks. Woods had probably been working the cards as a toddler, trying to keep quiet so he didn't anger some relative losing a crucial hand. Whatever allowed him to learn, it was a joy to see him manipulate the cards and Woods knew it. He grinned as he dealt, revealing his new state-bought veneers and singing a verse or two of "Kentucky Gambler."

"Just deal the damned things," Robison said. He fingered the small stack of colored construction paper used for chips. In the old days, the B-Unit boys had been allowed multicolored buttons to bet with, but someone had fired one out of a slingshot constructed with the torn elastic band from their Fruit of the Looms. The incident ended that privilege.

"In a minute," Woods said. "Can't get these to stop sticking together." He dealt the cards face up. A ten of diamonds, three of spades and the queen of hearts.

Terry sat alone at the other table. None of the boys offered to let him join the game, but Jason doubted if he'd have been interested anyway. The nurse in Medical spent most of the morning with Terry, and now he sat wiping his hands on his pant legs, eyes glazed and skin beaded with sweat. Plenty rode the withdrawals out, but something else was gnawing on the boy. Jason thought it might be his presence. Terry had been asking for him earlier that morning, but Jason didn't have the balls to go see him. So far, no one inside The Shell knew about their connection. Jason wouldn't lie if asked about it but wanted to keep things secret if possible. Most B-Unit boys despised him, and he didn't want to see that hate transferred to Terry.

"Mr. Felts," Terry said. "You got a minute?"

Jason sat down at Terry's table and prepared himself in case the boy mentioned the night in the morgue. All logic contradicted this. Terry didn't need another charge, but Jason assumed that he wouldn't be able to hide the truth. Behind them, Woods took up the chorus from "If We Make It Through December." The boy often sang outlaw country when gloating. Jason wished Huddles would get tired of being cheated and just hit him.

"What's up?" Jason asked. Jason readied himself for Terry to beg for pills, since he'd already been merciful in the morgue.

"I need to make a call," Terry said. His voice sounded like air leaking from a deflating tire.

"No phones right now," Jason said. "You'll get a chance to speak with your lawyer tomorrow."

"I need to know about my dad," he said.

The police had issued a report after Terry's father missed the arraignment. They went door to door in the community waking people before dawn, but no one seemed to know anything. It was as if the earth had opened and swallowed the man.

"I need to find out if Roscoe is okay." Terry began to weep. "It's my fault."

"Get this bitch a tampon," Woods yelled. He tossed a handful of cards at Terry. Most caught the wind and drifted down until clubs littered around their feet, but a single queen struck Terry below the eye. He jumped up to charge Woods, but Jason got his hand around Terry's sleeve and pulled him back. Woods' new teeth did nothing to improve his grin. Craters of black blight still spread across his canines.

"That's right, sit back down," Woods said.

Terry sank back into his chair. Jason turned away from him, embarrassed to see the boy crying harder. Nothing prepared him for moments when the posturing faded and he was reminded they were just children. He wanted to touch the boy, but staff had been warned against physical contact.

Huddles pushed his cards forward. "Shit, Woods. No need to be a dick constantly," he said.

Woods began to protest, but Robison leaned forward and began to pick up the fallen cards. "Let's just play," he said.

The shuffling began again. The sound from the cards not the previous swish, but a grind like bones rubbed together. Jason thought the friction might ignite the paper in Woods' hands.

"Tell me about Roscoe," Huddles said as he sat down beside Terry.

Terry seemed apprehensive, but Jason was used to watching boys shrink away from Huddles. "He's my dog."

Huddles didn't quite smile, but his lips ticked upward. "A big Dobermann? A Pit?"

"He's a mutt."

"West Virginia Brown Dog is what my brother calls them."

"He's about eight now," Terry said.

They went on talking while Robison won hand after hand of blackjack. The magic had abandoned Woods. He could no longer make the cards obey. The game broke after a few more hands, each boy drifting to his cell or congregating below the hanging TV in the Commons. Once the boys were distracted, Terry waved Jason over and shoved a folded piece of paper into his palm. He didn't say anything after the note was passed, just went to watch TV with the others.

Jason slipped the note into his pocket. The urge to read it nagged him as he sat in B-Unit, but he waited until he was outside The Shell in his truck. The note was two parcels: a crude map with minimal text, and a meticulously folded letter, considerably thicker and with more text. Jason sat the letter aside without reading it and spread the map out across the steering wheel. Just a list of directions really, descriptions of roads he'd need to travel, obscure turns Jason wasn't sure he could even find. He traced the route in his mind, got as far as the point where Terry had scrawled "on foot from here." He was lost after that, unable to conjure the images of the described trail. There was little explanation for the chosen messenger. Just a few lines at the bottom of the page.

His name is Davey Stanton. Please give him this. You don't owe me, but there isn't anyone else. Please.

Jason stowed both in the glove box and sat thinking for a moment. Who was Davey? Why was he so important that Terry risked passing a note in front of other boys? Secret communication with staff was forbidden, an unstated rule by which all the B-Unit boys adhered. Whatever was in the letter must have been worth the risk of being labeled a rat. Jason considered reading it, almost convinced himself he was owed more of an explanation if he were tasked with such an unwanted favor. Still, he kept the papers closed up in the glove box. He kept thinking about the small handwriting, the elegant loop in the cursive *P* of *Please*. It was capitalized, a single word followed by the dark blot of a period. Words were such fragile, imprecise things, but that please explained everything. It said more than any reason Terry could have offered.

As Jason waited at Cheap Charlie's Drive-Thru for beer and sandwiches, his mind wandered back to a boyhood night when Uncle Henry still owned the funeral home. This time, he recalled one evening when his cousin Ben found an X album among all the Springsteen and AC/DC records in Uncle Henry's collection. Jason and Ben weren't close, but they worked as pallbearers together sometimes. The job made both outcasts enough to force tolerance if not a bond. Jason worked to help Uncle Henry, but Ben got a real kick out of hauling the bodies. It offered him more of a chance to frighten people. So, when

Jason told him he wanted to listen to the records, Ben said he couldn't unless they went down to the garage and Jason opened the door to the morgue.

Jason had seen plenty of bodies, but only after all the fresh signs of death were erased. Corpses with the thick makeup already applied until they resembled dolls more than people. It wouldn't be that way on the metal table in the morgue. Down there, they'd look like the zombies on late-night TV.

"No way," Jason said.

"Anyone who don't wanna see the tits on Tracy Calloway is a fag," Ben said. He fiddled with a new stud in his left nostril. Ben kept begging to dye his hair Joker green, but Uncle Henry didn't think it decent for a pallbearer. He made Ben take the nose ring out whenever he worked a funeral.

"But she's dead," Jason said.

"Don't matter," Ben said. "Looking at tits is looking at tits. You'd know that if you'd ever seen a pair."

The garage was cold like always and cramped with the hearse parked inside. They had to squeeze around the bumper and could only crack the morgue door enough to slip inside. Tracy Calloway was naked on the table. Her chest had been cracked open like a giant crawdad, her rib cage hollow and showing the slick shine of her liver and lungs. Jason puked on his Chuck Taylors while Ben laughed and pulled a rubber glove from the dispenser on the wall. The latex snapped against his wrist.

"Nothing to be afraid of," Ben said as he reached into her chest and plucked out her heart. The organ was still in his hand, but Jason recognized it had once been part of something the way a pit was once part of a peach. Ben held it out like a heathen priest.

"Touch it," he said.

Jason ran into the bumper of the Cadillac and was heading back into the sanctuary of the funeral home, past the pulpit where Reverend Walker would preach about Tracy's virtue before sending her to the Lord. The memory made him think of Sheriff Thompson on the metal table, split open the same way. Jason told himself that later that night he might sip slow on a few beers and go touch the sheriff's heart, see what sort of courage Ben had gained from it.

Other men didn't have stories like these. People from tamer places carried more conventional traumas. Nothing more than the psychic equivalent of flesh wounds. None had ever held death in their palm or watched the top of mountains disintegrate in dynamite explosions so their families could eat. It made him feel like no one from the outside world would ever understand him.

Jason drove to Fuller Street. The power was back on, the houses glowing in the late darkness with such intensity that electricity seemed something just discovery. It wasn't the arrival he'd hoped for, his fantasy of all the houses dark with sleep and only a single low-hued lamp shining through one of Uncle Henry's windows. As he pulled into the lot, Jason saw the renovations were coming along. The old front porch had been torn down and the lumber lay piled in the lot ready to be burned. The new porch had yet to be constructed, so a stack of cinder blocks sufficed for steps up to the front door. The left half of the house was outfitted in new vinyl siding, but the right side remained stripped until the home seem as if it were shedding off dead skin. The lawn was absent its previous trash, any random litter now dumped atop the wood pile. Even the weeds were cut back until Jason wondered how many snakes Uncle Henry killed clearing the path.

Sharon Hendricks' Honda sat in the driveway. Jason remembered the first time he'd seen her and the car, a cold morning when she arrived at The Shell to deliver a bucket of fried chicken to her husband. Sir Hendricks had complained about the lack of coleslaw and slapped her ass, sent her down the hill without a kind word. Jason could recall how nervous he felt when her eyes stopped on him, how the cigarette smoke in his lungs felt warmer as she looked away and how he wished his short legs weren't swinging freely from where he sat perched on the smoke shack's hand rail, telegraphing how small he was.

Jason parked beside her car and took a moment to survey the neighborhood. Nothing moved on either side of the tracks. He shrugged into the overcoat he'd worn that day at The Shell, but the material itched the way it used to when he wore it for funeral duties. Jason took it off, laid the coat in his lap and touched the splitting stitches under the arms. The fact he still fit into the jacket seemed a cruel joke. It made him think about Huddles' insult. No doubt the boy was hard, but too many people were using him. His brother using him to run product, the guards and police using him to snare his brother. Jason understood why Huddles didn't have any trust left. He even admired the integrity it took to place your back against the wall, to refuse anything if every offer of assistance required some compromise or debasement in return. The boy was right about the coat anyway. Jason looked like a fool in the old funeral rag. He reminded himself that he didn't need to keep trying to impress Sharon, but assumed the extra effort was one of the things she found endearing.

Sharon and Jason had met for the second time in Boyle's Market. It was months after their first encounter, but she'd been on his mind as he walked through the produce section, enduring the stares of old men leering at his small size. He was contemplating leaving when she came by pushing a cart. Before, Jason had been struck only by her beauty. This time, he could see a sad contemplation in her eyes. Sharon's hands gripped the buggy's rail hard as the men and women in the store turned their gaze toward her. She hung her head, hair eclipsing her face. It was a gesture Jason recognized. He'd employed similar methods to hide his aversions for years until he finally decided to stare defiantly back at anyone who gawked. Only Sharon didn't look angry, just tired.

Such a woman simply didn't appear in a place like Lynch, and Jason knew he'd never forgive himself if he didn't at least speak to her. Just a smile from a woman like her would be worth the chance of repudiation or the ridicule of onlookers. When Sharon lingered next to the fruit, Jason struck up a weak conversation about kiwis. He was delighted when she admitted to never tasting the fruit. They traveled the frozen food aisles together, this tall woman and small man. Eyes continued to follow them around the store. Sharon's mother was of Sioux heritage and she retained the woman's dark hair, sharp cheekbones and bronze skin. The sight of two rarities became almost too voyeuristic a pleasure for the shoppers. Old women were no longer satisfied with furtive glances. Jason didn't mind it as he walked with Sharon. She calmed him.

It had been a long time since any woman took notice. So long, Jason began to wonder if there would be another love in his life. Maybe that's what allowed him to excuse his lust for a married woman. When guilt got the best of him, he often asked her why she'd continued talking with him, his eyes obviously unable to stop tracing her curves, his voice turning to whispers so that he might lean in closer for conversation. At the time, he'd thought it just luck that she stopped to stare at the fruit so long, but weeks into their affair, she confessed wanting to be close to him. "You intrigued me," she'd said. "I watched you handling the fruit so delicately, inspecting it, and I wanted you to touch me like that."

Jason had a hypothesis that all women who felt attraction to him went through a moment of revulsion. Not necessarily at his body, but at themselves for finding a pull towards something so unconventional. He knew that no little girl ever dreamed of growing up to be with a man so much smaller. This seemed to necessitate a reckoning with their feelings. A month into the affair, he finally gained the nerve to ask Sharon about this.

"I never questioned it," she said. "As soon as we began to speak, I knew what we were going to do. I don't have any regrets. I wanted a decent man and now I've found one."

Their conversation in Boyle's remained innocent but powerful enough for Jason to look her up in the phone book. Everything inside told him it was wrong, that this was the wife of another and she would never be interested in such a diminutive man as himself. He'd been beyond surprised to hear that she'd been fantasizing about the call. Jason couldn't imagine any woman fantasizing about him. He'd had a few other girlfriends, but romantic relationships in general seemed untenable. There was a cold war brewing between men and women. A silent acknowledgment that one gender had spent generations trying to dominate the other and now women were naturally wary of trust. Jason could feel the reticence in so many conversations, women waiting on the warning signs of some hidden aggression. He didn't blame them. Occasionally, the lust he felt mingled with a desire not just to covet or touch, but to own. Perhaps it was the weakness he felt around women, but he'd seen the same flaws in enough men to know the defect was shared. It made him wonder how couples ever got past it, how they could eventually trust and forgive enough to love. Considering it made him fearful about the future.

Jason climbed out of the truck and ascended the concrete blocks. The door was unlocked, so Jason stepped inside to the empty hall. His shoes crunched over bits of plaster. Uncle Henry had only furnished a single room. Just a mattress placed atop a bed frame and wrought iron headboard. It lacked a footboard, sheets or pillows. Only a quilt lay folded at the foot of the bed. It made him sad that his uncle had been living like this.

Sharon sat at the small table in the kitchen with a cup of tea. The pot boiled on the stove burner, and Jason was surprised Uncle Henry had the gas going already. All around Sharon, broken cabinets hung on the walls. The trough sink was full of shingles that had fallen through the holes in the roof. Uncle Henry often complained about starlings darting inside through the holes to snatch roaches foolish enough to stay exposed to the early dawn.

Jason took a seat at Uncle Henry's kitchen table while Sharon wiped away spilt tea with a rag and grabbed the kettle off the stove burner. She poured him a cup. Jason placed his palm over the mug's open mouth until the heat fill his hand.

"I know it was my suggestion," he said. "But is this really necessary?"

"I have neighbors," she said.

"Your neighbors wouldn't pay any attention to me."

Both knew it wasn't true. Jason had driven by her home the day before while Sir Hendricks was off swinging his battle-ax. Sharon's house was a tiny one story with a picket fence, the street littered with children Jason feared would remember his stature. Not even a ghost of Hendricks' hardness could be found in the yard. The absence of the man's presence made it easy to pretend, but he knew it was too dangerous for him to visit her there, just as it was too dangerous for her to keep coming to his apartment above the funeral home. The small borders of Lynch made secrets hard enough. It was Sharon who asked if he knew a secret place. Jason almost hadn't told her about Uncle Henry's. He didn't want to see her standing among walls ready to cave in and dirt generations old.

"You make this place look so much worse," he said.

She gave the sort of smile that said it had been too long since she'd heard such flattery. Jason wondered what her time with her husband was like. Did they just drift by one another in the house? He didn't understand how a man could ever take the love of such a woman for granted.

Sharon placed a hand over his on the tabletop. "I heard about the sheriff."

"We should get out of here," he said. "It's dirty."

She smiled again, but it was the sort of smile given to naive children. "It's time together. I wish you'd enjoy it."

Jason sipped his tea and felt her hand rub his leg beneath the table. Her fingers moved higher towards his scars.

"Tell me more about South Dakota," he said.

She'd told him in Boyle's Market that her mother lived on the outskirts of a town called Farina, in a small house she'd saved for years to buy. Sharon lived there until she was nineteen, came southeast on the chance to play softball for Marshall University, met Hendricks, got pregnant and dropped out. She miscarried the baby, kept the man, but couldn't remember why. Three years ago, she'd finished her paralegal degree and began working for a small criminal defense firm in town.

"Too wide open. Everything all flat. I drove through Kansas once as a girl after they'd just finished burning the fields. Black ash as far as you could see. It was like driving on a dead planet."

"I want to see things like that with you. I want us to make those kinds of memories."

"We will," she said, but Jason wasn't sure he believed it. She hadn't agreed to leave Hendricks yet.

Before Sharon's first arrival to his apartment, Jason worked hard to keep things in perspective. He stood in front of the full-length mirror in his bathroom and assessed himself wearing the Oxford cloth dress shirt he'd hemmed so that it didn't cover his knees. No woman would ever truly accept this, he told himself. This wasn't anything more than a momentary respite from being alone, but the night together made it harder to drown his hope. Sharon wasn't disgusted by his body or awed by it. Jason believed she had cataloged him in a new space, invented a specification that transcended his illness.

The first night they spent together, she pressed her body against Jason and let her fingers trace the scars on his thighs.

"Trying to fix them?" he asked.

She'd smiled with small, sharp teeth. "No. I like every part of you."

"You look tired," she said and pointed to his full tea mug that grown cold. "You didn't finish your tea."

"Too much going on at work," he said. He was ready to tell her everything about Terry and the letter, but she stood and pulled his head to the plain of her stomach, his forehead resting on the mound of skin that swelled with each breath.

"Come on," she said and pulled him to his feet, led him back to the bedroom where they laid hands on each other like faith healers.

CHAPTER TEN

THERE WASN'T MUCH of a bar scene in Lynch. Most remaining watering holes were the cinder block hovels located in Cherry Tree that drew customers in with nude dancers instead of drinks. Across the tracks was Hob & Millie's, a redneck joint that advertised itself as a sports bar, but had only one fuzzy pictured flat screen. The last hard drinker's establishment since The Mount Gay Lounge closed its doors was The American Legion underneath Lynch Lanes. Jason knew it well. He'd spent evenings inside as a boy during Uncle Henry's worst days. He carried his toys down into the basement where the old veterans shouted their stories over the crash of strikes from the Wednesday night's league echoing upstairs. The marine's wife tending bar always let him drive his Hot Wheels around the stack of napkins near his stool and kept him supplied with fresh Coca-Colas while Uncle Henry pounded George Dickel neat. He was pleased when Counselor Beverly suggested it for a drink after work. Sad as it was, it remained one of his favorite places from childhood.

Jason followed her straight from The Shell. They parked beside each other and stood next to their fenders, feeling the chill in the wind despite the warmth of the night. The whistle from a late train cut through the racket of men stumbling out of the bowling alley and going downstairs to have a beer before heading home. Jason looked over their jeans and T-shirts, buttoned his overcoat and considered removing his clip-on tie. Clip-ons were a necessity inside The Shell. A normal knot could get you strangled in a fight. Beverly shook her head as Jason began to remove it.

"You look sharp," she said.

"You do realize where we're drinking?"

At the foot of the steps, a man with his head covered by a black do-rag collected IDs. The bouncer held the door for Beverly and gave her a wink. She'd changed into different clothes before leaving work. Tight dark jeans and a sleeveless smock under the windbreaker she'd kept zipped up inside B-Unit while conducting group.

Group had been hard for Jason. Terry sat with his arms folded, refusing to participate. He didn't look as sick as the day before, but he kept looking at Jason, pleading with his eyes for information regarding the letter. Watching the boy sulk, Jason knew he should probably write Terry off. He was too far gone to be saved and to continue thinking otherwise was delusional. You spent time talking to the ones who were receptive, you let the others go on until they got a hard sentence or the life finished them. It was a cold but quick system of prioritizing and saving those you could. He was slowly learning that. Still, Jason wasn't sure how exactly one hardened his heart to such a point.

The bar hadn't changed much over the years. The back wall was still one giant cracked mirror pane. The reflection made the room look twice as large, as if the few odd drinkers ignoring the new laws against smoking indoors were a larger crowd transfixed by the middle-aged woman on the stage belting out a karaoke version of Loretta Lynn instead of just old men biding time. The dead marine's wife had been replaced as bartender by a woman in her mid-twenties whom the old leathernecks flirted with as they ordered. She already seemed aged by the surroundings, settled into the dangerous position sure to sap her of any vitality. The men turned on their stools as Beverly entered and looked hard before returning to their drinks. She chose a seat far from the row of pool tables while Jason fetched them a pair of drafts.

"We should make a habit of this," Beverly said when he returned to the table. "It's nice not running straight home after work."

"Sure," Jason said. He took a sip of his beer and watched her, but Beverly was looking at her reflection, her eyes searching the image as if observing a stranger. Jason knew she was on the verge of saying something important. He figured she'd be confessing by the time they reached the bottom of their beers.

"How did you feel about the one-on-ones today?" she asked.

Jason wasn't sure what she meant. Things had been routine. Woods was still pining over the same lost love. He'd shed a few tears, but that was nothing new. Robison was becoming more agitated, quicker to huff and curse over institutional regulations, but that too was to be expected. Part of their job meant allowing the prisoners to release their anger at incarceration gradually, to keep it from building until they assaulted an officer or each other.

"I think they went pretty good," Jason said.

Beverly ran a finger around the rim of her glass.

"I don't think we're getting anywhere with Huddles."

Jason knew what she meant. Huddles stayed quiet while Beverly asked questions and tried to pry him open with her smile. The boy was too sharp for any kind of kid gloves. If he had been running things, Jason would've promised not to bullshit the boy if Huddles remained honest. He was too good at being frozen, turning himself off before he even entered therapy.

"We just need more time," Jason said. "You know how his family works. He's not going to give anything up easily."

Beverly shook her head. "That's what I used to think. I think the best thing to do might be to get him out of The Shell. Send him up to Tiger Morton next court date, and let them see what they can do."

Jason had heard stories about Tiger. It boasted the highest number of violent offenders in the state. A guard had been cut there three years ago during a brawl in Commons and the place only had only become more severe in the aftermath. A larger staff was hired, more restrictions applied. Huddles might thrive in a place like that, but it wouldn't be something Jason wanted for him.

"You wanna give the kid another week or have you already started writing the report?"

"He's not just been truant at school or something. His brother has killed people, and they busted him with a carload of guns and drugs."

"Don't give me that tough love routine," Jason said. "You know sending him along is just passing the problem on to someone else."

A rowdy group of young men in cowboy boots and hats came inside. Women in high-waist jeans hung on their arms, the couples filling the bar with drunken laughter shrill as breaking china. They twirled in the space by the karaoke machine, bumping against nearby tables and almost spilling patrons' drinks with their dance. Jason found himself envying them. He could be moving across that floor with Sharon, his hands on her waist and her long hair dangling down on him like a living rain instead of advocating for some delinquent.

"Do what you like," Jason said. "You're the one writes the reports."

"You'll be burnt out, too," Beverly said. "Give it a few more years of seeing nothing change. Hearing how they leave and end up in one of the con-colleges upstate. You'll get sick of it, too."

They finished their beers, and Beverly decided to sing. She tried to lure Jason closer to the stage, but he stayed at the table, told her he preferred to watch from the corner. She went up front, signed the list of performers and took the stage to anesthetized applause. The young dancers gave her some whooping and whistles, then went back to the bar for refills while she began "How I Got to Memphis." The country crawled out of her voice as she leaned into the notes, the sound carrying across the silence without the assistance of a microphone. Jason listened until she neared the end of the song, then rose to go to the bathroom.

Only one of the light bulbs inside still burned, and his shoes stuck to the piss streaked floor. Waded paper towels lay littered around an empty trash can. A bearded man stood filling the nearest urinal, coughing as his bladder emptied. Jason went to the far end, unzipped and began to urinate along with the man who'd taken his hand from his prick and was scratching at the hair growing on his neck. Jason saw the digits were tattooed so that each finger bore a different playing card symbol. The tops of his hands were covered in more faded ink. Jailhouse work that climbed up to hide inside his sleeves.

The man zipped up and turned toward him. Jason waited on a remark about size, a reference to either his height or his cock. It wouldn't be the first time. Curious men often stole glances when he stood at a urinal. Jason supposed they wondered how such a small man were equipped. He'd always found his own penis unremarkable, and in some strange way loved it because of this. Some might view the average as more disappointing than overly small or large, but so much of Jason's body was remarkably different he felt great pride at such a normal appendage. The man continued to stare until Jason zipped his pants and turned to face him.

"You work up at The Shell, don't you?" the man said.

"Yes," Jason said. Whose relative might this be and what grievance might they try to avenge by drowning him in the piss or slamming his head against the porcelain? "I'm a counselor. Not a guard."

The man smiled. Jason noticed his teeth looked predatory, sharp and crooked as if accustomed to chewing through bone and gristle.

"It's jail," the man said. "If they let you inside without putting you in a cage, you work there."

Jason took a step towards the door. There was nothing between him and the exit, but he'd have to turn his back on the man to leave. He wasn't prepared to do that yet.

"Maybe you can help me," the man said. "I'm Ferris Gilbert. I'm sure you know my little brother."

"I know Huddles," Jason said.

Ferris reached into his back pocket, removed his wallet and began to count out several hundred-dollar bills.

"That's two thousand dollars," Ferris said. He slipped the money inside the pocket of Jason's coat. "I'd like you to do me a favor. You know he's got court coming up?"

Jason took the money and held it out to Ferris. "I'll help him if I can, but I don't need money for that."

Ferris smiled. "You have enough to turn down generosity? You that rich?"

"No, sir," Jason said. "I don't have much, but I don't need to be paid to help."

Ferris reached out and his tattooed hand swallowed the bills. "You would if you were helping me," he said. "Why are you being so rude? I'm being respectful here, not coming to your house, not bothering your uncle or that woman of yours. She is your woman, right?"

Ferris seemed to be waiting on Jason to speak, but Jason didn't have anything to add, just stood waiting on Ferris to dismiss him. He didn't want to let the alarm he was feeling transform his face red and hot with anger. If only he could be large once, he'd take this tattooed hick by the ears and bludgeon his head on the floor.

"I'm not going to do anything to hurt your brother, but I'm not going to compromise myself either. I don't care what you know about me or who you tell about Sharon."

Ferris grabbed the end of Jason's tie and yanked hard. The clip-on popped off his collar, and Ferris stood holding the lank silk like a dead snake. Jason waited to see what the man would do next, but Ferris just chuckled. He held the tie up, turned it in his hands as if it were some strange new marvel and dropped it into the urinal.

"You and I'll talk again sometime," Ferris said. "When you're more receptive."

When it was clear the man wasn't going to lay hands on him again, Jason turned and walked out into the wall of sound. A new crooner was belting out a song Johnny Cash sang at Folsom. The dancers were reverent now, their stomping finally ceased as they held each other and swayed. Beverly sat at the table, but Jason walked by her. He didn't want Ferris to notice her, to sit down and try to slip the same bills into her blouse. He went outside, climbed the stairs and stood in the lot listening as the cacophony of pins being bowled over mixed with the muttering from the basement.

CHAPTER ELEVEN

AT HOME, JASON listened to the cats. The strays climbed the steps to sleep beneath the swing on his patio or curled up into vibrating piles atop the plush cushions. He could hear them meowing from hunger most nights, sometimes hissing and fighting until he felt the urge to go kick them over the balcony. Whenever he went outside in the early morning, he caught only glances of the slowest slinking away. Mother cats swollen with the weight of kittens ready to be born or decrepit toms missing patches of fur, their scarred faces occasionally absent an eye from duels. The cats had been coming since he was a child. The current pride were the incestuous descendants of a brood that first appeared when Uncle Henry owned the funeral home. As much as Jason hated their racket, there was something reassuring in the idea that a generation of felines would remain long after he was gone.

Anyway, it wasn't the cats keeping him awake. It was the thought of Ferris Gilbert snatching the tie from his throat.

It had rained enough that evening to extinguish the heat. The soft drizzle making its rhythm on the roof sounded pleasant when Jason closed his eyes. In his loneliest times before Sharon, Jason needed things like rain or the cats to fall asleep. In the quiet of the small apartment above the mortuary, his mind would fill with doubts about the future unless he could focus on monotonous noise. He usually slept better now, but Terry's note taxed him until he rose from bed to retrieve the map, tracing fingers over the indentations made by a pencil in the cheap construction paper. The words begged to be read aloud. The please at the bottom of the page more urgent than anything ever asked of him. Eventually, Jason got dressed.

He opened the nightstand and took out his grandfather's pistol. As far as he knew, the gun had ended three lives. Uncle Henry liked to recite a story about a night when a few of the stray cats snuck into the back lot where the children kept ducklings they'd received as Easter presents. Jason's father woke to the sound of frantic screams, grabbed the revolver and came outside in time to see the strays dragging the ducks down. He killed a fat calico with the first shot, missed with the second and third before chasing the fleeing cats around the side of the building. One of the animals hid under a neighbor's porch, but Jason's father shot the cat between its glowing yellow eyes. The final bullets were reserved for their wounded ducks. Uncle Henry had to pull the trigger. Jason's father couldn't manage. He'd only been ten years old.

It was one of the few stories Jason knew about his father, and somehow it remained more vivid than his actual memories. Jason couldn't recall much other than the old man's anger. He was kind, but always seething under the surface. Even an odd philosophical musing, the sort of question a child might ask about the ways of the world, would cause a huff to expel from the man. His father didn't like knowing the answers to hard questions Jason was already beginning to ask. Perhaps he wanted to keep the boy ignorant to all that trouble for a few more years of innocence, but Jason's condition had never really allowed for much of a childhood. That was something else for his father to be angry about. Nothing is implicit. Things like justice, peace, or love aren't inherent. Humans only tried to build some order out of chaos. If Jason ever forgot that, all he needed to do was look at his shrunken legs.

THE TRUCK BEGAN making its strange noises as he approached lower Bradshaw, so Jason turned off the radio, leaving the cab silent until he could listen to the engine strain. A bad grinding, but the truck had been doing that all month. Lower Bradshaw consisted of collapsing homes that looked uninhabitable. Standing water filled the ruts in the poorly paved road, puddled in the yards until the tall unattended grass was nearly submerged. Water rolled off the gutterless roof of a small one-story house. The cascade pounded the porch until Jason was sure some runoff must have seeped inside the home.

Ahead, the road ended in a spot just large enough to turn around in before the hillside started its gradual slope up the mountain. A battered Chevy pickup sat parked just off the road. It was slathered in mud up to the door handles, the paint job on the hood nearly hidden by bug carcasses and grim despite the rain. Jason couldn't imagine what anyone else would be doing out here. Maybe this was a sign to turn back, but he pushed past that paranoia.

Jason pulled over and stepped out into the downpour, the sheet of water stinging the back of his neck and his cheeks. A few foot trails wound their way through the trees, but the water ran downhill and filled these paths. It was a hard trek in the dark, so Jason ascended the mountain slow, often clinging to the nearest tree trunk as he tried to gain purchase. The beam from the flashlight he'd brought shone weak, unable to illuminate more than a few feet in front of him. He kept the dull light trained on his feet. As his path began to level off, Jason found himself walking through ankle-deep mud, minding his footing as he stepped around tree roots hidden by dead leaves.

Eventually, he reached a clearing in the flattest part of the thicket where a small cabin took shape among the few remaining oaks. The wooden door looked rotten, the lower section clawed as if animals had begged entry each night. One of the windows had been covered by sodden cardboard, and a candle burned behind the other, its light muted by the thick frosted pane. If it weren't for the light inside, Jason would have believed the building abandoned.

He spread the map across his wet knee and searched it with the flashlight, but the rain weakened the paper until it withered in his hands. It must be the place. There could be no other bootlegger cabin in these woods. Something foreboding about the structure made Jason want to slip back down the mountain. It wasn't just the childhood fear of haunted pines with their spectral apparitions. Something more substantial made him take the pistol from his coat and check the cylinder again. The exposed brass of the bullets became drenched with rain. Jason wiped them on his shirt, closed the cylinder and slipped the gun into the back of his jeans.

Closer, he could see the door was ajar. Jason gave a push that sent it creaking open.

"Hello," he said. "Davey Stanton?"

The room was too dark to see much aside from shapes. The few candles by the window burned low, ready to snuff out. His eyes had yet to adjust and the flashlight was beginning to strobe, the beam flickering until he hit the back of the case and the light gained a moment of life. He saw a crumpled form in one of these brief flashes. A large man lay on the floor by the wood stove, his face turned away and the back of his head slicked by rainwater. Jason bent low, ready to roust the man from sleep.

"Davey, I'm a friend of Terry's," he said.

The man didn't move. Jason took another step forward and felt the wooden floor under his feet change. Something slick robbed him of traction, thinner than the mud outside and warm through the soles of his boots. Jason smacked the flashlight and it burst into bright life. Davey lay on his side, open eyes staring eternally out at the dirty floor. His throat had been slit. The far wall was flecked by an arterial spray.

Jason's knees went weak, and he almost sat down in the puddle. It was the same as that distant night when his cousin Ben held aloft Tracy Calloway's heart. Only Ben hadn't split the girl open to acquire it. Jason leaned down, placed his hand to the still warm flesh of the body. Soft and free of the waxy tactile experience he'd become accustomed to during his pallbearer duties.

The warmth set off alarms in his mind. Whoever did this would still be close by. Jason remembered the truck and retched, his stomach clamping down in fear as he turned to sprint for the door. This maneuver made him slip, his ankle twisting in the puddle until he tripped, hit his left knee hard on the planks and had to regain his footing before clearing the door. He was already in the yard when he heard the door swing wide on its rusted hinges. The tree line was far away, the gun jostling in the back of his pants. Every cell inside screamed for him to continue running, to hit the thick underbrush and slide down the mountain toward the truck. Behind him, his pursuer was huffing hard, gasping as they splashed through the slop of mud.

Jason reached the trees and began to run diagonally down the mountain. He stumbled a few times, but continued moving. The sound of the man chasing him seemed closer, the smell of blood and body odor filling his flared nostrils along with the night's musk. A crack like the breaking of a tremendous tree splitting echoed behind him. Jason hit the low brush, crawled forward as he fumbled for his gun. Once the weapon was free, he turned and pointed it out at the darkness.

No one stood behind him. The flashlight was forgotten in the cabin, so Jason squinted his eyes and stared hard on the gunsights, readied to fire on the first sign of movement. His eyes were adjusting when something cold pressed against the back of his neck.

"Drop it," a voice said.

Jason tightened his grip, tried to decide if he could turn before the bullet entered his spine. The barrel pressed down harder into his flesh as if anticipating this thought.

"Toss it, and we can talk," the voice said. "Otherwise, we can end it here."

Jason let the hammer down on the revolver and dropped it into the weeds between his feet.

"Stand up slow," the voice said.

Jason had trouble getting to his feet. Even before the chase, his joints had felt fused by the cold rain, his muscles sore from the hard hike. His hips were in a state of deterioration and the run had made them ache. He hobbled up to his full height as the gun pressed into his neck.

"I'm gonna take this gun off you," the voice said. "Then you and I are gonna walk back up the mountain. If you think about running, remember that this thirty aught six is only a foot from your back. Understand?"

He was beginning to recognize the voice. The same mocking timbre as earlier that night. It seemed ridiculous, but Jason knew before he turned that he would be looking at Ferris Gilbert. The hard barrel of the gun poked him in the rib.

"Understand?" Ferris said.

"I understand."

"Good. Now, nice and slow. Up the path."

From the first step, Jason didn't think he could make it. His hips sang in pain, feet heavy and swollen as if he'd been marching for years, but knowledge of the gun pushed him forward. He focused only on the next step, then the one after that, while behind him Ferris complained.

"Running down the mountain. What were you thinking? That those little stumps could carry you somewhere fast?" Jason heard the man spit a lungful of phlegm to clear his throat. "You should have seen yourself."

The cabin was in sight. Jason told himself just to clear the threshold. After that, he could collapse. Plans for escape seemed too optimistic. Inside meant death, but he was too weak to attempt anything. Any gesture would just bring a quicker end, and Jason found himself ashamed at how much he wanted each additional second of life, how important it seemed to continue to draw each burning breath and feel the needling pain in his knees.

Ferris pushed Jason inside the cabin and closed the door behind them. Jason got his first look at the man. Different clothes than at the bar. A dark wool peacoat and straight leg jeans, motorcycle boots caked in mud. Ferris wore a pair of wooly gloves and a large bone handled knife on a sheath attached to his belt.

"Sit down," Ferris said. He pointed the rifle barrel toward a table and chairs in the corner.

While Jason collapsed in the chair, Ferris stepped over the corpse, took a dying candle and set it as the table's centerpiece. Ferris looked strange in the candlelight, his cheek cast ghoulish in the low light like a child telling stories by a campfire. He took another chair, straddled it and sat with the rifle absently trained on Jason.

"Well, this is pretty goddamned surreal," Ferris said. He rested the rifle butt on his thigh, dug in his pocket for a cigarette and offered one to Jason. Jason accepted and leaned forward to let the candle flame kiss the tip of the cigarette.

"What are you doing up here?" Ferris asked. "You left the bar in such a hurry, I figured you had something worthwhile to go do. Even left behind that tasty singer."

Jason kept his eyes on the table. It was the same as his early days with the bullies, times when he learned that the blows were coming regardless of resistance or pleading. Back then, he decided that he'd always fight back, throw the first punch while the larger kid was menacing him with threats. If he couldn't do that, he'd take the beating as quiet as possible. They wouldn't get the satisfaction of hearing him beg.

"Course that singer isn't your woman, right? We've established that earlier. Can a woman be considered yours when she's already married? I mean, times are changing, but it seems like some things stay the same." Ferris let the smoke roll out of his nose and envelop them. "Aren't we going to chat?"

Jason nodded towards the body. "Why'd you kill him?"

"Him?" Ferris pointed with the cherry of his smoke. "I wasn't really after him. You still haven't told me why you were coming up here."

"Fuck you," Jason said.

Ferris pressed the rifle barrel against Jason's inner thigh. "I'll ask again, and you'll be polite unless you want your dick blown off."

Jason crushed his cigarette out on the tabletop. "Somebody gave me a letter to deliver. I was bringing it to Davey."

"And how do you know him?"

"I don't. It was just a favor."

Ferris let the barrel slide down, the steel caressing its way to Jason's knee. "You got this letter on you?"

"In my pocket."

"Take it out slow," Ferris said. "Keep in mind I've got no problem stacking you on top of the pile."

Jason rose off the chair, went into his back pocket for the letter and dropped it on the table where Ferris scooped it up. Ferris struggled unfolding it with one hand, the other still busy aiming the gun. For a moment, Jason considered grabbing a candle and swinging while Ferris was occupied, but what would be the point of a single strike? Ferris leaned close to read in the candlelight, his lips mouthing the words as his eyes traced down the lines. After he finished, he sat back shaking his head.

"You read this?" Ferris asked.

"No."

"Bullshit, you read it."

"I don't read things that aren't for me."

"So, you have no idea you were carrying a confession?"

Jason shook his head. "I don't know what you're talking about."

"That little bitch you and your Uncle Henry employ killed Sheriff Thompson. This is his confession."

Jason scoffed, but he was remembering the night in the morgue, Terry sitting in the floor near the sheriff's body, the bottles of chemicals swaddled in his lap. He knew Ferris had no reason to lie. Especially if he was likely to be shot in a moment. Still, his mouth denied it. "Bullshit."

"You wanna read for yourself?" Ferris let the paper hover over the candle flame. "Last chance."

When Jason didn't respond, Ferris touched the paper to the fire. It lit quickly, the orange flame licking its way up toward his fingers. Ferris held it until the flames looked ready to creep across his palm, then let it sail down to wither and blacken in front of them on the table.

"Do you know why he killed the sheriff?" Ferris asked.

"No."

"Because I told him to. If he hadn't, he'd be like this one over there," Ferris pointed to the dead man in the corner. "Now, have you figured out what I needed from you earlier tonight?"

"You want me to do something for your brother," Jason said.

"You seem willing to be a delivery boy. I want you to deliver something to Huddles."

Jason shook his head. "I'm not bringing anything inside. I don't care about the consequences."

Ferris smacked him hard across the face. The man's open hand left a stinging in his jaw, and Jason could taste the blood from his split lip. He spit on the table, and Ferris leaned forward to strike him again. The force nearly made Jason topple from his chair.

"You aren't the only one you have to worry about. Little sawed-off shit like you might be ready to die, but what about your drunk Uncle Henry? What about Sharon Hendricks? You're gonna leave here tonight under contract. Otherwise, my next stop after leaving you rotting on this mountain is her house. Do you understand?"

Ferris closed the distance until Jason could smell the man's breath, those unblinking gray eyes locked on him, the tattooed hand rising as if longing to hit him again. Jason swallowed a mouthful of blood and looked back to Davey's body. He didn't want to die in this cabin, but he was more concerned with Sharon and Uncle Henry. Make the deal, he told himself. Make the deal, and then figure some way out of it.

"What do you want me to bring him?" Jason asked.

"Nothing much. Just something to use on Terry Blankenship. Now I know what you're thinking. You think you owe the boy something, but that ain't so. He got you into this mess. Get my brother the gear and it's all over. Understand?"

"I understand," Jason said. He could barely breathe, his chest heavy as if some unimaginable weight were crushing down on his diaphragm.

Ferris stood, took Jason by the collar and pulled him to his feet.

Ferris held up Jason's revolver. "I'm gonna hang onto this," he said, then pointed down the mountain. "After you."

Jason led Ferris to his truck. Both men were tired, sweating from the hike down the mountain. Still, Ferris looked more resilient, stood tall while Jason hunched over feeling as if his bones might be reduced to chalk. The ache was an arching wave now. Something that originated in his joints and radiated outward through him until even his digits throbbed.

"I'll have the package waiting for you tomorrow morning," Ferris said. "One last thing to remember, any calls or any attempt to get in touch with that uncle or girlfriend, well it might save one, but I'll get the other. Understand?"

Jason sucked at his swollen gums. "I'm not stupid."

"Good to know. It'll be on your patio tomorrow morning. Remember, I'm watching."

Ferris climbed into his truck, sat watching until Jason put his own truck in gear and drove home.

CHAPTER TWELVE

EARLY MORNING RAIN had saturated the mountains until the runoff washed into the low lands, filling the valley roads and turning the ground into a soup of mud. Jason hadn't slept, just watched the rain out his bedroom window, thinking about it pouring through the holes in the cabin roof to wash Davey's body clean of evidence. It was still a surreal experience. His mind felt unsure it had really happened, but the scrapes on his palms and the tender places where Ferris slapped him made it undeniable. So did the parcel, which he'd found right where Ferris said it would be. A small bag stuffed under the cushion of his porch swing. He sat on the deck, the package unopened on his lap and watched his neighbors fret at the slow swell of the creek that ran behind their homes. Downstairs, mourners congregated to pay final respects to Mrs. Cole, an elderly woman who finally passed in her sleep during one of the week's wet nights. The men and women huddled close under the awning in their sodden coats. It was a solid turnout considering the early hour and the rain.

Before Uncle Henry lost the funeral home, Jason would have been out there with them, a loaned pallbearer since Mrs. Cole had outlived all her male relations. Jason wondered how many evenings he'd spent as a boy wearing an itchy black suit and carrying strangers to their grave. Pallbearers who weren't kin seemed an odd custom for people who buried their dead in such private plots. Hill people liked to carry their own, but too many graves were located on the mountainside, a trek up a steep incline with the casket braced on a few young shoulders. Now, people bought plots just off the freeway. Jason drove by them some nights, looked out upon the rows of flat headstones that could be mowed over easily and found he missed the hard clay and overgrowth of secret family cemeteries. When it was his time, he wanted planted in the woods. This sentiment made him think again of Davey. How long before the coyotes or mountain cats drug away his bones?

Jason hadn't mustered the bravery to open Ferris' package. He simply turned it in his hands, gave it a shake and judged the weight like a child with a Christmas present. Whatever was inside seemed small. It rattled around with a metallic tinkling. All he knew was that it would be dangerous. It might as well have been a box of spiders.

Jason left it sitting on the swing, stood to hold the railing and considered if he could actually go through with this. If he did, he'd be responsible for two young lives ending. Terry would die, and Huddles would be forever damned to either prison or the will of his brother. Jason had no doubt Ferris would use the boy up, but he tried to justify it, to tell himself he didn't owe the boys anything. Terry's life was over anyway. He'd gotten Jason involved in his crimes and would likely be discovered as the sheriff's murderer. Still, this was only a way of deflecting blame. If he took whatever tools were in the package to Huddles, Jason knew he might as well be murdering both boys with his own hands.

He pulled on his overcoat and went downstairs to start the truck. When the mourners glanced in his direction, Jason offered a weak nod of condolences. They turned back to their cigarettes and coffee, conversation about how fine Mrs. Cole looked in the casket. The truck wouldn't start. Jason turned the key several times with only the weak straining of the engine. He pumped the gas until the engine flooded and the whole lot smelled of the combustible fluid. The old men on the porch watched him. A few seemed ready to offer advice, to roll up their sleeves and go under the hood, but Jason went back upstairs before any could approach.

In the kitchen, he called Beverly and told her he needed a ride. She agreed to be by in fifteen minutes. This left little time for a decision. Jason went back on the porch, sat in the swing and unwrapped Ferris' package. It contained a single dark vial a clear, odorless liquid. Jason turned the item over in his hand. The poison looked harmless in his palm. It could probably travel safely in a pocket, but he stuffed the vial inside his sock where it lay against his ankle. He went into the bed-room and dressed quickly. Blue checkered shirt, black slacks, and a new clip-on. His favorite tie was still floating in urine at the bar.

After a few more minutes of watching the mourners mingle, Bever-ly's car came up the road. She parked the Chevy away from the wake's traffic and Jason ran down from the porch, splashing across the deep puddles in the road.

"Thanks," he said as he climbed inside the car. The interior smelled of leather protectant. The back seat lay full of spare clothes, a few pair of jeans and empty water bottles. "I appreciate this."

"No worries," she said. He should've formulated an excuse in case she asked why he left the bar so quickly, but Jason's mind was else-where. He was watching the runoff from the mountain fill the ditch beside Ralph Fortner's trailer. The water would be in the man's yard by noon if this kept up. Ralph stood on his porch, sipping beer and wait-ing as if he'd already lost the place. Jason thought it might be the smartest attitude. No sense combating uncontrollable elements.

"You remember last time when the creek flooded?" Jason asked.

Beverly squint her eyes as if she were trying to visualize the day. "What about it?"

"It trapped a widowed woman and her two babies on the roof of their trailer. I'd been out with Uncle Henry helping Bud Richmond evacuate people. Two miners wanted to risk a trip across in an old john boat with nothing but a troweling motor. Bud tried to talk them out of it, but they went on anyway. Only one washed up. They found him a quarter of a mile downstream."

"Shit, "Beverly said. She dried her hair with a towel from the back seat. The rough fibers brought out her natural curl until the damp tangle spilled around her head like wild roots. "What happened to him?"

"Found him clung to a big tree stump. All his clothes had been sucked off by the current. He was shivering and praying when they pulled him out. I remember wrapping him in a blanket while Clayton Briggs plowed his brand-new Ranger into the trailer's front door. He got the woman and kids out, and Bud cussed the woman before she got a foot on dry land, told her she'd been warned to have her country ass out days ago. He said that she'd drowned a good man."

"Bud always had a temper. He used to run with Doc Foster and those other hellions."

"That must have been the bravest thing I've ever seen."

"Pretty selfless out of Clayton, too. I know how much he loves fishing those tournaments."

Jason shook his head. "Those first boys, I mean. The ones in the john boat."

Beverly snorted. "Stupid if you ask me."

"Clayton knew he could get across and be a hero. Shit, people still buy him drinks. Those first boys, they might as well have been hitting the beach at Normandy."

Beverly looked over the few mourners sharing cigarettes. One man fiddled with a camera, his large fingers struggling to replace the digital chip.

"All you redneck men admire martyrs too much," she said. "See a couple mine shafts collapse, a couple OD's and start getting strange."

She pulled out onto the road and offered the towel to Jason. Her bangs still dripped, but she only brushed them off her forehead. Jason took the towel and folded it over his knee. He could tell her everything, make her drive straight to Sharon's so he could see she was okay, take them both to the police station and confess what he knew. It wasn't too late, but he just sat back and listened to the tires surge through the puddles, to Beverly humming quietly as he thought about those old floodwaters.

AT THE SHELL, Jason followed Beverly straight to Control. Malcolm was in the middle of another apocalyptic tantrum. Both Fitzgerald and Sir Hendricks stood by his cell door, trying to reason with him as he slung his body headlong into the far wall. His tiny frame would go limp right before he collided into the painted cinder blocks, body dropping back as if boneless. He sucked in a breath, climbed to his feet and ran at the wall with another scream. At some point, he must have bitten his tongue. The gaps of his teeth were full of blood.

"You need to go in," Jason said, but Sir Hendricks was already on the mic, requesting assistance.

While the rest were concerned with Malcolm, Jason stopped in the employee restroom. He sat on the closed toilet, took the poison from its hiding place and dropped it inside his coat pocket. His hands were trembling, lungs burning like the oxygen in the room were on fire. The urge to cry filled him, a swelling in his throat he hadn't felt since adolescence when the bullies would circle like wolves. It wasn't fear like those days, but shame that made his eyes well. He stared in the mirror for a long moment, whispered lies to himself that things were fine, then splashed some water on his face and went to B-Unit.

The boys were riled up. They lined the main entrance, clamoring and hoping for news of Malcolm's latest battle. Holding couldn't be seen from the main floor, but Malcolm's caterwauling came loud enough for his voice to echo throughout the whole facility. Woods, Callan, and Robison debated how many officers it would take to bring him down.

"Little shit ain't big enough to be this much trouble," Callan said. His eye was still bruised from Sir Hendricks' tackle. When he saw Jason passing by, he snorted. "Oh shit, sorry bro."

"No worries," Jason said. "Just remember, it only took one to floor you. Guess the little shit has you beat."

Robison and Woods cackled.

"Where's Huddles and Terry?" Jason asked once they caught their breath.

"Terry's in Medical," Woods said. "Says he's sick."

Down the corridor, Jason saw Huddles' door ajar. The boy sat on his bunk, a book lying open across his knee. Huddles always looked strange in his cell, his muscles tensed beneath the quiet demeanor, only docile in the way a jungle cat seems relaxed to observers at the zoo. His eyes surveyed the room, eyebrows arching high as Jason nudged the door closed.

"We gotta talk," Jason said. He came forward and sat on the edge of Huddle's bed.

Huddles didn't move or ask what this was about, but Jason could see the boy knew it would be more than another discussion about his grief over Shane. Understanding filled Huddles' eyes with the speed of a bug colliding into a car windshield. The world unquestionably one way, then irrevocably another. Jason could feel the judgment, the boy's surprise that his brother snagged someone who'd seemed incorruptible. He expected Huddles to lord it over him, to use the reversal of power in some sadistic way, but Huddles seemed a little disappointed, like he'd been hoping for something to finally destroy his cynicism.

"So, you're the one he found to bring it," Huddles said. He pushed himself up on his elbows.

"Not my idea," Jason said. "He threatened my family."

Huddles dog eared the page in his book and set it aside.

"Let's see it," he said.

Jason took the vial from his pocket and laid it on the bed. Huddles slid it beneath his mattress.

"When did he tell you?" Jason asked.

"The other day at visitation."

"Do you know why?"

"I know."

Jason didn't believe Huddles was as cold as he tried to act. Beneath the posturing, there was reticence in the boy, some fear in taking things so far. Running guns and dope was one thing. Murder in a public place, he wouldn't be able to come back from that. It occurred to Jason that in some ways their relationship was more honest now. The truth of this made him consider the futility of The Shell. How could a man help children with all these games of trust?

"You don't really want to do this, do you?" Jason asked. "I mean, your brother knows you can't get away with it. All the main corridors have cameras." Jason pointed to the mattress where the poison was hidden. "Even if you manage to get him alone, that's going to show up in an autopsy. You won't be able to blame it on somebody else."

Huddles leaned back against the concrete wall and squeezed his eyes shut.

"What choice do I got?" he asked. "Look what happened to Shane."

"Maybe there's another option," Jason said. "We could get you sent to Tiger."

Huddles didn't shrink at the mention of Tiger, but Jason could read the worry in his brow.

"You know what will happen to me up there?" Huddles asked.

"I know you won't be a convicted murderer and I won't be an accomplice."

Huddles stared at the ceiling as if some answer might manifest there. "I don't want to hurt him. Shit, I like the kid. I lent him my shoes the other day." Huddles wiped his eyes and looked at Jason. "Assuming this could work, how do we do it?"

"Lay low a few days. Refuse Education and just ride it out in here. Your next court date is four days away. I'll write the reports on how you need to be sent somewhere more secure."

"So, you railroad me in court? Great. What if it ain't enough? I could bust Woods in the nose or something?"

"No, no more violence. Just lay low, stay in your cell as much as possible and we'll get through it."

"I'm trusting you," Huddles said. "But remember, you brought this shit in. You try to deviate from the plan, I start talking."

"No need for that," Jason said.

They sat in silence, the pact hanging over them while Jason tried to think of a way to seal it. Perhaps they should shake hands, slit their palms and mix their blood.

"You dump that shit in the toilet," Jason said. "I'm trusting you. Anything else you need?"

"Time alone," Huddles said and picked his book back up.

Jason left him be, stepped outside and watched as the B-Unit boys began another game of spades.

MEDICAL ALWAYS REMINDED Jason of hospitals from his youth. There was no real resemblance. The hospital that preformed his surgery was tailored to children. Friendly cartoon animals were painted on the exam room walls and a game room had been established where he first played Nintendo during his rehabilitation. Later, he learned to beat all comers at air hockey even sitting in his wheelchair. The staff tried to make it a place without fear, but underneath all the amusements lingered the antiseptic smell of sickness, of broken bones recently set in hardening plaster, vomit expunged from pain-filled stomachs and the sweat of parents who hadn't slept or been home to wash in days. The smell of Medical was the same. It triggered some olfactory memory that made Jason feel phantom pains in his thighs as he walked in.

The exam rooms in Medical held no cartoon animals for these kids. The walls and linens in the main ward a stark white that let every stain on the sheets stand out. A tired nurse slouched at the front desk. Her eyes heavy lidded, blinking incessantly to stay awake. Jason didn't bother to speak with her, just walked past the beds lined up like the sleeping quarters of some barracks. Terry lay in the next to last bunk with IV tubing dripping fluid into his arm. His gown was too large. The open neck exposed his collar bones.

Jason stood at the foot of the bed until Terry looked up from his lap. His eyes were heavy with the effort of consciousness.

"Did you see Davey?" Terry asked.

Jason spent the morning wondering if he could successfully lie. He never bothered to weigh any other options. The truth was untenable, but he still didn't know if he could make the fabrications work. The complete silence of the infirmary didn't help. It was as if Jason could hear the miniscule processes that kept the bodies alive. Still, the truth would carve out any resilience left in Terry. Under different circumstances, he might have told him about the plan with Huddles, might have let him understand the danger they were all in, but not with such weakness seeping off the kid. The less the boy knew in this state, the better. He'd need to sell the lie hard.

"He was gone when I got there," Jason said as he sat on the edge of the bed.

"They've got him." Terry signed, ground his knuckles into his eyes. His breath became a shudder that tried to hold back tears. "What about the letter?"

"I read it," Jason said. "After that, I burned it."

Tears welled up in Terry's eyes, but he didn't sob. It was as if he were too exhausted even for that.

"I was so afraid to tell anyone," Terry said. "What would he think of me?"

Jason reached out and took his hand. Tubing and tape kept him from being able to clasp it tight, but Terry didn't pull away.

"You need to tell me who else knows," Jason said. "I can't help you otherwise."

Terry still wouldn't look at him. "Why are you doing this? Why didn't you just turn me in that first night?"

Jason had asked himself, but never managed to articulate it. Maybe because no one would have done it for him. Maybe because no one cared enough for him to cry the way Terry was weeping now. Maybe just because he was in too deep to dig his way out. An accessory to so much that he might as well go tether a rope from the rafters of the funeral home.

"Who else knows?" Jason asked again.

"Just Ferris. I didn't want to do it. I'm sorry."

The levy broke, and Terry began to tremble. He pulled the sheets high until he was bundled in them, face hidden in the starched folds. Jason patted Terry's impaled hand, squeezed his cold fingers.

"It's gonna be okay."

"He'll kill me," Terry said. "As soon as I'm outta here, he'll kill me."

If he'd been a decent man, Jason would've explained the plan. Let him know about Huddles' orders and their scheme to circumvent them, but he couldn't trust Terry with it.

"You can only guess at what he knows."

If Terry heard, Jason couldn't be sure. He'd receded into his grief, all choked sobs with the sheets shielding his mouth.

FERRIS GILBERT WAS waiting when Jason got home. He sat in the swing on Jason's porch, rocking slow as he pushed the glider back and forth with the heel of his boot. The neighbors had all retreated inside, but Jason doubted Ferris would kill him on the porch. In Jason's childhood, moments of violence became so frequent he learned to anticipate them, to almost feel the electric charge in the air, a stiffening of the hairs on his arms and an ache in his balls before the first punch was thrown. None of this emitted from Ferris. He just sat swinging where the package had rested that morning.

"Wanna invite me in?" Ferris asked.

"Not particularly," Jason leaned his back against the railing. "I did what you asked."

"I knew you would." Ferris reached into the pocket of his coat and came out with a roll of bills secured by a rubber band. He snapped the band off and let the bills unfurl so Jason could see the amount.

"I don't want that," Jason told him.

Ferris shrugged and lumbered to his feet with some effort. He stuck the bills in Jason's shirt pocket.

"You did the work, you have to take it," he said. "I'm insistent on this point."

Money overflowed from his pocket like an obscene handkerchief. Jason transferred the bills to his pants. For a moment, that seemed to be the end of business, but Ferris opened his coat and pulled out Jason's revolver from the night before. Ferris opened the cylinder to show it was unloaded and handed it over. The gun felt wrong in Jason's hands, tarnished by the time it spent traveling in Ferris' coat.

"I thought you'd want that back," Ferris said. "It looked like an antique."

"It was my grandfather's," Jason said.

"I know all about the importance of heirlooms," Ferris said. "I've got an old shotgun that was my father's. It'll belong to Huddles when I'm gone. Passing things down is important. When you own a thing used by generations before you, that thing carries the imprint of its previous deeds. I know that's the case with my daddy's gun."

Jason considered how many felines the revolver had laid low. He closed the cylinder, felt the heft of the dangerous, beautiful thing and wondered why he couldn't feel the echo of all those dead animals, of the times his grandfather had used the pistol in anger or self-defense.

"You believe that?" Ferris asked.

Jason shook his head. "I don't guess I do. That or maybe I just can't feel it."

"You haven't done anything to make it yours," Ferris said. "It's still your grandfather's in your mind. Once it's yours, then you'll feel the history."

"How do you make it yours?"

Ferris smiled. "It's a gun. I'd say best way is to shoot something."

Jason didn't want to hold the pistol anymore, so he stuck it in the front of his pants. The barrel poked his leg, the heavy piece making his pants sag.

"Are we square?" Jason asked. "I need to know my family is safe."

"We're square. Long as you keep things to yourself. I get even a hint you're talking, I'll burn that shithole of your uncle's down and scalp your bitch. I promise."

Ferris stepped past him and began descending the steps, but stopped to linger on the middle flight.

"Remember what I said about that iron," Ferris said. "Make your own notch or else it'll never be yours."

Jason watched Ferris all the way down to the street, hand on the butt of the gun as he climbed into his truck and drove back towards Lynch.

CHAPTER THIRTEEN

THE HEAT IN the motel room left an electric tingle on Jason's bare skin, the clinging fabric of the sheets molding to his stomach as he sat up in bed smoking the stub of a Camel while Sharon preened in the vanity mirror. Something transfixed him when watching her like this. The way she massaged concealer under her eyes, brushed her lashes with mascara and stared at her own reflection felt like the sort of private moment that no man should witness.

When he was able to be honest with himself, Jason knew unguarded moments like this were important because he'd believed he would never have them. Sex never worried him. Even in his strange body, some women might go to bed with him out of pure curiosity. Certain women looked at him with what he thought of as carnival lust, a sort of sideshow greed that came from wondering what it would be like to wrap their legs around a body so misshapen it might feel inhuman against their own and, while embracing the grotesque, would make them feel better about their own, casual imperfections. If not those women, then there were the whores who prowled the night in Cherry Tree. Sex he could get, but this was different. Something in people made them want to touch the taboo, but not love it.

Sir Hendricks was away for the night at one of his fairs, competing in the broadsword tournament with the other false knights. Jason and

Sharon had taken the opportunity and rented a room on the outskirts of Lynch, halfway between Huntington and Charleston. For once, they'd be able to fall asleep together, wake tangled in bed sharing morning breath and tousled hair. After seeing Ferris that evening, Jason felt fortunate to have another night, especially one like this.

"What are you thinking?" Sharon asked. She didn't turn, just kept watching her reflection as she fluffed her hair. The muscles in her back contorted as she leaned close to the mirror.

"Nothing much," Jason said.

Sharon turned to let him know she recognized the lie and then went back to her reflection.

He'd been considering his discussion with Huddles. The boy hadn't even looked scared holding the poison. The longer he lived in the world of The Shell, the more it changed him. A cynicism stronger than he could have imagined in his youth was beginning to sap the last of his idealistic nature. Maybe that was what made Sharon's nude body so hard to accept. In a world where children were contracted to commit murder, how could moments like this exist? Then he reminded himself that she belonged to another man and things began to feel proper.

A part of him wanted to tell her everything, but he knew it would only cause fear. Ferris had promised to leave her out of it. Maybe it was only selfishness, but he convinced himself there was no reason to ruin one of their few nights.

"I suppose I'm worried," Jason said.

"About Randall?" she asked.

Hearing her husband's first name irritated him. Jason preferred Sir Hendricks. It fit more than Randall, which seemed the moniker of a simpler and safer man. Sharon perched at the foot of the bed, crossed her legs and let her long arms rest on her bent knees. When Jason was a boy and the casts were still on his legs, his worst fear had been that one night he might wake and see the devil seated at the foot of his bed. He never worried that it would be the Halloween horns and bifurcated tail. He imagined whatever it was might look beautiful as Sharon did now. A tempting mirage that could make him hand over his soul for a single touch.

In a way, he was readying himself to lose her. Even if she loved him, it seemed unlikely that she would leave Sir Hendricks. The two were chained together by something unnamable. Jason knew the tragedy of it would be that life would simply go on. There would be no apocalyptic upheaval. He would go back to being alone, but now with the knowledge of what he was missing, would grow old and become the sort of man others assumed had always been alone. No one would know he'd ever had nights like this, and without the public knowledge of what he'd lost there would be nothing romantic in his sadness.

Her touch brought him out of these thoughts.

Sharon furrowed her brow in imitation. "This deep worry," she said. "Let it go for a bit."

He tried, but doubt kept breaching the mental walls he erected. There were things he wanted to say. He wanted to tell her that he'd been clay when she found him and she had molded him into something of substance, but words would've been inadequate, his internal poetry without meter.

"He's going to be in trouble at work," she said.

"Hendricks? How so?"

Sharon took the burning butt from Jason's hand and dropped it in a half-full Solo cup of flat Coke. It went out with a hiss as she rubbed his chest.

"He was talking about it the other night. He really worked one of the kids over. Now, he thinks they'll file charges on him."

"But they haven't yet?" Jason asked.

"No, but he feels it's coming. That's usually all that matters."

Sharon once said Hendricks was a man of superstition. He might not read signs in chicken entrails, but his belief was dictated by gut feelings. The kind of man to taste change on the wind.

"What was it over?" Jason asked.

"He said the boy refused to hand over a book. He's lost it over less. It's all wrapped up in this code of his. This bullshit macho knight stuff. It's exhausting watching him try to be a man. That's one of the things I like so much about you."

"You like that I don't meet the requirements?" Jason said it like a joke, but he nervously awaited her response. He'd never understood fully what she saw in him. Hopefully, he wasn't only a refuge towards weakness after years with a man preoccupied by violence.

"Is that what you think about yourself?" she said. "If anything, you're luckier than most men. You didn't feel like you could meet all the rules, so you didn't have to find out the truth the hard way."

"What truth is that?"

"The rules are all impossible. Society's version of manhood, it's a rigged game. You've gotten to be a man on your own terms. What could be better than that?"

How could he explain that others still held him to that standard? He tired of walking the halls of B-Unit where even adolescents pitied his inability to grow tall and straight. The idea that someone had excepted this, and that someone was as exceptional a woman as Sharon, still seemed impossible. Jason had to fight the idea that it would all be revealed as a cruel cosmic joke.

"It isn't easy," he said.

"I know. That's what makes you brave."

Sharon stretched out on the sheets beside him. Jason wanted to touch her, but knew there was more she needed to say. Sharon scooted forward until her back rested against the headboard.

"I want to go away somewhere," she said. "Would you take me?"

Jason thought about the money Ferris forced him to take. More money than he'd ever had in his life. Enough to escape Lynch and The Shell.

"Where?" Jason asked.

"Anywhere else."

"Back to South Dakota?"

"Well," she said with a grin. "Anywhere, but South Dakota."

Jason indulged himself for a moment with daydreams of buffalo grass and flat land rolled out as far as he could see, of winters with snow so deep a man might look out at the endless ice and forget his way. A place where the only possibilities weren't cheap hotels and quick rutting hidden among his uncle's renovations. He told himself this offer of leaving wasn't legitimate. It was foolish to believe it. Things would run their course and end as expected. He didn't know why this was so ingrained in his mind. He knew Sharon could read the doubt on him and a part of him thought she was owed an explanation, only he couldn't explain it. Even if he managed, he would be telling another man's wife.

"I'd like to see where you come from," Jason said. "You've seen where I grew up. I want to know everything about you."

"Can't I just tell you?"

"It's not the same as seeing someone in their home."

"I got you a present," Sharon said. She reached underneath the bed and pulled out a large box wrapped in golden paper.

"When did you sneak this in?"

"When you were in the shower earlier. I've been saving it for days."

With the parcel in his hand, Jason could only think of the package Ferris forced him to deliver. He closed his eyes, breathed in and began to tear away the golden paper. Inside, secured underneath a layer of gossamer tissue paper, was a leather jacket and a gray denim shirt. The jacket's nickel belt buckle jingled as Jason held it up and slid his arms inside the cool sleeves.

"I thought of you when I saw it," Sharon said. "I was so worried it wouldn't fit. Do you like it?"

"I love it," he said. Secretly, Jason had wanted a leather jacket ever since he saw *The Outsiders* as a kid. He'd never found one that fit and hadn't been able to afford something tailored that wasn't for pallbearer duties.

"I hope you didn't spend too much on this," he said.

Sharon ran hands over the leather shoulders, pulled the coat closed and carefully zipped it up. The leather clung around Jason in a slick embrace.

"You're a new man. You need a new look."

He wanted the jacket to be a symbol of something, for the two of them to be creating happiness that just once wouldn't dissipate like train smoke. Sharon peeled the coat off him, then began to slide under the covers where their skin rubbed together.

IN THE DAYS of Huddles' isolation that followed, Malcolm's constant war whittled the staff down. Everyone inside The Shell operated in irritation. Even Beverly refused to smile anymore. If any of this were a victory for Malcolm, he didn't ease up to celebrate. He spent the early mornings screaming and pounding the walls until the team suited up and restrained him for the first time that day. Breaches had become such ritual that they put the gear on without comment, each man helping the other with their buckles and waiting solemn by the cell door as if they were about to receive communion.

The outbursts made the guards more creative. Hendricks' trick with the cartoons hadn't even lasted a week, but that small cease-fire made the group believe there must be some answer to fixing the boy's behavior. Beverly tried sitting in the floor outside his cell and reading picture books. Her voice slipped easily into the croak of talking toads or the excited cadence of puppy dogs. Jason enjoyed watching her crouched by the cell window asking "See, there he is" as she pointed out the illustrations. Malcolm listened to three or four books in a row before going back to screaming and beating the walls.

Fitzgerald brought his grandfather's fiddle. His bowing was awkward, but he managed a few ballads, the strings whining high and lonesome in the otherwise empty corridor. Jason listened through the door inside Control. Eventually, even the fiddle lost its hold on Malcolm. Weeks ago, Beverly had already turned to the more productive method of expediting Malcolm's transfer to a psychiatric hospital for juvenile offenders in Ohio. Even with all the momentum, Jason knew it would take months. By the time bureaucracy allowed action, Malcolm would have buried any resolve they had left. Already men were slow to respond to his wailings. Jason found himself sitting in Control watching the boy scream for full minutes before he keyed anyone on the intercom.

ONE MORNING, JASON heard water spilling against the tile floor. The sound came muted through the Control door, but loud enough to know it wasn't just a slow trickle. Malcolm must have plugged the toilet again. Jason went to the dark window and looked out at the holding cells. Malcolm wasn't visible from where he stood, so Jason popped the door to Control and went for a closer look. He found Malcolm kneeling in front of the stainless steel toilet. His small fingers clasped the rim of the bowl as he lowered his head into the water. Jason expected Malcolm to emerge quickly after the first douse, but the boy held himself under longer with each descent, pushing his face deeper until only his hair floated on the surface. Just when Jason thought it impossible for someone to hold their breath that long, Malcolm pulled his head out and looked up at him. His eyes opened in small slits like a cat's and the whites were a mass of busted vessels. They held each other's gaze for a long moment, and then Malcolm's head slipped back into the water.

"HE'S GOING TO die," Jason said. Sharon sat across from him in the vinyl booth. They were forty miles outside of Lynch on one of the rare trips into public they allowed themselves. Hendricks hadn't returned from his tournament yet, but Sharon said he called and had won second place in the archery contest. He'd be home by Friday, the day they were scheduled to take Huddles to court. The diner was named Monroe's, an old double-wide trailer with concert bills for dead country music stars papering walls left smoke stained from the twelve-hour slow cooked brisket served most Saturdays. A jukebox sat in the corner. Garth Brooks was the newest artist available the last time Jason bothered to look.

"Why would you say that?" Sharon stirred her cup of chili and sipped her sweet tea. "All those people around. Medical staff on site. I don't think anyone is going to die."

Jason nodded, but kept seeing Malcolm's head dipping into the toilet like an obscene baptism. The deliberate way he exhaled all the air from his lungs before letting the water cover him. Malcolm had been placed on suicide watch, but that didn't change anything. He was already in the cell reserved for monitoring, already receiving mandatory checks every thirty minutes from the guards. All they could do was outfit him in a green paper pickle suit that offered no hems strong enough to fashion a noose.

"I can't explain it, but I don't see him lasting much longer."

Jason gouged a slice of apple pie with his fork, took a bite and pushed the plate away. The warmth of the diner made him unbutton the collar of the shirt Sharon bought him. The thick fabric wasn't suited for summer, but he wore it anyway to please her. It was the smallest size the men's department carried and he'd tucked it into his jeans to hide the way its tail fell low against his thighs. He didn't have the heart to let her know how poorly the gift fit. Eventually, he'd hem it the way he did all of his clothing. Sharon ate his slice of pie while Jason stared out the window.

"What are your plans once this is over?" she asked.

It was her way of hinting at leaving again. There wasn't anything holding him to home. There was no opportunity left in the hills. With the mines shutting down there wouldn't be much left of Lynch in ten years anyway. Just empty storefronts and the few families left behind without jobs, becoming more isolated as the economy collapsed. Jason guessed everyone would pull up stakes eventually or be forced into the regression of a frontier barter system and poaching. He needed to leave with or without Sharon, but the mountains were all he knew.

"You wouldn't be taking anything from him, Jason," Sharon said. "I haven't loved him for a long time."

* * *

Malcolm began biting his forearm that night when Jason arrived to work a late shift. Jason found him during a routine check, his small teeth sunk deep into the pale skin and his head twisting as the blood oozed out around his lips. Whenever pain overtook him, Malcolm would suck at his teeth and bite down again, attacking the wound at a new angle. Jason reached for the radio he didn't have, then began to pound on the nearby Control door. The officer inside opened up, but remained seated behind the board, his eyes dark as if he'd been sleeping.

"Call for assistance," Jason said. "We need Medical to Holding."

The officer looked confused, but began to reach for the intercom button. Jason brushed past him and smashed the button on the console.

"Officers and Medical to holding," he said.

On the black and white screens, Jason watched as men looked away from their magazines or television and began to sprint. He pushed buttons as fast as he could, unlocking as many doors as possible before the guards reached them. On-screen, Fitzgerald stood trapped at the exit to Education. He shifted his weight, hopping from one foot to another before he burst through the door hard enough to trip and sprawl across the floor.

Still, Fitzgerald was the first inside the holding cell. He grabbed Malcolm by the scruff of his neck and pried his mouth from his arm. Gore hung between the boy's teeth as he snapped at Fitzgerald's fingers. Fitzgerald wrapped his hands around the wound in an effort to staunch the flow while other officers gathered outside. Most stood still at the sight of Malcolm's flailing while Fitzgerald tried to hold the boy down. One of the nurses from Medical pushed past the crowd and came into the cell.

Jason left Control, and moved close enough to smell the metallic scent of the blood in the air. Fitzgerald held the boy down while the nurse worked. Two other guards held Malcolm's legs. The boy was slowing down, his body no longer racked by violent tremors as he fought against them. Eventually, he went limp in the mass of hands. Malcolm's bloody lips curled up into something near pleasure as the men and women held him. A gloved hand wiped the smeared blood from his chin, the latex making a squeak as it rubbed against the boy's exposed teeth.

CHAPTER FOURTEEN

HUDDLES DIDN'T LEAVE his cell much after talking with Jason. The first day was the hardest, the minutes dragging by until he thought time might cease its movement altogether, but the hours eventually passed. Mostly he drifted, neither entirely asleep nor awake. It wasn't quite the corridors of memory Ferris talked about. He'd lost the ability to access a specific moment for his past like turning to a page in a book. Now, memory came in sporadic flashes. He could be down at Ferrell's Pay Pond skewering chicken liver on a treble hook to catch catfish or have his hands covering Melissa Thornton's breast, his thumb rubbing the bud of her rising nipple through the thickness of a sweater. He saw a night from when he was ten years old, sneaking downstairs to watch Megan shimmying off her clothes to a Lynyrd Skynyrd song while Ferris sat at the end of The Cat's Den's stage, his empty eyes moving over her.

Whenever these moments receded, his brother always took precedence. He would see Ferris when he first came home from prison, outside in the July sun filling a garbage bag with the water hose. His brother pumped water into the bag until the thin plastic swelled nearly to bursting, then he would dead lift the bloated weight, water sloshing until it looked ready to breach the plastic's thin membrane. Ferris never tired or grunted, just emitted easy and calculated breaths through the gaps of his teeth. Sweat dripped from him, diving off the cliff of his nose without being wiped away. The image left Huddles cold. He would squeeze his eyes shut hard and force himself to remember something other than his brother's orders. Sometimes it worked, sometimes he just thought of Shane.

HUDDLES LAY ON the bed and thought about killing Terry. He'd never truly harmed anyone, but had watched Ferris do it. One night when he was fourteen, they drove out to Hatfield Bottom and parked the truck outside Aaron Mounts' place. Huddles sat in the middle, his small hands gripping the barrel of a Winchester to keep it from clattering around the cab.

"Wait here," Ferris said.

Huddles watched Ferris and Shane cross the yard. Even alone in the cab, the car still smelled like the men's whiskey sweat. Huddles' eyes squeezed shut and when he forced them open Shane already stood on the porch, knocking on the door while Ferris disappeared around the side of the house. Mounts came outside rubbing sleep from his eyes. He was shirtless, tattooed across his chest in markings Huddles couldn't decipher from such a distance and his stomach covered in wiry hair. They were talking, but Huddles couldn't hear anything.

Ferris stepped out of the darkness behind the house. Aaron saw him and tried to run as buckshot peppered the porch, sending splinters of wood flying, but he tripped down the uneven steps. Ferris shot him twice in the yard. Aaron's head came apart the way rotten Halloween pumpkins exploded whenever Huddles and Shane placed M-80s inside them.

The men stank of gun smoke when they climbed back in the car. A few specks of blood dotted Ferris' jeans. Huddles wanted to wipe at them with his hands. The shooting kept him awake for a week. When Huddles finally asked Ferris why he took him along, his brother sat on the edge of the bed scratching at his beard, his eyes on the ceiling as if the answer might materialize from the shadows.

"I needed to know I could trust you," he said. "One day, you'll be the one telling Shane what to do."

At the time it frightened Huddles, but after nights of replaying the shooting until he felt comfortable seeing Aaron's blood covering the grass, it began to make him proud. This pride disturbed him more than watching his brother kill the man. It was the first time he became aware of just what kind of power Ferris held over him, and while he never fully understood why or explained to himself where it came from, he knew it as absolute. Shane had been a testament to that. Even if he didn't want to hurt Terry, Huddles knew he couldn't tell his brother no. At best, he might be able to stall. Court was only days away. He could avoid Terry and bide his time until Jason shipped him to Tiger Morton.

TERRY CAME TO see him on the third day. He stepped inside the cell with caution, awkward eyes searching the corners rather than look at Huddles straight on. The neck of his jailhouse T-shirt had become a misshapen ring after so many washes and this allowed Huddles to see the purple bruise climbing up his collar bone.

"Why are you refusing class?" Terry asked.

"I don't feel like being out there."

"We got another game going today. We could use you on the court."

"I bet," Huddles said. "Which of them boys gave you the bruises?"

Terry hung his head. "Woods. He checked me hard when I went for a layup, but he didn't mean anything by it."

"He did it because you're gay. Woods is a homophobe."

Huddles thought Terry needed to know the truth, but he also wanted to test the waters of their relationship, to see if Terry was ready to share this secret with him. A bond seemed to be forming, but if Terry lied, it might mean that Ferris was right not to trust him.

"You won't tell anybody, will you?" Terry asked. "I'm not ashamed, but I'm scared in here."

"No, I won't tell anybody, but I need you to keep your distance for a few days."

"Because you can't be seen hanging around a queer?"

Huddles shook his head. "It's not like that. I need you to keep your distance because of something I gotta do and I don't want you to be involved in it."

"Is it for your father?" Terry asked. For a moment, Huddles thought the whole truth might come out. They were at least approaching the point where speaking about these secret connections seemed plausible. It would be a relief to tell the boy, to let him know what he'd been commissioned to do and how he didn't want to follow through with the task. Still, Huddles kept quiet. Better to remain vague.

"Yeah, it's for my father. Just keep clear a couple days. And stay away from Woods."

"I can handle Woods," Terry said.

"No," Huddles said. "I got that, too. Just waiting for an opportunity."

"Thank you," Terry said. Huddles couldn't be sure, but something deeper than the problem with Woods seemed to be hidden in the gratitude. A silent acknowledgment that both knew more than they could say.

HUDDLES DID LEAVE the cell one time that week. He exited to walk over the card table, lean down behind Woods and whisper in the kid's ear. He placed a hand on the boy's shoulder as he hissed out the insults, squeezed a little to let him feel the strength in his hands. Woods wanted to recoil from the hot breath in his ear, only Huddles kept him rooted in place until he'd finished his threats. Afterward, he mussed the boy's shaved head. On the way back to his cell, he stopped to give Terry a solemn nod. The boy had been silently watching the exchange.

CHAPTER FIFTEEN

JASON CAME IN early to ride on the transport to Huddles' court date. Once Control buzzed him through the outer doors, he walked onto the main floor and strolled by the ping-pong tables towards B-Unit where the boys sat playing spades. Pick-up hands of poker or blackjack came and went, but the spades tournament was a never-ending cycle. New players joined a continuous game that helped bridge the days together. Whenever a boy would be released, another simply took over the empty seat as if it were a requirement of his incarceration. No money was permitted, but the boys kept a mental tab of wins and losses. No doubt some of them would try to collect when they hit the streets.

Huddles was partnered with Woods. The small thief's eyes squinted as if trying to see some hidden truth in the cards. Sir Hendricks sat nearby with the newest edition of *Guns & Ammo* open on his lap. His forearm was marred by a long laceration Jason suspected he'd received during his recent tournament. Lately, he'd been trying to remain civil, but it was hard to separate his feelings for Sharon from their interactions.

"New Beretta?" Jason asked, pointing at the magazine.

"Yep. Getting one." Hendricks took out his earpiece, dug into the canal with his pinkie and put the earpiece back in. "We're leaving at oh-nine hundred hours to take Huddles to court. He's gotta be in his orange in fifteen, which means he and Woods best hurry."

Hendricks' radio gave a squawk and he turned the volume down. From the other side of the facility came Malcolm's familiar animal howls.

"Kid should be executed," Sir Hendricks said.

After the biting, Malcolm spent the night in Medical. Repeat outbursts forced the staff to keep him in restraints and eventually medicate him for the night. Now, the boy lay strapped to a hospital bed they'd wheeled into the Holding cell, a guard monitoring him around the clock.

"How often?" Jason asked.

"Every hour for the last three," Hendricks said. "You know, Fitzgerald tells me he likes it when they put him in The Wrap."

Watching Malcolm struggle in The Wrap, the fabric rippling as if he were being consumed by some beast made of canvas, Jason didn't see how anyone could enjoy such suffocation. Beverly came onto the unit wiping at the front of her windbreaker with a damp cloth. Her face was flushed and her hair had fallen from its tight bun until it clung against her neck. She sat next to Hendricks to watch the game.

"I just can't figure out what it's gonna take," she said.

"Ain't no excuse to act this way," Sir Hendricks said. He rubbed a finger inside his mouth, probing his upper gums. Jason heard him complaining to Officer Fitzgerald about small sores where he deposited his Copenhagen. It made him wonder if Sharon knew. Would she be devastated if her husband came home with a cancer diagnosis? Shameful thoughts emerged that Hendrick's death might leave her an available widow.

"We can handle him," Sir Hendricks said. "Just gotta get a little harder."

"I'm not going to court," Beverly said.

Hendricks sat forward. "What do you mean? You write the damned reports."

Beverly checked to made sure she wasn't keying her mike. "They gave me mandatory training in Fairmont. Boss says I have to go."

Jason had read the session reports. Beverly recommended that Huddles be shipped off to Tiger Harris. He'd done the same in his own notes, but it wasn't a place anyone went to lightly. Judge Wallace was one of the few barristers who hated to see troubled kids sent to harder facilities. He thought such confinement turned them into real criminals. However, he also carried a personal hatred for Ferris Gilbert. If he couldn't punish the older brother, any member of the clan might suffice. The judge would have to decide to keep the boy close under his thumb or send him on to a harder punishment. Either way, Beverly's absence would be an issue. Jason just hoped the reports would be enough. He'd promised Huddles he could get them both out of this.

If Huddles overheard their conversation, he didn't have anything to say about it. While the other inmates were busy spinning lies about criminal achievements or just mouthing off, Huddles had become quieter. All week he sat alone in his cell whispering. Jason recognized some murmurs as excerpts from *The Day of the Locust*. Huddles liked to recite passages just before lights out.

Another howl echoed from holding, followed by a squawk as Hendricks' radio came on. Jason could hear the fighting bleed out over the line, the hiss of Officer Fitzgerald saying, "Somebody grab his legs."

"Should just take that kid out and shoot him," Hendricks said. "Shoot all these little wastes."

Beverly pretended not to hear. Woods played a Joker and scraped the last hand of cards to his side of the table. His new teeth were already fuzzy with plaque as he smiled.

"Hell, we ain't worth a bullet," Woods said.

Jason and Hendricks waited by the outgoing desk while Huddles pulled the orange jumpsuit on in the bathroom. Officer Fitzgerald came waddling off the main floor. He still wore the padded chest protector that only covered the center of his sternum. Right about where a bull's-eye would be in his girth. He sat next to Jason, wiped his bald head and flicked sweat against the far wall.

"How's it going, Fitz?" Sir Hendricks asked. He was attempting to untangle the massive knot the leg irons had twisted themselves into, but every tug made the chains tighten around each other like coiling snakes.

"Living the dream," Fitzgerald said.

Hendricks continued to struggle with the chains until Fitzgerald took them from him and began to unravel the knot with his fat fingers. The chains fell apart with the gentle nature of his touch.

Huddles came out wearing the orange and placed his palms flat on the far wall. He spread his legs a shoulder's width apart. Fitzgerald squatted down and shackled his feet, then ran the belly chain around his waist and secured his cuffed hands to the chain.

Another scream came from the holding area, followed by the loud crack of something solid hitting the cell walls.

"He's strapped down," Fitzgerald said.

Jason walked down the corridor towards the holding cells. Malcolm lay flat on the hospital bed, secured by a series of thick leather straps. He fought against them, wriggling like a maggot as he made growls deep in his throat. He wore a helmet with a grid of metal covering his mouth. The surface lay scraped from previous fits as if it had skidded across a quarter mile of asphalt. The helmet seemed too heavy for him to completely lift his head, but Malcolm rose the few inches he was able and repeatedly drove back into the pillow hard enough to make his teeth rattle. Jason stepped closer to the glass and peered inside. Malcolm's bare feet were the only part of the boy that still seemed human. They protruded from the end of the sheets, twitching in time with the blows of his head. Jason wanted to lay hands on them, to preserve them in some way from becoming like the rest.

"Felts," Hendricks yelled from around the corner. "Give the freak show a rest. We're rolling out."

Malcolm began a low chant. His mouth quivered as the words poured out in an unconscious stream, fighting to be released from the prison of his mouth.

"Someone touch me," he said. "Somebody please just touch me."

EVEN THOUGH HUDDLES hadn't been outside The Shell in over a month, he asked for very little. At one point he requested the radio be changed to classic country. Another time he asked if the air-conditioner could be turned down a notch. He sat as far towards the edge of the seat as his chains would allow and laced his fingers through the wire mesh that separated the prisoners from the driver. Hendricks sat in back beside him, spitting Copenhagen into a Styrofoam cup. Drops of the liquid stained the collar of his shirt. Jason rode up front, watching the hills roll by as the transport van crossed the mountains. As much as he wanted to speak to Huddles or reassure him with some silent gesture, it seemed easier to ignore the boy. Huddles followed his lead.

Fitzgerald lectured as he drove. He told Huddles this could be the last chance to save himself. He needed to turn away from crime and do whatever was necessary to make a real change. He should find Jesus. He should go to Narcotics Anonymous, even if he'd never used, to see the effect of his product on others. He needed to stop living his life as a human parasite that profited on the misery of others because it was immoral and only made him weak and dependent, created a symbiotic relationship of pain. Huddles nodded in the right places. Jason just tuned out. It wasn't that Fitzgerald was a blowhard. He believed what he said and hoped that the stock speeches would be enough to change the mind of just one. Maybe it was, but Jason didn't see the point. No kid going to court was ever in the right mind frame for an epiphany. The smell of fresh cut grass along the highway couldn't permeate the stink of the van. No beauty would shine through the dark tinted windows. The ride was more waiting for the inevitable.

Despite his fear, Jason wanted to close his eyes and rest, but he'd gotten into trouble for falling asleep on transports before. The administrator considered it reckless. The kids respected it, decided that it meant Jason didn't have any fear of them, but that wasn't true. He'd just been tired.

Fitzgerald exited the interstate and soon they were downtown. Hendricks unfastened Huddles' seatbelt while Fitzgerald parked in the reserved area behind the courthouse.

"Beverly should be here," Fitzgerald said. "The judge is gonna raise Hell."

Hendricks helped Huddles out of the van. The leg shackles had little slack, and on more than one occasion inmates had tumbled out and busted their teeth against the pavement. Hendricks gripped Huddles behind the right elbow as they walked through the backdoor, past the elderly guard on duty who only looked up from his paperback long enough to wave them around the frame of the metal detector. In the hallways, raw-boned tweakers leaned on the benches in baggy, borrowed suits.

Huddles' attorney looked hunched in his rumpled seersucker blazer, but alert with eyes that surveyed the room while the prosecutor shuffled papers in a panic. The attorney pulled Huddles close, whispered directly into his ear. Jason strained to hear, but couldn't make anything out over the white noise of the proceedings.

The casual nature of a courtroom before a trial had a way of belittling the serious event that was about to take place. Bailiffs snickered with cops. Prosecutors discussed politics with representatives from state agencies. There was no reverence. It reminded Jason of the wakes he used to work. A room full of people socializing, their enjoyment only coming to an end when it was time to line up and pass by the bereaved and their departed. Jason had interned for a defense attorney while studying for his undergrad degree. He'd accompanied the lawyer to a trial where a man suffered a seizure while testifying. Afterwards, the counselors waited in the judge's chambers until the paramedics took the man away, and the judge, an ex-cowboy who wore pounds of turquoise jewelry, reenacted the fit by tossing his body about the room while he made tittering noises. Everyone laughed except Jason.

Judge Wallace was not the sort of man to have such a sense of humor. He took the stand to silence, stiff posture and straight faces. Huddles seemed calm. Most fidgeted or were unable to stand tall, but Huddles could have been carved from marble. Jason tuned out the initial protocol. He was focused on Huddles' lawyer, who sorted through a pile of papers, searching for something that might save Huddles from a few years up at Tiger.

"What does the prosecution request?" Judge Wallace eventually asked.

The prosecutor looked the part with his charcoal three-piece suit and expensive haircut. He cleared his throat before launching into well-rehearsed elocution.

"In light of The Shelby Juvenile Center's report, your Honor, the prosecution requests that the court consider the recommendation of Counselor Beverly McGrew and remand the defendant to the custody of the Tiger Harris Detention Center."

"Where is Ms. McGrew?" Judge Wallace asked. "I want to hear from her personally regarding this recommendation."

Fitzgerald and Hendricks stared at one another. After a long moment, Hendricks stood, smoothed the front of his shirt and spoke up. "Your honor, Counselor McGrew isn't available to appear in court today."

"And why not?"

"She had a mandatory training session in Fairmont, sir."

Color drained from Judge Wallace's face. "You mean to tell me that Ms. McGrew has suggested this young man by locked away in the hardest facility in this state and is not going to be here today to discuss her decision? Is that something you want to tell me?"

"No, your honor, but she said the report should—"

"I have read the report. I wanted to speak with Mrs. McGrew in person about this matter, but it appears she had more pressing issues than my court." He stopped to read Hendricks' name tag. "Do you think my court is trivial, Mr. Hendricks?"

"Of course not, your Honor."

"I want one of you to please exit this courtroom and attempt to contact her at this training."

Fitzgerald was on his feet and out the door before Hendricks could move. Hendricks started to sit, but thought better of it. He remained standing, waiting to be dismissed while Judge Wallace turned his attention to Jason.

"Mr. Felts, have you been present during Mr. Gilbert's sessions?"

"I have, your honor."

"What is your impression of Mr. Gilbert?"

Huddles faced forward, eyes locked on the judge as if the verdict couldn't touch him.

"I consider him to be an exceptionally intelligent young man. I believe he shows great future potential if he were to give up his criminal pursuits. I don't, however, think he would be willing to do that. He has a history of violence inside our institution, manipulation in counseling sessions, crimes outside in public life and his background suggests continued involvement in antisocial behavior."

"Does he belong at Tiger Harris?" the judge asked.

"I believe Mr. Gilbert belongs in Tiger as a high security risk."

"You feel confident in this?" Judge Wallace asked.

"Who feels confident about anything?" Hendricks whispered.

When they returned from court, Sir Hendricks tossed Huddles' cell. All the boys were clamoring with questions, but Fitzgerald ignored them by turning on the TV. He surfed channels at such high speed each image only flashed a second on the screen. The quick bursts of picture and sound made Jason think of subliminal messages.

"Where's he at?" Woods asked. His hair had recently been buzzed by the barber who came in once a week. Each head was styled in the same quick sheering as soldiers preparing for war. "Sent his ass on up to Tiger, didn't they? It's hard time from here on out."

"He's changing out of his court clothes, you dumb shit," Robison said.

"You know what I really want?" Fitzgerald announced to the room. "I just want time to sit back and think. I've never heard so much talk with no real purpose." He paused on ESPN long enough to watch Detroit blow their chance at a two-point conversion.

"We got plenty to say, man," Woods replied. "You just ain't listening."

Fitzgerald's radio went off. The voice over the line was indistinct as if someone were speaking submerged in water.

"New record," Fitzgerald said. He rose up and handed Jason the remote before leaving the section. Jason passed it to Woods and went to see about Sir Hendricks.

The sheets were off Huddles' bed. Hendricks, his hands encased in latex gloves, canvased the fabric in motions accustomed to muscle memory, tossing open each fold in a search for contraband. Panic caused Jason's breath to catch and his stomach to roil, but he closed his eyes to calm himself. Huddles would've disposed of the gear.

After he finished searching, Hendricks tossed the sheets in the corner of the room and began to look through a stack of folded clothes. He reached into the pockets of Huddles' standard-issue khakis, then shook out the recreation sweats.

"I got a problem," Hendricks said. "I got a real problem with the way you handled the judge. You made us look weak as a facility."

"What makes you think that?" Jason asked.

Hendricks laid the pants on the mattress and crossed his scarred arms over his chest. Sharon had told Jason that the worst scar was from when a foil managed to slice through his cheap fencing vest, back before he started training with a shield and bastard sword, before his colleagues began to refer to him as Sir Hendricks. She'd been lying naked on the bed in Uncle Henry's house, staring up at the ceiling where a few holes let the moonlight pour inside. The mention of her husband's body hurt Jason, made him think how strong the man's limbs must be compared to his own. The thoughts caused him to pull her close and guide her hands to his erection. Afterward, he was disgusted at himself for fucking her harder not out of passion, but to prove he wasn't weak.

"We work as a team here," Hendricks said. "When you say something that makes it seem like we can't handle a problem, like you did in court today, you jeopardize us. Not just me and Fitzgerald, but every man working on the unit."

"I said what I thought. That's all I'm ever going to say, regardless of the outcome."

Sir Hendricks leaned in close enough for Jason to smell the mint Copenhagen on his breath. His chest puffed like a fighting cock, trying to make Jason shrink as he stood in the man's shadow.

"Then you don't have any business here. We got no use for spoiled midgets. Especially ones without loyalty."

Hendricks bumped Huddle's worn paperback copy of *The Day of the Locust* off the edge of the bed. The smell of decaying paper filled the cell as the book's spine cracked open. Hendricks picked it up and squinted trying to read the evaporating print.

"You're the reader," he said. "What's this about anyway?"

"About all these people in Hollywood who have dreams they weren't able to realize."

"How's it end?"

"With a riot."

Hendricks dropped the book onto the floor. "So, a bunch of ass-holes throw a fit because things don't work out?"

There was another scream from Holding. Hendricks pressed a finger into his earpiece. "I'm on my way," he said.

Jason stood looking at the bare walls of the cell, the way the fluorescent lights cast their beams down on the pile of wrinkled sheets. He reached out his toe until it touched the door and gave it a slight push. It swung on the heavy hinges, nearly closing before it came to rest.

"Around quitting time, Todd Hackett heard a great din on the road outside his office," he whispered.

JASON CALLED SHARON as soon as he stepped outside. They had rules against this. No calls to her home and no calls within the vicinity of The Shell, but after court, Jason needed to see her or at least hear her voice on the line.

"I want to come by," he said.

He could hear the world around her over the line. The television loud in the background as a sitcom laugh track played, cars passing on the street and children playing outside.

"You know you can't do that," she said.

"He's not coming back for hours," Jason told her. Hendricks had showered after Court, and Jason saw him standing in the break room wearing a civilian T-shirt, talking about going to someone named Maurice's gym.

"I can meet you somewhere," Sharon said.

"No," Jason said. "I want to come by. Please."

Another beat of silence and then she answered. "Okay."

WHEN HE ARRIVED, Jason saw the wild children of Sharon's neighborhood riding circles on their bikes, rusted chains groaning and half-flat tires cutting through the gravel lining the sides of the street. The oldest child rode shirtless with an air rifle on his handlebars, the barrel pointed ahead of him like a lance. In his free hand, the boy held a dead crow by its feet, wings spread and blood dripping a trail behind him. Jason knew his stature would be remembered, so he turned off down an unpaved alley behind one of the neighbor's homes and parked his truck where weeds had been allowed to grow high. Once he reached Sharon's back gate, Jason took another look at his truck. It wasn't quite hidden, but he told himself it looked inconspicuous in the coming dark. Pride wouldn't let him sneak in the back, but it didn't matter. The street was empty. No neighbors on porches, no more packs of children on scrap metal Schwinn's.

Sharon opened the door and ushered him inside. She wore a cotton house dress with fabric so thin he could feel her heat radiate through the cloth.

"What's wrong?" she asked.

Since he couldn't tell her about failing Huddles or his fear over whatever retribution might be coming, he just collapsed into one of the kitchen chairs, tilted his head back and tried to cough as the air-conditioning cooled him.

"I'm all right," he said, but it was all bluff. Jason wrapped his hands around her waist, burying his face against her. She stroked his hair, separating the strands of gray with the rake of her fingers, and took him to the bedroom.

Afterward, they sat at the kitchen table. Sharon's gaze continued to drift towards the door to see if it was still locked. Jason knew they were being careless, but the kitchen was just too comfortable to rush. The room felt the way a kitchen should with its overused stove and table that had weathered a thousand late-night conversations. Evenings of chatting as a couple stuffed checks into envelopes so the bills could be mailed in the morning. He could imagine them discussing family issues. Hopes for the future and fears of the present. It should have made him feel guilty, but all Jason managed was stifled envy. Hendricks got to have all this while he went home to the apartment over the funeral home with nothing more than a nook for cooking, little room for even the small table where most meals were eaten microwaved. A bed where no woman ever shared the sheets.

It made him wonder if Sharon really wanted him, or just wanted an alternative to life with Sir Hendricks. Maybe love was simply gratitude towards whatever saved you. If he'd been a normal man, he wouldn't have worried so much about this, and sometimes it helped to remember women carried similar insecurities. He recalled watching the shy way schoolgirls hovered around the boys they admired, floating just outside their proximity and waiting to be chosen over whatever pursuits kept the boys' attention. Jason couldn't fathom how those girls didn't understand they had the power to pry any boy away from their beer and bullshit, to make them ache for their bodies with just the right look or touch. He'd told Sharon this once, but she'd only smiled at him.

"Admit it," he'd said.

"Maybe. But girls aren't that way. At least not at that age."

"Just because you all haven't figured it out yet." He was hoping she'd confess to knowing what sway she held and swear to never use it against him. Sharon only smiled.

"You boys best hope we never figure it out."

Some sound came from the front yard, pulling him from the memory. Sharon went to the window and pried the blinds back with her fingers.

"Probably just that Bluetick Coonhound you were telling me about," Jason said even though he recognized the rattle of Sir Hendricks' truck. He noticed for the first time how unkempt he was, shirttail still untucked and hair mussed from Sharon's petting. He made adjustments as he opened the kitchen's screen door and stepped out into the night air. Sir Hendricks came around the house with a wooden bastard sword in one hand and a wooden claymore the length of Jason's body tucked into his left armpit. The claymore's blade knocked against a shield strapped to his forearm.

Jason stopped when Sir Hendricks saw him. Hendricks didn't speak, just stood looking at Jason as if his mind couldn't comprehend the sight of the disheveled man leaving his home. He walked past Jason without a word, stepped up onto the porch and pulled the screen door open with the bastard sword still gripped tight in his hand.

"Hold up," Jason said.

Hendricks came off the porch and tossed the bastard sword and shield at Jason's feet. They clattered together in the burnt grass.

"Pick it up," Hendricks said.

Jason toed the sword away with his boot and raised his hands in surrender. He wanted to let Hendricks know he wouldn't be humiliated. If he wanted to take the claymore and break every bone in his body, Jason couldn't stop him, but he wouldn't let Hendricks turn him into some mockery, a child-sized man brandishing a wooden sword and shield in real violence.

"Pick it up," Hendricks said again.

Jason gave a snicker. "She ain't a goddamned trophy."

Hendricks took the claymore out from under his arm and adjusted his grip. His feet spread as he raised the sword high so that each strike could rain down atop Jason's head.

"Home early," Jason said. "Ferris Gilbert told you, didn't he?"

Sir Hendricks didn't answer. The man was crying, tears of rage flowing down his cheeks, but he wouldn't loosen his grip on the sword to wipe his face.

"I'm going to stove your fucking head in," Sir Hendricks said.

"Just know you're being used." Jason bent and picked up the shield. He fumbled for a minute as he tried to figure out how the straps went around his forearm, but sudden shame filled him as he bent for the sword. Jason left it in the grass.

Hendricks struck the shield with a downward swing that reverberated through Jason's arm until the stinging could be felt in his ear. Jason didn't have the strength to lift the shield again, so he scurried forward, snatched up the discarded sword and thrust it at Hendricks. The man took a step back and smiled, amused by the tiny combatant trying to fend him off.

As he moved in for another assault, Jason jabbed Hendricks in the upper thigh. The gouge made Hendricks stagger, but his next strike connected with Jason's sword arm. The blow knocked Jason's weapon across the yard, breaking the skin and releasing a trickle of blood from the base of the swelling wound. The pain brought Jason to his knees, but Hendricks didn't let up. The claymore connected with Jason's right shoulder and took him to the ground.

Hendricks stood over him. "Little bastard," he said, raising the claymore again.

Jason managed to force his shield up. Hendricks' strike shattered it completely, pieces of debris flying off as the wood separated, two shards hanging from the straps around Jason's arm. Jason knew instantly his arm was broken.

The screen door slammed, and Sharon crossed the yard barefoot. Hendricks lowered his sword as she approached. Sharon pulled it from his grip and tossed it hard against the fence.

"Are you crazy?" she said. "Are you seriously fucking crazy?"

Her hands canvased Jason's sternum for broken ribs, her fingertips prodding at his wounded arm until his vision blurred and he screamed so loud Sharon jerked away from him. His nerve endings sang out in agony. Jason tried to move his arm, but it wouldn't respond. Sharon took him around the waist and helped him stand.

"I can't believe this," Hendricks said. He pointed his finger as Jason slumped against Sharon. "I can't believe you'd fuck this thing."

"My arm's busted," Jason said.

"It's okay," Sharon told him. Her grip tightened around his waist. A small grunt expelled from her lips as she lifted him, his feet leaving the ground as she cradled him in her arms like a bride carried across a threshold. Jason wrapped his unwounded arm around her neck. He could've walked. In fact, each step jarred his broken arm and when they reached the wooden gate Sharon jostled him painfully trying to figure out how to unlatch it. Still, he liked the idea that she'd carry him. It was his only victory over Sir Hendricks.

"Where did you park?" Sharon asked.

"Just down the way," Jason said.

"Where are your keys?" she asked.

"They're in my pants pocket."

"I've got to put you down," she told him.

She sat him on the ground, and Jason felt her dig through his pocket until she found the keys, then helped him into the passenger seat. Hendricks stepped out of the yard and grabbed the sleeve of her dress. Sharon recoiled back against the truck's hood and swatted at him.

"Don't touch me," she said. "Don't you dare fucking touch me."

Sharon climbed behind the wheel and drove off with Hendricks standing in the road. Jason could hear her crying. His palms ached from the swords rough grip and his forearms seeped around the splinters of shield buried under the skin. He tried to dig one of the slivers out with his fingernails, but Sharon wrapped his hand in hers and rested the clasped pair in her lap as she turned down the narrow road toward town.

PART III
THE WAKE

CHAPTER SIXTEEN

TERRY CARRIED THE borrowed shoes to Rec. He hadn't kept them on purpose, just neglected to return them before being admitted to Medical. With Jason suddenly absent, the shoes became a chance to have a conversation with Huddles, to weigh if there was real danger there or if it was only paranoia keeping those thoughts in his head. After all, there was no evidence his father or Davey's disappearance was related to the Gilbert's. Terry assumed his dad was simply on another bender, and Davey's absence likely had an even simpler explanation. His man left heartbroken when Terry didn't return. Why stay isolated in the woods when he could venture out, get his fix and commune with others? No doubt he'd desire companionship after being jilted by a lover. As much as it hurt to imagine Davey betrayed by the misunderstanding, Terry preferred it to the alternative. Davey dead in the woods, leaves filling an open, breathless mouth.

The B-Unit boys were split into factions of Shirts and Skins. Robison and Callan stood shirtless, sweat drenched until they glistened under the bright lights. Making Robison play skins seemed especially cruel. His tits jiggled as he ran, the layers of fat smacking together as if offering applause. Woods chuckled at the sound even as he covered some new boy who'd come in for stabbing his brother with a screwdriver. Everyone in B-Unit was impressed with his charges until they learned the attack was only on his brother's leg. After all the details came out, the boys started calling him Flesh Wound.

Huddles hadn't picked a team yet. He sat off to the side against the far wall, tying the laces on a pair of green Converse. The tongues lolled out and one loose sole flapped. A previous owner had tried to improve their appearance by smearing the toe caps with Wite-Out, but none of it did much good. They'd probably disintegrate as soon as Huddles started running.

Terry offered the loaned Jordans to Huddles. "I'm sorry I kept them so long," Terry said.

Huddles didn't speak, just examined the contours of the shoes, eyes tracing over a long scar down the toe of the left mate.

"Scuffed them to shit," Huddles said. "Keep them."

Terry licked his finger to buff the scrape. He massaged until the black smear evaporated, but the leather was still marred.

"They aren't that bad. Still better than those borrowed ones."

Huddles pulled his shirt over his head. Small tufts of black hair sprouted from the center of the boy's chest. Terry's own chest was still as smooth as before puberty. This curly patch made him think of Davey's chest, always tarnished with acne bumps he could feel under the thick pelt. Terry averted his eyes before Huddles caught him looking.

"If they're fucked up, I'd like to at least get you a new pair." Terry offered.

"How you gonna do that?" Huddles asked. "You got nobody to deliver them."

The quick insult reminded Terry of his father, but Huddles' response to the awkward silence eerily mirrored the old man. Huddles just sighed, wiped his face with his shirt and offered a bitter smile.

"I'm sorry," he said. "That shit was outta line. Look, I don't give a fuck about the shoes. Just keep them."

"Sure," Terry said.

"Naw, seriously," Huddles stepped forward so that Terry would have to look at him. "I meant it. I'm sorry. You've been a good friend in here. You didn't deserve that."

"It's okay," Terry said. He was acting more wounded than he felt, performing just like he used to do with Davey. He hoped that Huddles meant the apology, and not just because he was afraid Huddles might be used as an instrument of retribution by Ferris. There was something lonely about him, desperate for friendship that made Terry sympathize.

"I just want us to be cool."

"We're cool," Huddles said.

On the court, the shirts were winning. Callan covered Woods hard, posted up until his chest pushed at the smaller boy's face. Damp tangles of hair fell over his eyes as he worked under the rim, snatching rebounds that bricked off the backboard. Robison huffed along behind while the guards lined the wall and discussed who would win to stave off boredom.

"You bitches playing?" Woods called as he traveled up the court.

Huddles looked to Terry, pointed at the shoes he held. "You in?"

"Sure," Terry said. He pulled his shirt off, a bit self-conscious over his bony ribs. The game paused for them, and Robison took the lull as an opportunity to suck some oxygen back into his lungs. Terry hit the court fast, snatched the ball from Callan and drove toward the basket where he sunk an easy layup. The guards were watching him. He could hear them whispering, speculating on where a scarecrow of a boy found such speed.

They pushed up the court. Robison lagged weak on his feet, each awkward stride like the thunderous echo of stampeding hooves. Woods tried to slap the ball away while Huddles crossed him, dribbling between his legs in assured movements. Terry wanted the game to last forever. If they could stay on the court, nothing would matter but the moment they existed inside. If the game became eternal, he could be free of prior mistakes and the weight of their consequence. He would never grow full of regret like his father. He tried to hold onto these thoughts, but in his mind, Davey ran beside him keeping pace, his stride long and his arms pumping easy. The apparition wasn't reality, but it didn't make any difference. It kept him from fully submitting to the fantasy.

CHAPTER SEVENTEEN

SINCE COUNSELOR FELTS had disappeared, Huddles spent the following days thinking of murder with the vial stowed in his underwear. He'd promised Jason that he would dispose of the it but kept the vial in case the plan to send him to Tiger fell through. Just carrying the poison could mean further charges and isolation in Holding, but the moment when he might be alone again with Terry could occur any time. Besides, Mitchum had made things clear after court. Huddles would poison Terry, or else he'd answer to Ferris.

His first real opportunity came during Education. Terry asked to be excused to the restroom and Officer Fitzgerald escorted him to the small bathroom beside Mrs. Miller's class. Huddles sat near the door and might have been able to slip out while Fitzgerald read his magazine full of articles on secret desert warfare. Mrs. Miller would probably have seen him leave, but he could pretend to browse the large shelf of paperbacks outside, sneak into the bathroom and leave the bottle on Terry. Guards would question how he obtained it, but a suicide wouldn't be much of a surprise. In the end, Huddles just waited to hear the flush.

He liked the kid even if he couldn't decide on exactly why. Terry wasn't particularly interesting and a few of his habits annoyed Huddles.

The guy asked too many questions, never allowed a moment of reflection on the events they were witnessing. If someone said something funny in group, Terry would repeat the joke, break the phrase down until any enjoyment was sapped from the exchange.

Still, Terry made meal time easier. Huddles began eating with him for the chance to spill the poison on his food, but something about sitting alone at those steel tables with his ass on the cold metal bench made Huddles feel eternally lonely even in a room filled with the sound of forks scraping plastic trays. The guards' eyes were on him, making sure he didn't pocket any of the plastic flatware, but it felt like they were looking right through him. Terry alleviated that.

Huddles couldn't quite weigh the level of his resolve. Certain moments of the day he felt compelled to carry out the task. The boy couldn't be trusted. Better to just get it over with, protect himself and Ferris from such weakness, but in those moments, Huddles thought of Terry willowy and thin on the basketball court, gaunt ribs looking ready to tear through skin as he moved up and down the floor, or on the first day, sulking in shoes too tight and more worried on the fate of a mongrel dog than himself.

Whenever Huddles decided he couldn't dose him, images of Ferris always entered his mind to fight that belief. The smell of his brother something physical in the cell, the wet and rotten reek of his breath harsh as Huddles' first sip of bourbon. He remembered the tattooed hands flat on the tabletop during Ferris first visit. Hands that absent their ink mirrored Huddles' own hands. Every time this happened, Huddles resisted the urge to go outside and force the poison down Terry's throat. He tried meditation to remove these warring thoughts of murder or friendship, but they never left completely, simply sunk back into the recesses of his mind.

The Shell just felt different with Counselor Felts gone. Whenever the rumors stopped swarming, a profound silence settled in. The guards almost too ashamed to keep bullshitting with one another. Everyone shuffled in the halls. Two days into Jason's absence, Huddles caught Counselor Beverly crying outside B-Unit. She was braced against one of the ping-pong tables, sobbing until Officer Fitzgerald led her away. All of them stood on the precipice of something, a moment that would forever alter Huddles' world, but he was unable to know whether the event would help or hinder. Alone at night he examined the small bottle, it's glass reflecting the only fragment of light in the cell's darkness.

HUDDLES CHOKED DOWN as much meatloaf as he could manage during dinner, but Terry couldn't stomach it. He complained that it filled his guts like cement, so he only picked at the cold peas and finished a bruised granny smith apple. Huddles' stomach had never fully recovered from his court date. Five days had passed, and the fear still coiled inside him. What he needed was a distraction. Luckily, the guards were organizing a basketball tournament for later in the week. It happened every few months and the boys who'd been around long enough to lose a few rounds took it seriously. Teams were chosen pick-up style, but negotiations were held in secret days before, favors exchanged for some of the more valuable players.

Terry talked about it all through chow, excited at the chance to prove his worth.

"What about a fourth man?" Terry asked.

"I don't know," Huddles said. "Robison's too fat to get down the court, but he's solid under the rim. Some of the boys from A-Unit will be contenders. Maybe Flesh Wound?"

"I guess so." Terry speared a pea with his fork.

If Huddles were forced to pinpoint a moment when they first connected, he knew that it was on the court. The one hour of Rec was the only real opportunity for physical contact, and even than The Shell's exercise routine stole a lot of time. The B-Unit boys lined the wall and finished their exercises dictated by a deck of playing cards. Afterward, Officer Fitzgerald tossed out the balls and half of the boys pulled off their shirts to play as skins. Huddles preferred to play skins. He liked the feel of the air-conditioning on his exposed chest. Since he let Terry keep his shoes, Terry played for his team as if the gesture required some sort of permanent allegiance. The borrowed high-tops gave the other team plenty of ammunition for shit talking, but it was worth it to have Terry on the court. All the passivity he usually carried left whenever Terry touched the ball. His legs weren't long, but his feet danced around the defense and his arms swatted away shots with such grace Huddles began to realize what beauty might mean. Strange that he should find it here. He'd never discovered it in the mountains.

Huddles wished Terry could continue this dominance off the court, but weakness wafted from him most other times. He cared too much in education, devoured the lessons and Mrs. Miller's words. Huddles scolded him about it, told him that if he didn't get some hard bark on him one of the B-Unit boys would bash his head into a concrete pillar, but it wasn't something Terry seemed to grasp. He still cried at night, but not in the same breathless rasp of the first days Huddles had overheard. Just a soft whimper now. Only audible because Huddles listened for it. In those late hours, the poison seemed like it might be a mercy, but those thoughts vanished with daylight, leaving Huddles with the same old indecision. He'd never really had a friend before and couldn't quite fathom what it meant for his future if he killed his first one.

"Any news on your dog?" Huddles asked.

Terry exhaled as if rabbit punched. Weakness again, caring to the point of agony. Huddles wished he could just carve it out.

"Better to know," Huddles said.

Sir Hendricks came onto the floor as Huddles took the last bite of Terry's meatloaf. Hendricks looked beaten, abrasions mapping his crossed forearms, eyes raw from nights without sleep. His normally pressed uniform had lost its starch.

"Huddles, come with me," Hendricks said. "Your lawyer is here to see you."

Mitchum coming unannounced meant that Ferris needed to deliver a message that couldn't be relayed over the phone. Terry's eyebrows rose, but Huddles shrugged his shoulders. Hendricks escorted him to the door, waited until Control buzzed it open, then walked past Education towards the visiting rooms. Inside, Mitchum sat at the table wearing one of his seersucker blazers. A paisley tie several decades out of style was fixed to his shirt with a diamond-studded tie tack. Onyx cuff links sagged from underneath his jacket sleeves.

"How you doing, son?" Mitchum smiled, showing his dentures.

"I'm still in the clink."

The good nature went out of Mitchum's posture as soon as Hendricks stepped outside. He leaned back in his chair ready to be serious. Mitchum took a deep breath that made his chest rattle.

"We're doubting your resolve."

"Have you taken a look at how many cameras are in this place?" Huddles said.

"I wasn't sent to listen to fucking excuses." Mitchum's voice raised a decibel until Huddles could see some of the fire from his youth, the sort of man who didn't operate only with good old boy charm. "This sort of thing could put Ferris away the rest of his goddamned life."

"He won't talk," Huddles said. "He hasn't yet."

"Do I have to go back and let him know you turned me away?" Mitchum asked.

Huddles closed his eyes and saw his brother the way he always saw him, bare-chested and running through the woods the first year he came home, remembering him crouched on the ground rubbing dirt between his fingers. The bits of earth soiled his hands until the dirt looked a part of him. He stared at the poor soil with such appreciation it seemed Ferris had lived a life surrounded only by concrete.

"You'll have the week," Mitchum said.

CHAPTER EIGHTEEN

WHEN OFFICER HENDRICKS said the new sheriff had come to see him, Terry knew he was caught. This realization set off a strange internal throb that split his mind and body. The flesh in a panic, the soul full of complacent understanding. No more waiting on the inevitable, of expecting the confrontation at any moment. Resolution was finally here. Whatever punishment the murder warranted could be administered. At least that's what he thought. As soon as Sir Hendricks led him to one of the rooms reserved for group sessions, Terry knew the meeting was about something else. The group therapy room was a soft place for bad news. The pastel walls covered in motivational posters where eagles soared through pillows of clouds and affirmations like A HEALTHY BODY MEANS A HEALTHY SPIRIT screamed at him in large block font. They wouldn't take him somewhere so meek to sweat him. They were hoping to soften a blow.

The new sheriff stood when he entered. She wore her black hair pulled back into a thick rope of braid that fell between her shoulders and her face was clean of any makeup. The only feminine flourish she allowed herself was a gloss coat lacquered on her short nails. Even the uniform buttoned all the way up to a tight collar. She looked more capable than Thompson. While the former seemed to be all bluster and charm, this woman carried a real aura of authority.

She motioned to the seat across the table. Terry sat down knowing what she would say before the words emitted from her lips. She clasped both hands together to hide their tremble.

"Mr. Blankenship," she said. Terry felt odd to be spoken to like a man after so much time being treated as a boy. "My name is Eliza Hood."

He was already near tears. His throat tight at what he knew was coming.

"A deputy found your father this morning inside his truck at the end of Bradshaw Hollow. I'm sorry."

Terry pictured his father slumped behind the wheel, a bottle between his clenched knees, palms open in his lap with the fingers curling up like the legs of some decaying spider. Dirt would cake those digits and mud would fill the grooves of his boots from climbing out of the cab and sloughing through the wet ground to piss in a ditch. Terry wanted to think that his father had only passed out and asphyxiated, perhaps got the tail pipe clogged in mud and drifted off as the fumes accumulated inside, but he couldn't help thinking it was something else. He wondered if Ferris Gilbert was sending a message, wanting Terry to know that he'd come to the same end.

Terry didn't know how to feel about his father's passing. His memory was filled with days of sitting together in the backyard while Roscoe paced circles around them, snapping at bumblebees that glided by. They'd listen to the song of crickets as dusk crawled over the mountain to shadow the grass. Terry could also remember the man slumped drunk in his chair, the nights he'd muttered about rather having a dead son than the current disappointment. It was nearly incomprehensible to think that neither version of the man remained.

"How long was he out there?" Terry asked.

Sheriff Hood adapted quickly to his candor, took on a business tone as soon as she saw that Terry wouldn't descend into hysterics. Sympathy didn't seem her strong suit. "A few days. There were a lot of beer cans in the car. An empty fifth of vodka."

"Car is always full of cans." Terry had been kicking empties under the seat to fool police since he was six years old. A lot of things might have killed his father, but drinking himself to death wasn't in the old man. If he wanted to die, he'd have finished the bottle and put his .38 under his chin. It had to be Gilbert.

"Was my dog with him?" Terry asked.

Sheriff Hood squint her eyes at the question. "Nobody found any dog," she said. "We've ordered an autopsy."

"I don't see no reason to cut on him," Terry said. "If you wanna help, find my dog."

"How do you know there's no reason?" Sheriff Hood asked.

He stood to excuse himself, but Sheriff Hood stood with him. She was shorter than Terry and had to crane her neck back to look him in the eye.

"I'm gonna be back in a few days to check on you," she said. "You think on whether or not you have something to tell me."

THE GUARDS TOOK pity on Terry after the news and let him take another shower. They said Counselor Beverly would be by later that evening to discuss the possibility of furlough. If she cleared it, he should be able to attend his father's funeral. Terry wasn't really concerned about that. He just wanted to get clean. Cry a bit where no one could hear him.

On his first night, Terry expected the showers to be nothing but rows of rusted nozzles where a mass of young bodies stood underneath, each one trying to scrub fast and get away from the weak pressure and cold drip. The idea of sharing that bareness with so many other men had frightened him. What if his body responded? It brought to mind prison movie scenarios where guards watched while the other inmates beat him until the drain clogged with blood, but it was nothing like the movies. The shower became one of the only moments of the day Terry still looked forward to.

Each housing unit contained a room with a stainless steel stall where an inmate could wash alone. A guard stood outside the door while Terry took his allotted five minutes. It didn't seem like enough time to rinse the shampoo from his hair, but things slowed down inside the shower's womb. Whenever Terry closed his eyes, he saw his father dead in the truck, the flies on his bloated face and his swelling body ready to burst. It should have sickened him, but there was something serene in it. Better than imagining him drunk behind the wheel, Roscoe scared in the passenger seat as his father swerved and discarded empty road beers out the truck's open window. Roscoe was the only worry the water couldn't ease. Terry couldn't stop thinking about the dog's mangled ears. Once he was clean, he toweled off and slipped into his sweats.

When he returned to his cell, Terry found Huddles sitting on the bunk. An open book rested atop his hairy knee. The Air Jordans were on the edge of the bed.

"I heard about your father," Huddles aid. "I wanted to say I'm sorry."

The condolences seemed sincere, but Terry knew he couldn't afford trust. He wondered if Huddles' kindness might have always been a way to get close, just a test to see whether or not he would remain silent. Maybe this was punishment for not confessing his involvement with Ferris right away, but Terry had thought it best to keep Huddles out of it. After a time, he'd wanted a friendship with the boy. Now, he understood that circumstances wouldn't allow him such luxuries.

"Is that really what you're here for, or do you have something to ask me?" Terry said.

Huddles slid down the edge of the bed. "I want to know what you did for my brother."

Despite how long Terry had rehearsed lies for the question, he didn't feel the fear he'd expected. His feet held steady and his stomach didn't sour. Instead, he focused on the water trickling down the crevices of his body the towel missed. So much of him still felt damp all he really wanted to do was finish drying.

"Did you think I wouldn't find out?" Huddles asked. "Did you think I wouldn't have obligations to my brother?"

Officer Fitzgerald would come running if Terry screamed. Only he didn't want to scream. He wanted to finally say the words.

"I shot Sheriff Thompson," he said. "Your brother asked me to do it."

The book clattered to the floor as Huddles stood.

"Who else knows?"

Terry bent to pick up the book and felt Huddles rub his hands through his wet hair. His grip tightened, and he jerked Terry forward by the tuft.

"Why'd you let yourself get picked up, asshole?" Huddles whispered.

Terry glanced outside the cell. The day room was full of boys watching cheerleaders bouncing on television. Officer Hendricks sat at the table, his legs crossed and a magazine open in front of him. Huddles wrapped his free hand around Terry's throat.

"Do I have to worry about you?" Huddles asked.

Huddles loosened his grip enough for Terry to croak out a response.

"You bastards didn't have to kill my father."

"My brother didn't have anything to do with that," Huddles said. "Now, who else knows?"

"Jason Felts."

Terry's knees went weak. He slumped to the ground, kneeling before Huddles as his eyes began to water and his vision blurred.

"You told the dwarf?"

"I asked him to deliver a letter. He just put it together."

Terry gasped in a deep breath. He coughed as if his throat were still constricted, but his airway opened, and he felt hot air fill his aching lungs. Rather than pull himself up, Terry just sat up and waited to see what Huddles might do to him. If the hands were going to clasp his throat again, Terry wanted Huddles to have to feel his bare skin growing cold, watch as the organs stalled and his body faded blue.

"Will he talk?" Huddles asked.

Terry shook his head. He tried to speak, but didn't have enough oxygen yet. Earlier that day, he'd heard the guards spreading the rumor about Sir Hendricks. Apparently, Felts had been fucking his wife. After that point, the rumors got complicated and opinions varied. Some said Jason was staying at his uncle's, some said he'd left Lynch entirely.

"He ain't even coming back," Terry said.

"You really believe that?" Huddles asked.

"He helped me before."

"Why?" Huddles asked.

"I don't know. I helped his uncle with his house and he was just nice to me afterwards. He feels responsible or something."

Terry tried to stand, but his legs felt weak. All he wanted to do was lie on the concrete floor, feel the cold block against him damp body. Huddles bent down over him, produced a small vial. Terry knew the liquid inside would leave him frothing and dead in moments. He waited on the immense fear, but it didn't arrive. Instead, he felt the last of his resolve taper off, the urge to open his mouth and swallow the poison.

"Go ahead," Terry said. "You fuckers have taken everything else."

Huddles pressed the vail against Terry's lips. Terry opened his mouth, closed his eyes and waited on the liquid to touch his tongue, on the sudden and complete silence to begin his eternal nonexistence, but he could still feel the cold glass against his chin. He opened his eyes to Huddles retreating. The boy knocked the Jordans off the bed and sat on the edge.

"I'm supposed to kill you," Huddles said. "I was supposed to kill you two weeks ago."

"Just make it quick," Terry said.

Huddles picked up one of the shoes, turned it in his hands. "I like you, Terry."

Huddles put the shoe back down. His left hand still held the bottle and he tapped it against his kneecap. "I never had a friend before, and I don't wanna spend the rest of my life in here."

"If you don't do it, Ferris will kill us both," Terry said. "He killed my father. I know he did."

"I know," Huddles said. "Counselor Felts was supposed to get me to Tiger, keep me away from you."

The proximity was the problem. Terry could see that as long as he remained this close, their options shrank to an inevitable outcome. Ferris loomed too great and, eventually, he would prove an influence that couldn't be denied. Terry looked at the cinder block walls. Just outside them were dogwoods and hills, the smell of cut grass and sap. Despite all he'd lost, he wanted to be among those things again.

"What if I was gone?" Terry asked.

"I think that's the point," Huddles said.

"No, I mean gone from here. I might get furlough for my father's funeral. I can escape and never come back."

Huddles shook his head. "You're in worse shape out there. Ferris will bury you alive. He'll burn the whole funeral home down to get at you. Besides, I'll still have disobeyed him."

"Then I'll kill him," Terry said.

Huddles stabbed a finger in his direction. "That's my brother you're talking about."

"A brother who wants you to commit murder. Neither of us are safe with him alive."

"You couldn't do it anyway," Huddles said. "Little bitch like you wouldn't have a chance."

"I've done it before."

Huddles shook his head. "Better to run if they do let you out. You get on your own as soon as you can. You can't trust anyone. He'll be hunting you."

Terry walked to the edge of the bed. Huddles wouldn't look up at him, just kept staring at Terry's bare feet.

"He's still my brother," Huddles said. "I can't tell you to hurt him."

COUNSELOR BEVERLY CAME by later with her condolences. Terry was afraid she'd sense the scuffle that had taken place in the cell hours before. He kept reminding himself not to rub his neck, kept worrying the blossom of bruise would flower in front of her. Huddles had tucked the bottle into his waist band, but Terry still felt himself combing the corners of the room, expecting to see it lying with the corpses of insects. He wore the Jordans over his sockless feet.

"I've been on the phone with the funeral home," Beverly said. "They have the services planned for Thursday and Friday. The wake Thursday night. I may not be able to get you outside for both."

Beverly tapped her pen on her notepad to secure his attention.

"If it has to be one," Beverly was saying. "If it has to be one, which do you prefer?"

"The wake," Terry said.

"Less people," Beverly said as she wrote her note.

Night, Terry thought.

CHAPTER NINETEEN

BEVERLY MET HUDDLES alone for his session. No Counselor Felts this time to stare at him. Just Beverly, the yellow notepad braced on her knee, foot swinging at the end of her ankle. She seemed to have broken her habit of tapping her pen or chewing on the cap, but Huddles couldn't stop watching the constant swish of that shoe.

"How do you feel?" she asked.

Huddles just shrugged.

"I don't know," he said. "Is the dwarf coming back?"

Her eyes flared like she wanted to lean across the table and strike him. Huddles wondered what it would take to make that professional mask slip. It seemed considerably less than he'd anticipated.

"I guess I'm not surprised."

She scribbled something down. "Tell me why not?"

"He spent every day fighting."

Her eyes widened as she took notes. "Elaborate a bit," she said.

Huddles thought of Shane, his head broken in by Bradshaw boys up the hill. He thought of the way Ferris' body gradually lost all the jailhouse muscle after his first-year home when the High Life helped pack soft flesh over his midriff. How everything wears down, the mountains themselves eroded by time or blasted away by men. Soon the hills would be nothing more than gravel, tiny particles of something that once eclipsed the sunlight as it tried to shine into the valleys. Nothing left behind but chemical waste dumped by the companies in abandoned mine shafts, poisoned well water and bones of animals preserved in slurry ponds.

He thought of the weak plan he'd forged with Terry. Pitiful grasping because he'd finally learned to care about something other than the loyalty owed to blood.

"I mean things change."

He watched her write that down, too.

CHAPTER TWENTY

THE LOT OF Felt's Funeral home sat nearly empty. Just a few pickups parked up front beside the hearse. A handful of mourners filed in past the undertaker who greeted each visitor before letting them cross the threshold. Watching this sad congregation through the transport van's fogged windows, Terry had the urge to ask Sir Hendricks to take him back to The Shell. It didn't surprise him that his father's wake garnered a paltry attendance. Drink had isolated the old man from everyone except the hardest imbibing friends. Laid off miners and fraudulent disability drawlers, previous homeowners turned creek bank dwellers who wouldn't darken a church under any circumstance. Not that the wake would be a denominational affair. Since his father died godless, the funeral home even removed the crucifixes flanking the front door. These accommodations surprised Terry in such a God-fearing town. It seemed the one thoughtful gesture.

Terry sat behind the cage wearing a three-piece suit Counselor Beverly had delivered. She'd forgotten to remove the price tag, and it embarrassed him that some good Samaritan spent so much on clothes that would never be worn again. If his plan succeeded, he'd have to shed such identifiable clothing in the woods. The cornflower blue tie knotted around his neck would be the first thing discarded. It had been choking him since they strolled out of B-Unit. Unaccustomed as he was to dress clothes, Terry liked the shoes. Black wingtips that made him feel like a man of substance. Too bad their soft leather would be chewed up climbing the mountain. Still, the outfit was the nicest he'd ever owned. Black wool with a subtle blue pinstripe to match his tie. The jacket had even been altered so that the shoulders didn't swallow him. It made Terry wonder who guessed his measurements.

"I'm gonna let you out of those chains," Sir Hendricks told him. "But you have to promise no bullshit. Fair?"

Hendricks' uniform would still give him away as an inmate, but Terry was touched by the gesture. There'd been a change in Sir Hendricks ever since Jason disappeared. A softness none of the B-Unit boys could have previously fathomed. He'd even let Terry remove the coat and folded it across the empty passenger seat to avoid wrinkles before securing him with the belly chain.

"No bullshit," Terry said. "I give you my word."

Hendricks opened the cage and unshackled him. Terry took a moment to rub his sore wrists before slipping back into his suit coat.

"A boy shouldn't have to do this wearing chains," Hendricks said.

The mortician who greeted them wore a tight buttoned overcoat that strained to hold back the shelf of his gut. His handshake lasted a beat longer than was needed and came with a silent squeeze meant to remind Terry he wasn't thrilled about a convict in his sanctuary. Of course, the mortician was too polite a man to mention this aloud in a time of bereavement, but Terry got the message. Afterward, they stepped inside to the smell of donation flowers. The interior was a flood of scents. Citrus candles burned on sconces fixed to the walls, mingling with potpourri poured into the small copper bowls resting on the sitting room tables. A few of the mourners saw Terry coming and looked away. Just a cluster of old men who must have worked with his dad in the early days. They weren't the same group he'd labored alongside. His father's temper and drinking had scared that lot away. Terry could feel the shame radiating from them. The judgmental whispers as Hendricks followed behind him, the keys on his tactical belt ticking together in the relative silence.

Sir Hendricks lingered by the door to the chapel. "I'll let you go from here," he said.

Terry stepped through the men huddled around the door of the viewing room. The pews sat empty, the space silent aside from the somber organ being piped in from hidden speakers. Terry didn't recognize the hymns. It was all wrong. Strained strings might have been more appropriate, something like the fluttering of a mandolin that made less of an attempt at holiness. His father's casket sat surrounded by a multitude of floral beauty. Chrysanthemums, tulips, and wildflowers that had already began their wilt. The dry stalks sagged as if in supplication while Terry crossed the wine-colored carpet to peer inside.

The body looked bloodless, his father's face sunken as if the skin were that of an older man. He wore some blazer and secondhand slacks much too large for him. Terry supposed the undertaker kept clothing on hand for the indigent dead.

"Should've buried you in jeans," Terry said.

The sight of the body set off some indecipherable clash inside him. An internal upheaval that wanted him to reach out and grab the cold hands, press them to his face and beg for the answers to questions he never got to ask. Deeper, under the raw and childish pain that surfaced, something reminded him of all the cruel words. The disgust, slaps, insults and shaming. With time, the two emotions might blend into something not quite forgiveness, but for now all Terry could manage was to reach out and clasp one of the waxy hands. He'd have nights of hate and days of longing, but in this moment things felt simpler. The dead hand made him wish for a final moment with his father. Say what you need to say, he thought. Lean over and whisper it into this dry ear. Only he didn't have anything to say.

Terry surveyed the room for Sir Hendricks. When the guard was nowhere to be found, his attention turned to quick exits. The sanctuary and viewing room were in the back of the building. He'd have to go out into the hall and risk being spotted to reach a possible side door. What he needed was to find access to the morgue. There had to be some quick passage to the embalming room, a way to transport the body from the slab to viewing area with little fuss.

Terry resisted the urge to slink as he entered the empty hall. Left was the front door, but he'd never make it out and across the parking lot without being noticed. Right led further into the mortuary toward a private office and unisex bathroom. Terry ducked into that restroom. Low lights, a single sink and nearby toilet with stacks of old magazines on top of the tank. He searched for a window, but there was nothing overtop the toilet aside from a yard sale quality painting of a sailboat.

Someone knocked on the door. "Terry, you in there?" Hendricks asked.

Terry strained his throat, tried his best to make his voice sound choked by a sob. "I just need a second," he said.

"Take your time," Hendricks said.

Terry sat on the closed toilet lid to formulate a plan. The hallways sounded quiet through the thin door. He'd give it three or four minutes, step out and see if he could exit through the office. If the door was locked or if Sir Hendricks stood outside, he didn't see any alternatives.

At the three-minute mark, Terry opened the door. With no one in the hall, he crossed to the office and tried the handle. The door opened into a cluttered room filled with a long desk covered by papers. A giant portrait of Jesus carrying a lamb hung over a computer. At the other end of the office was a back door. Streetlights from outside shone through its small glass portal. Terry was moving toward it when a hand clutched his shoulder.

"Stop," Hendricks said.

Terry slung an elbow into Hendricks' neck, but the man didn't flinch. He slammed Terry on top of the desk. The wind rushed from Terry's lungs and his head cracked hard against the glossed mahogany. Something burned in his back as Hendricks wrapped hands around his throat. The pressure came slow, increasing each time the man expelled a hot breath onto his face. Whether it was calculated or just rage, Hendricks wasn't going to let up. Terry's hands combed the desk in panic, grasping for anything to strike out. His fingers gripped the telephone just as his vision began to blur. Terry bashed Sir Hendricks in the nose with the receiver.

The first blow did nothing but make Hendricks strengthen his grip. The second broke his nose with an audible snap, the cartilage cracking until the right nostril lay flat against his cheek. Hendricks released him to guard his face, and Terry hit him again in the forehead.

He was out the door and across the parking lot before looking back. When Terry saw no one in pursuit, the idea that he might have killed Hendricks filled his mind, but it didn't slow his legs. They were still pumping, the tie around his neck flapping behind him like a kite's tail as he hit the hillside and climbed high into the safety of the mountain-side for cover.

BY THE TIME Terry reached the cabin, he'd discarded most of his mourning clothes. His tie forgotten in the brush at the crest of the last hill, his jacket draped over his arm and vest unbuttoned after the sweltering work of climbing the mountain. The slick bottomed wingtips made the trek difficult, but he kept reminding himself of Davey.

The fantasy evaporated as soon as he saw the cabin. The lights inside were all extinguished and the door hung ajar. Animal tracks muddied the entryway, and claw marks covered the doorframe where some varmint forced its way inside. The emptiness of the cabin was palpable, a thing Terry could feel as solid as the ache in his feet. Inside, the stench enveloped him, forced him to his knees as the rot replaced all oxygen. His eyes refused to focus in the new dark. Terry reached out, touched the cold shape in the shadows and knew his hands felt a body. Even if his eyes seemed adamant in sparing him the sight, Terry let his hands trace the shapes, feel features bloated by internal gasses, tiny bites rendering facial features absent. If Thompson's body had left him in confusion, finding Davey broke him with grief. The pain rending him until he collapsed on the floorboards in the dried blood and lay close to the body he'd held so many nights. The solid arch of shoulders once strong now gone soft with putrescence, the sound of scavenger's claws reverberating through the floorboards as they scampered away.

"I'm sorry," he managed. "I'm so sorry."

Terry couldn't be sure how long he lay before eventually rising to his feet. The taste of sickness in his mouth was so strong he had to rinse it down with water from their warm wash bucket. The stagnant water tasted like something collected from a puddle. Terry sat down in a chair, looked at the corpse and tried to decide what next. There would still be pills in the hiding place. He could eat a handful, lay down and go to sleep next to Davey. The idea had some appeal. A chemical-induced slumber from which he would never have to wake. Two things kept the option at bay. He still needed to know about Roscoe and he wanted to kill Ferris Gilbert.

Terry covered Davey with his suit coat. The man was large, only his upper torso hidden underneath the fabric, but it was as close to a burial shroud as he could offer.

Outside under the canopy of maple and beech, Terry weighed his options. He couldn't leave without seeing about Roscoe. It was stupidity. The same sort of mistake that got him incarcerated in the first place, but at home he could also arm himself and arrive at The Cat's Den just before closing. Ferris would be ready for sleep, unguarded after a late night of watching the dancers. Terry could just shoot him down at the bar. Not much of a plan, but survival seemed unimportant now. Terry started down the mountain in the direction of home.

THERE WERE NO cars on the road. No sign of police cruisers roving around his property. Most nights Roscoe walked the perimeter of the yard, constantly moving up and down the fence line like a shark that would die if it ceased prowling. The stillness was a bad sign.

Terry hoped the fence, crossed the dark yard on his way to the front door. Inside, all the lights were out. The living room looked like the discarded stage from some domestic play performed long ago. Dirt that his father must have abided lay heavy on the end tables. Elaborate cobwebs woven into the high corners of the ceiling.

Terry checked the bedroom, but no dog lay on the unmade sheets. He knew by the smell in the house that Roscoe hadn't been there for days. He opened the night stand drawer, found the Ruger .45 that his father used to pack in the truck when he ventured deep into Bradshaw on jobs and feared the late-night exodus back home. The holler boys had stopped more than one car late in the night. Rumor was they sometimes fell trees for roadblocks during Halloween.

There was little money in the house. Terry searched under the mattress, his father's sock drawer, any random place where a few bills could be stashed. If he lived through his assault on The Cat's Den, he'd need cash. Eventually, he found thirty bucks in the kitchen junk drawer, then poured himself a glass of nearly spoiled orange juice and took a seat at the kitchen table. The night's events had sanitized his palate, but the cold liquid felt good going down his sore throat. Hendricks' throttling had done more damage than he first noticed.

From the kitchen table, Terry could peer into the living room and see the pillows where Roscoe laid during his last visit. He wanted to see the dog a last time, missed the feel of wet tongue licking his palm, of fur warm in his hand as Roscoe jumped against him panting.

The sound of bootheels echoed from the front porch. Terry stood from his chair, began moving toward the back door, but the creak from the warped back steps forced him down the hallway instead. He retreated to his father's bedroom, locked the door and hunkered down at the foot of the bed, pistol trained on the door. His finger tensed on the trigger. The silence allowed him to hear the intruders. At least two men. Too quiet to be police. No announcement of their presence, no shouting for him to come forward. Maybe if he stayed hidden they'd overlook him, but Terry remembered the cold glass of juice on the kitchen table. Stupid and sloppy.

The footsteps grew louder as the men came down the hall. Their pace remained languid, but Terry knew it was patience born from having quarry trapped. The bedroom door handle jiggled and Terry fired two shots into the wood.

"Fuck," someone screamed on the other side. The unmistakable sound of a shotgun breech opening came over the cursing. Terry lay flat under the bed as buckshot ripped a chunk out of the door, nearly blasting the weak wooden frame away. Ferris Gilbert stood in the hollow space, pumped another round into the chamber and fired again. The pellets peppered the bedspread, opening the door the rest of the way. Behind Ferris, Terry could see the pale man who lay bleeding in the hall.

"Toss it out, Blankenship," Ferris said.

Terry fired twice in reply, but Ferris had already taken cover. The rounds hit the wall above the pale man's head. The shotgun erupted again. The wall behind Terry exploded. As he rose to take aim, Ferris came forward, turned the gun and bashed him in the teeth with the stock. Terry tumbled back feeling his front teeth loosen, his incisors chipped from the hard walnut. Ferris kicked the fumbled pistol away and pulled Terry to his feet only to strike him again.

Terry tried to rise, but Ferris struck him in the back with the shotgun. He lay still afterward, feeling the hot pain of something inside shattered by the final blow. The man in the hall was crying, shouting for Ferris to help him. His feet lay in the doorway, boots kicking as the blood pooled across their laces. Ferris picked up the pistol and placed it against Terry's temple.

"Don't you move," he said. "Understand?"

Terry nodded. Ferris stepped around the bed and went into the hall. Jason heard him fire two shots. The boots stopped their swimming, the pale man's previous groans replaced with the blast of silence that follows a gunshot. Ferris walked back into the bedroom, tossed the pistol atop the pillows and pushed Terry to the floor.

"I didn't really think you'd be here," Ferris said. "Hendricks was sure of it, but I didn't think you would be so stupid."

Ferris perched on the edge of the bed, rested the gun across his knees.

"You surprised by that? Hendricks knowing you so well."

Terry shook his head and coughed until blood filled his mouth. Each breath was a labor now. Something inside him was filling, a heavy weight accumulating that pulled him down until he was sinking on dry land. He began to wheeze.

"So why did you come back?" Ferris said. "You were smart enough not to get in the car after you shot Thompson. Smart enough to talk my useless brother out of gutting you." Ferris leaned across the bed and picked up the pistol. "You planning on shooting me?"

"Was waiting till daylight," Terry managed. "Shoot you in your bed."

Ferris smiled at that. "I'm never that easy to find. Except tonight. Came out special for you."

Ferris sat the pistol next to his thigh. He rubbed fingers across the stock of the shotgun, tracing the woodgrain the same as when he'd given Terry the pistol to kill Thompson.

"Lots of places to get a gun," Ferris said. "I think there was something special about here. What was it?"

Ferris leaned in close, nearly pressing his ear to Terry's bloody lips.

"I had to see about the dog."

Ferris pointed the gun at Terry. The barrel poked his chest, but all fear had left him. Already he'd begun to drift, his peripheral vision blurring. Each time he blinked, his eyelids fought harder to open. One more minute and they wouldn't be able to stay wide. Terry sucked in a ragged breath, thought of Davey cold on the cabin floor, his father swaddled in the casket. For some reason, Huddles entered his mind. The way they moved together on the court, that last interaction in his cell when Terry thought he could feel Huddles' wanting to reach out and touch him. So much desire and no courage to act.

"Your brother," Terry said. "He loved me."

"My brother is a coward. Too afraid to get his hands dirty. I'll deal with him."

"It wasn't about fear," Terry said.

Ferris pressed the barrel to his forehead, but Terry didn't feel it. Already he'd began to grow warm with the passing, his final breath leaking out between clenched teeth.

CHAPTER TWENTY-ONE

TERRY'S DEATH WAS considerably hard on Huddles. He got sick the night he found out, spent the early morning hours before dawn hugging the steel toilet and heaving his stomach empty at the thought of what Terry's final moments must have been. There was no reliable consensus on the exact cause of death. The same jailhouse rumors. Everything imaginable from Columbian neckties to decapitation. Those extreme examples might not be the case, but all the anger Ferris accumulated while Huddles procrastinated would have been unleashed on Terry. Ferris would have made it last, taken his time for all the trouble Terry caused him. It scared Huddles. Scared him more than the way the other B-Unit boys looked at him afterward. If he asked, most would have licked his shoes clean out of obedience.

Huddles wondered what Terry told Ferris. Whatever he wanted to know most likely, but specifically about the way Terry offered to protect them both by killing Ferris. Terry probably never realized it, but Huddles had never been more grateful to another person. Whenever he tried his meditations, that moment in the cell kept interrupting. The sight of Terry not entirely dry, shivering as Huddles held his hair by the root. The boy looked so beaten, all Huddles wanted to do was reach out and smooth those assaulted locks until they lay flat to his scalp, to apologize for humiliating him and clinking the poison vial against his teeth.

Disturbances weren't isolated to his meditative practices. Huddles' dreams were filled with Ferris. Ferris performing innocuous tasks. Ferris frying eggs in the kitchen. Ferris smoking at the table. Ferris watching the dancers swing around the pole with a grin on his face. Despite the normalcy of the images, something ominous lurked underneath. Even inside the dream, Huddles waited on the smoking Ferris to extinguish the butt in his eye, the Ferris flipping eggs to bash his head with the hot skillet. At the end of one dream, Ferris stood under their skinning tree at the cabin in Pocahontas County, a field dressed buck strung up above him, entrails coiled around his boots and blood dripping from the flayed backside. As Ferris sheared the fur from the animal's flank, Huddles began to imagine Terry hanging in the tree, the knife carving deep into his white side, stomach open and hollow from the lost organs. Bits of meat hung in Ferris' beard as he rounded the tree. Huddles knew after his brother finished with Terry that he would be next.

The dreams and visions prompted an entire evening of sitting in the cell, wondering if Ferris would really send someone for him. It seemed the bond of brotherhood should save him, but he'd underestimated how little Ferris cared for Shane. While they never shared the same blood, Ferris had treated Shane like family. Huddles knew he couldn't count on the safety of kin alone. He'd proven himself disloyal. For Ferris, there was no worse crime. He'd be foolish if he didn't at least consider a coming retribution.

THE B-UNIT SPADES tournament was a three-day event running from Monday morning to Wednesday night. The tournament had been tradition for as long as the guards could remember, started in the early days of Administrator Roberts, a fat gambling fanatic that thought it might be good sport to let the boys have a card game and secretly open a book of odds on the delinquents. After his suicide over debts, the new administrator kept it going out of habit and a sense of honoring the old card shark. There was talk of canceling the game after Terry's death became common knowledge. Eventually, Officer Fitzgerald saved the proceedings by advocating that distraction was the best solution to unrest. Huddles wasn't sure he saw any unrest. Most boys took the news easy. Cracked a few jokes and went on grateful it hadn't been them.

In Terry's absence, Huddles paired with Flesh Wound. The kid was garbage at Spades. Often led with low cards sure to be defeated. Always bid for more tricks than he could handle, forced Huddles to bet low and pick-up for his partner's excess. This was complicated by Officer Fitzgerald's new rule. Any trick won that the players didn't bid on would count as a bag. Ten bags and you lose a hundred points. Of course, they found themselves down a hundred.

Woods sang more outlaw country as he won. Johnny Paycheck this time, lyrics about how he was the only Hell his momma ever raised. Fitzgerald let him gloat. Security on B-Unit was slack in Sir Hendricks' absence. Even forced to wheeze through a splint and bandages, the administration suspended him for removing Terry's chains and losing the boy while in state custody. Huddles would have given up the light rules just to listen to Hendricks struggle for air, the wet sucking as each breath traveled in and out of the ruined canal. It pleased him that Terry at least got the chance to tarnish the knight's ego.

Flesh Wound played a Jack of Hearts before the Queen had been thrown. Woods played the queen and took the hand.

"Another stupid play like that and I'll beat you till you bleed from the eyes," Huddles said.

Flesh Wound mouthed a sorry.

"Can't do worse to him than I am," Woods said. His smile spread wide and he laughed until Huddles could see the fresh dental work on his back molars, great crevices patched with silver fillings. The state must have put thousands into the boy's mouth. "I think you was better off with that little bitch. Rest his soul."

Huddles slipped his free hand below the tabletop. He crossed his legs and began to slip the sandal off his right foot. The plastic was floppy, but the bottom surprisingly thick. Huddles lamented breaking the vial and disposing of the shards. They could've been useful.

"Wonder if they got cards down in Hell," Woods said.

"Enough," Fitzgerald said. "Turn in your cards and get back to your cell."

"Like you're all broken up over it," Woods said.

Huddles stood and struck Woods across the jaw with the shoe. The blow knocked him back in his chair, sent the cards sailing down in a lazy rain as Huddles reached across the table, grabbed the boy's shirt front and slammed his face onto the tabletop. Tremors from the impact reverberated through the steel, the table making an oddly musical note in the fresh panic. Fitzgerald was lifting his girth up from his chair as Huddles slammed Wood's head again. The anger was gone now, the rest of the attack just a methodical process of dismantling the body before him. Huddle made sure to slam Woods face on the corner of the table and heard the desired crack as the new state-bought teeth shattered. Woods spit small white pebbles of enamel as Fitzgerald wrapped his arms around Huddles.

Huddles turned his focus on Fitzgerald. The officer dodged the punch and slammed Huddles hard on the floor. Huddles felt the weight of a knee against the small of his back. He reached back, trying to get his hands on either ankles or balls, but Fitzgerald struck him on the back of the head. The guards picked him up and carried him to holding.

Counselor Beverly came to see him within thirty minutes. Huddles felt grateful to her. The cell they tossed him in had belonged to Malcolm and he could still feel the lingering presence of the boy. Even his absence contained an amplified quality, a silence that seemed to blast as loud as the previous lunatic screams.

Beverly sat on the floor outside the cell. She had her standard yellow legal pad and tapped rhythmically on her kneecap with a pen.

"Aren't you gonna ask me about Woods?" she said.

"Did I kill him?"

"No."

"Then I don't much care."

Beverly made a small note on her pad. It seemed too fast to be of any real substance. Huddles considered that maybe she never made real notes, that somewhere there was a stack of legal pads with doodles and sketches, the mindless movements of a bored pen on paper.

"You fractured his jaw and orbital socket, knocked out all of his front teeth, broke his nose, and gave him a concussion. He's very fucked up."

"He was too rude to deserve new teeth," Huddles said.

Counselor Beverly nodded as if this made perfect sense. "What he said about Terry was vile but we need to talk about proper ways to cope, Huddles."

She chewed at the end of her pen, seemed to remember that it had been in strange places inside the jail and removed it from her mouth.

"It's hard, but if you can't fix it, you just have to bear it."

Huddles considered the phrase. Ridiculous. As if the incorporeal could be carried along in a physical sense. It didn't work that way. It wasn't something separate that could be set aside for a moment of rest. How was someone supposed to bear something without the possibility of relief?

"I want you to send me to Tiger," Huddles said.

"Why?"

"I want you to write a report that says I'm dangerous and that I need to be in a stronger facility."

Beverly stood, walked close to the cell glass. "Tell me why? What are you afraid of?"

"I'm not afraid of anything," Huddles said. "It's just true. If you don't send me to Tiger, I promise I'll just do it again."

THEY RELEASED HIM from Holding three days later. Huddles made good on his promise by hitting Robison from behind. He stomped the squishy rolls of back fat until one of the guards tackled him. The combination of Robison's padding and quick action managed to save the boy from any serious injuries. Still, they took him at his word after that. Huddles went into Holding and stayed there while Beverly arranged the transfer.

CHAPTER TWENTY-TWO

ANOTHER CAST. THE same plaster smell that infused with Jason's sweat and the incessant itching like when he was a boy, only now adult fingers couldn't slip inside to scratch. Eventually his muscles would shrink and provide opportunity for some real relief, but that was weeks away. Until then, the itching was too intense, a constant prickling like insect legs crawling up and down his arm. Jason reminded himself it was all temporary. He adjusted the sling around his neck so that the cloth would stop digging into his neck and listened to the drone of tires on the blacktop.

Days before in the hospital waiting room, Jason asked Sharon again about her mother's home in South Dakota. He needed words to take his mind of the steady throb. Distractions to keep him from thinking about what they were planning. She stroked his hair and told stories about growing up just outside a town named Farina. A little community of around two thousand. It was a hard sort of life to imagine. The mountains inspired comfort in isolation, protected their inhabitants by making the rest of the world an impossibility. Jason imagined gazing toward the horizon on such a vast expanse of flat land and wondered if knowing just how alone you were could grow unbearable. Still, the openness might be inviting. Seas of corn and soybean giving way to rugged buttes, red rock the color of frozen fire. They'd decided to leave as soon as the doctors finished with him.

The only thing more miraculous than Sharon's ability to drive for hours was the Honda. Despite the rebuilt transmission and 18,000 miles, the engine never faltered on their journey. The car seemed equally determined to put Lynch behind them. That first night they drove through Kentucky, Indiana, and stopped in Illinois at a small motel off the interstate. Sharon parked the car in front of the office and came around to open Jason's door for him. He thanked her, stretched his legs and breathed in the chlorinated scent of the motel pool. It was pleasant after hours inside the Honda.

A young black man sat behind the counter in the office reading a magazine. The muted television played a sitcom where actors mimed a dinner scene and taxidermy animals hung from every wall. A deer killed before it could sprout more than the nub of antlers and a rainbow trout with its colors dulled by death. Even a jackalope sat on the counter ready to thrust its tiny antlers forward at guests. They paid with little conversation and passed the pool on the way to their room. An old couple lay relaxing in lawn chairs by the water's edge and a tired mother, her face hidden behind a paperback, glanced over top the book long enough to yell at her children. The three boys swam in a school, splashing waves out onto the concrete. The room smelled of Lysol, yet had the stale quality of all rented spaces. Low lights and cheap furniture. Carpet you wouldn't want to walk on barefoot. The television remote lay bolted to the nightstand. Muffled sounds from next door leaked through the thin walls. Sharon dropped her purse on the bed.

"I'm gonna take a dip," she said. "You could just wade a bit."

Sharon purchased a green one-piece in a Wal-Mart outside Pikeville, Kentucky where they'd stopped to grab a few supplies. She told

Jason even though they were heading in the wrong direction for the ocean, every vacation required swimming. She bought him a pair of black trucks from the children's section despite his protests.

"You go ahead," he said.

Sharon gave him a quick, almost chaste kiss on her way to the bathroom. Inside, Jason could hear her shucking off clothing. He wondered why she'd needed the door between them to change, if it indicated some level of discomfort, but then she came out wearing the tight green sheath, its fabric so clinging he believed it might wash away once she dived into the water. The reveal made him thankful for the discretion.

"Sure you don't wanna go?" she asked. "It's better than sitting here and worrying."

She kissed him again, this time allowing her lips to press into his more forcefully. Jason knew he should follow her to the pool. They could swim a few laps and touch each other in the secret depths of the deep end. It would feel good despite the old peoples' stare. He just couldn't muster the energy. The weight of what they'd done pressed down until all he wanted was to huddle under the bedsheets.

"I'm fine. You go have fun."

He could read her disappointment, but Sharon didn't say anything. Just walked down to the pool with a hotel towel draped over her shoulder. Jason needed to call and tell the administrator he wouldn't be back. Even if the circumstances were crazy, leaving The Shell had been the right decision. He wasn't saving anyone. Nearly all of the B-Unit boys would be back to hustling. Some might get jobs in the mines, but the coal boom was over, the days of making a living at it finished. Five more years and not a seam of rock would be extracted from the earth. That inability to adapt had put many of the boys inside in the first place. The world had moved on leaving Lynch and towns like it behind. It was the right decision, but Jason felt ashamed that he'd done the same.

Out the window, Sharon swam languid laps. The rowdy kids had moved their splashing to the shallow end, their mother sitting on the edge with her feet in the water. Jason's wounds began to ache, but the beating hadn't left him as broken as it might have in his youth. Such a defeat would have left him hopeless before, sure the violence was the sort of thing that happened to men too ill equipped for survival. In the darkest hours on the road, when the radio was either static or the distorted thunder of some southern preacher's voice fighting the weak signal as he tried to save souls, those thoughts still slipped in.

Jason took out his cell and dialed Beverly. She answered immediately.

"Christ, Jason." A twinge of fear filled her tone. Jason already regretted the call. "Where are you?"

"I'm fine. I'm on a sort of vacation," he said. "I just didn't like taking off without saying goodbye."

"Jason, you need to tell me where you are. Everybody's talking here."

They all must have known about Hendricks. Publicly or secretly taken sides in the affair. Jason assumed most were against him. No real reason allegiances should lie anywhere else.

"I'm okay. Really. I just felt like I should thank you," Jason said. "I'm not coming back to work, and I appreciate how kind you were to me."

"Jason," she said. "Hendricks told us everything," A bit of the fear left her tone and it was as if he were speaking to her inside the confines of Control or out in the smoking hut as she checked to see if she were keying her mike. Outside, Sharon rested her arms on the side of the pool as she conversed with the mother. The woman gestured with her book, turning it in her hands as if the movement might help her articulate the story.

"I never felt comfortable throwing stones, but you know this can only end one way. It's not that she's Hendrick's wife. It's that she's anyone's wife."

There wasn't judgment in Beverly's voice, but Jason felt she was having the same realization he'd watched whenever a woman began to understand that he was filled with the same desires as other men. It always registered as disappointment. As if they'd found something pure and were sad to see it rendered as base as everything else.

Jason hung up and lay fingering the scars on his thighs. The heat in the room became suffocating, so he cranked the AC unit by the window and marinated in his sweat until Sharon came inside wringing water from her hair. He rolled over on his belly so that she wouldn't see his face. His eyes were open against the wet fabric of the pillow, but all he could see was darkness. Sharon lay down beside him, pulled him close until their damp skins sealed. He could feel the constant rise and fall as each breath cycled in and out of her.

"When you got hurt, I was so scared I'd lost you," she said.

DOWNTOWN FARINA WAS three well-paved streets lined with tiny storefronts. A throng of midday shoppers passed by on the sidewalk, women in sundresses carrying parcels and laughing with one another. Jason looked past them at the manikins on display. The female silhouettes wore dresses that left their plastic shoulders bare. The headless males clad in plaid blazers. At the intersection, they passed a bakery with a bench outside where two old men sat smoking and sipping coffee from Styrofoam cups. High school kids waited under the marquee lights of a small movie theater to buy tickets. Patrons came and went from the bakery, biting into bear claws or popping doughnut holes into their mouths. Farina was what Lynch must have been years before. It felt like proof of something, as real a relic of the past as a fossil from the earth. Jason wondered what made this place different. Why was it able to survive while Lynch disappeared?

Sharon turned down a side street. They rode past a steakhouse called the R-Bar and a Chinese takeout.

"You hungry?" she asked.

He wasn't, but Jason nodded. "Sure."

Sharon parked in front of the R-Bar and they went inside. It was mostly empty, full of darkened corners illuminated by strands of poinsettia shaped Christmas lights that hung from the ceiling. A juke-box rested at the end of the mahogany bar where two men sat swigging from longnecks and eating porterhouses, asparagus, and baked sweet potatoes dusted with cinnamon. Cowboy hats rested on the stools beside them. There was a small stage at the back of the bar where a woman performed a karaoke rendition of "Jolene" to an empty dance floor and the few couples drinking in nearby booths. A sign over the bar advertised the R-Bar as Farina's only liquor store. It listed prices for bottles.

"I went on my first date here," Sharon said. "Jacob Harvey. He was a chubby kid, too shy to kiss me goodnight."

Jason could imagine Sharon as a teenager, the sort of beautiful girl who was still trying to understand why boys became so awkward in her presence. If they'd grown up in this town together, would he have had the courage to bring her here instead of Jacob Harvey? Would the younger Sharon have seen whatever it was she saw in him now, or did people need time to mature in order to find the things they needed?

He considered this while the red poinsettia Christmas lights shone against Sharon's dark hair.

When the food arrived, Sharon cut Jason's steak into little cubes for him. He skewered it with his fork, but didn't really taste the meat. Despite the tender nature of the moment, the foolishness of their endeavor was beginning to show.

"Are we gonna talk about it?" Sharon asked him.

"Nothing much to say," Jason said. "It's done."

"It's got to mean something to you. It has to hurt."

There was nothing he could say to articulate his fear. The dream of their time on the road had been the stuff of fantasy, and now that he had a woman like her after so many years of longing, he didn't think he'd ever been so afraid of losing something. That wasn't an easy thing to admit when he weighed their odds. Half of relationships fizzled out under the best of circumstances. They'd started this thing with such hardships, he didn't know how long they'd be able to hang on, or the damage it would do when the love expired.

Jason sipped from his glass of lemonade. He really wanted a beer, but something about that seemed inappropriate before going to meet her mother. He almost smiled at the thought of an adulterer worrying over beer breath.

"Nothing I say is going to change it."

Sharon furrowed her brow until he could see that she had meant something else. Jason reached across the table and placed his hand over her wrist.

"Everything will be fine," Sharon said. "I want her to see I finally found someone like you."

She went into her purse for cash. Jason shook his head and took a fifty from his wallet.

*   *   *

THEY WERE OUTSIDE of town, driving across the plains with cattle in the distance, men on horses in the field removing their hats to fan away insects. Sharon kept sweeping her hair from her eyes, glancing into the rearview as if someone might be following the trail of their dust.

Ahead, Jason saw a small cluster of houses. Two white ranch-style homes with screened in porches, another yellow house with an old TrailBlazer parked out front. A man in a work shirt with the sleeves rolled up carried a bucket overflowing with suds to the vehicle. Sharon parked in front of the white house and climbed out. The screen door opened, and Jason watched a small woman in a yellow dress come out onto the porch. The resemblance was immediate, the woman's lips and mouth the same as Sharon's even as they pulled back into a wrinkled greeting. She came down the steps and wrapped her arms around Sharon.

"I didn't know you'd be here so early," she said.

Jason hadn't climbed out of the car yet. Sharon had told him that her mother knew, that she'd always despised Hendricks, but he wasn't sure what to think. Something about the scene seemed too quaint and wholesome for their situation. Even if the mother could accept the circumstances, could she accept him when he climbed out on his stunted legs, unable to extend his broken arm to offer his hand? He forced himself to open the door.

"Momma, this is Jason Felts," Sharon said.

He forced himself to look up from the dirt. The old woman had been hunched and shrunken by age, but she was still taller than Jason, looking down into his face as the wind blew her long gray hair. She reached out an arthritic hand and grasped his shoulder. He could feel the cold flesh through his shirt, but it wasn't an unpleasant coolness.

"It's a pleasure to meet you," she said. "Come on up to the house."

THEIR MORNING SHOULD have been perfect before the call. After breakfast, they sat out in her mother's field in sagging lawn chairs. Jason could have stayed there all day with the wind against his face, the wide expanse of sky moving lazy cloud patterns overhead. Perhaps they could have constructed a small tent, built a fire and slept outside on the darkening prairie.

They'd been talking about grass before the call. A pheasant had taken wing, and Sharon pointed to the tall growth from where it ascended.

"I used to know the names of all these different strains," she said. "I've forgotten."

"I'd just call it weeds," Jason said.

"Seriously, I need to remember. Knowing the words for a place allows you to live in it." She shielded her eyes as she turned to him. "I'll teach you."

He scooted over in the chair, and she slipped in beside him until her hips pressed against his, her back resting in the concave of his chest. Her hand brushed his thigh and she gripped the hard square of the cell phone in his pocket.

"It's vibrating," she said.

AFTER THE CALL, Jason went straight to packing. Sharon didn't question him. Jason knew she'd overheard enough to know it was another dead boy, and rather than pressing for details she lingered outside his proximity, circling as he tried to fold his shirts with one hand.

"Let me," she said and took the shirt from him. She folded each one fast and placed it inside the suitcase that lay open on the unmade bed, careful to fit them all. The leather jacket she'd bought him was inside, stowed away because of the weather and his preference for the shabby old overcoat.

The bed sheets were still balled from where they'd spent the morning warming them. They'd been sharing the bedroom, but most of the things were Jason's. His books rested on the nightstand, deodorant and shaving kit on the nearby desk and his overcoat draped over the matching chair. Sharon picked the coat up and brushed lint from its sleeves. The child-sized garment didn't even cover her torso. She tugged on one of the loose hanging buttons, inspected the gaping lining inside.

"This thing is starting to grow on me," she said as she adjusted the lapels. Jason reached to take it from her, but she shook her head. "Turn around," she said.

He offered his back to her and she slipped his arm inside one of the sleeves, let the garment hang over the wounded appendage in its sling. Once the coat was on, Sharon wrapped herself around him as if her body were a continuation of the cashmere cloth. She rested her face in the crook of his neck, and Jason felt her breath as she took in the scent of him from a day without showering. She'd told him she enjoyed something elemental about it, pure as placing sandstone on your tongue.

"Is this the boy with the dog?" she asked. "The one who worked with you and your uncle?"

"Yes," he told her.

"And you have to go back?"

"Yes," he said.

"You know I won't," she said.

"I know." His voice was full and final. No thought in it.

"I've been confused before in my life, but I see it very clearly."

"You can't think in such absolutes," he said.

"I love a man who loves a broken thing," she said, but Jason didn't believe she was speaking to him.

The clock on the wall continued its eternal tick. Through the house, the front door opened, and Jason could hear boots on the wooden floor in the living room. Sharon kissed his neck and zipped up his suitcase.

THE NEXT MORNING, the Honda wouldn't start. Sharon cranked the engine and listened to it knock until she climbed out and kicked the tires. Jason stood in the yard growing envious of the machine. It had the luxury to die when the task became too hard. He'd spent all night thinking of a way out of his obligations to Terry, but he couldn't see a way clear. It wasn't as if he owed the kid anything. He'd given him the chance to escape, given him money and tried to help him keep the job working on Uncle Henry's renovations. As far as Jason knew, he might have been the only one who gave a shit about Terry, but he'd also put the tools in Huddle's hands.

They drove to the airport in the neighbor's TrailBlazer. Several men nearby owned trucks in better condition, but Sharon's mother said she only knew one neighbor closely enough to feel comfortable asking for the favor. He was a stout man with a buzz cut that looked wrong on him. He'd been pleased to meet Jason, shook hands with his great mitt swallowing Jason's own large hand and stood watching with Sharon's mother as they pulled away. Shrinking in the rearview, Jason saw the man place an arm around the mother's shoulder. It made him wonder if some more intimate relationship existed between the two.

Antelope grazed in the fields on the ride. A few bucks standing in the low grass, snorting in the warm air. Sharon slowed the car, turned Dwight Yoakam down on the radio and waited as the beasts shook their heads, muscles trembling along their flanks. She pulled the car to the shoulder and they watched for about five minutes in silence. Finally, the animals walked on and left the fields bare.

"My mother told me that I was a good woman for being with you," Sharon said. "Said I was kind to be able to see something in a man like you."

Jason had suspected as much. The old woman had been polite but looked on him with a certain shock. It was as if she were watching a small goblin pet her daughter and walk around the kitchen sipping coffee.

"I'm not too surprised."

"You know what I told her?"

A part of him was afraid to know. "What?"

"I said that any woman who couldn't see it was a fool. With or without you, I'm not going back there, but I'm going to rent a place in town. It'll be waiting for you."

Jason nodded and squeezed her hand. He hoped it was true.

They parked in short term parking, and Sharon helped him inside. The extendable handle on his luggage was too long for his short frame, so the bag rolled behind at great length, stalking him across the floor. Their stop to watch the antelope left them with only a few minutes before boarding. Jason tried to take her hand near the gate and for a moment he thought she might pull away. His long fingers wrapped around her hand until their appendages seemed chained.

"A week at the latest," he said. "Then I'm on the next flight."

He knew she didn't believe him. Men sitting nearby watched them over their newspapers. Women walking by slowed to stare. An airport should have added anonymity, but this small terminal wouldn't let them be lost in a crowd. Jason glanced at his watch as the PA began to make calls for flights and Sharon leaned down to kiss him, his hands burying in her hair and drawing more scrutiny from the passengers milling about.

"I love you," he said.

Jason gave her hand a final squeeze and went to the security gate where the TSA woman reminded him to take off his shoes. Jason bent over and untied them, handed the old Oxfords over. The woman held them in her hand, marveled perhaps that a men's size nine could be pried off such a small man's foot.

CHAPTER TWENTY-THREE

Tiger lived up to its reputation. Everything inside screamed maximum security. Each cellblock was cramped with over thirty offenders. So many inmates that the security staff, double that employed by The Shell, were significantly outnumbered. Huddles went from the one bunk privacy of The Shell to sharing a room with two other boys. One a tattooed kid from Morgantown with a dead left eye, perhaps once an ocean green, but now dulled by a milky white film. The other a small black boy who refused to look at anyone who spoke to him. Bright brown eyes perpetually cast down at his shoes. He cried and screamed in the night, ensuring the wrath of the dead-eyed cellmate would be directed at him. Huddles felt somewhat fortunate.

Getting used to the differences was hard. Extra sets of doors to be buzzed through and more cameras hanging on the ceiling. The walls were absent The Shell's pastels. All of them coated in an institutional white until he felt lost in the banality. When his cellmates slept, Huddles tried to close his eyes and preform his meditative exercises, but the noise of so many young men locked into one building suffocated him. All that stifled life became like a radio signal hidden underneath static that bled into his quiet concentration. Whenever he did manage to mute the sounds outside his cell, Terry was all he could see. Other times, it was Ferris.

Huddles remembered the ride to Tiger. Fitzgerald stopped on the interstate to piss at a gas station that sold COAL T-shirts. A group of hunters gassed up a pickup in their blaze orange jackets, rifles slung over their shoulders. Huddles remembered fretting over whether it was actually hunting season. It seemed possible that one of the men might walk over to where he sat chained and execute him with a bullet through the window. Even in the locked womb of Tiger, he never felt safe from Ferris.

There were other things to fear. The wolves were more plentiful here, their violence more potent. At least one boy had been raped in the communal showers since Huddles arrived, and according to the rumors, one was just as likely to be beaten or fucked while lying drugged in the infirmary.

Even the conveniences inside Tiger brought with them a double-edged sword of heightened danger. The onsite dentist's drill had once been utilized in an assault on a boy. The idea of a constant dentist employed by the institution shocked Huddles, but apparently the state shipped inmates from seven different counties to have their oral needs met. Huddles had personally destroyed the man's work when he beat Woods. He tried to imagine a man tasked with the job of cleaning only inmate teeth. What would such a man do to get though the endless days of telling angry little men to preserve their molars? The concept was so surreal sometimes his meditation became a close-eyed consideration of his own mouth, tongue prodding each tooth for looseness or weakness, but they were storng. Even when the dead flesh was peeled from his head by carnivorous insects, the teeth would be preserved in a skeletal smile, privy to some eternal joke none of the living knew.

Jason's letter arrived after Huddles' first encounter with a wolf. A larger boy with a mountainous geography of spiky red hair cornered him outside of his cell, demanded that Huddles buy him items from the commissary. Huddles tried to explain he had no people to put money on his books, but the boy hit him before he could finish. The fight was quick. Two jabs to Huddles' mouth, then the hot taste as his split lips bled on his tongue. The guards tackled both of them to the ground. Huddles spent two days in solitary that he welcomed.

The letter was waiting when he returned. No long-winded correspondence. Nothing about the clandestine agreements they'd made or the secrets they kept for one another. All Felts wanted was to be added to the visitor's list. Huddles sat on the bunk, looked at the South Dakota address and considered what would bring the man so far. No one in Huddles' entire life had offered something without expecting a favor in return. Not that he'd expected anything less. Regardless of what all those naive people preached from the Sunday pulpit, the real human instinct was to exploit. Huddles tried to imagine what Jason might want. Maybe the man just needed reassurances that his secrets would be kept.

In the end, Huddles added him to the visitors list without really understanding why. Maybe he wanted to see what he could get Jason to do for him. A couple of dollars on his commissary books or a little bit of info on Ferris. Maybe he just did it because he wanted to see someone who knew him when his name carried some respect and he had the fear of the B-Unit boys.

JASON ARRIVED A week later. The visitation room allowed no contact. Prisoners sat on one side of a pane of glass with a black phone against their ears, listening to mothers, sisters or anyone else who was still coming. Conversation hissed across the lines like whispered prayers.

Huddles sat at the end of the row in a baggy orange jumpsuit, his hair shaved to a scabbing scalp, eyes wet behind bruises from his fight with the red-maned wolf. The glass between them was streaked with palm prints from all those who's pressed against it hoping the smooth surface could suffice for flesh. Jason took a seat and picked up the phone. Huddles expected the tiny man to be diminished by worry, but he looked better than ever before, back straight and eyes alert with a sort of exuberance few men obtained. It was a pleasure to be near, but also made Huddles envy whatever allowed the man such peace.

He raised his receiver from its cradle. "What's the dwarf want?" Huddles asked. The animosity was only half sincere. Huddles smiled and showed gums gone raw. The cracks of his teeth bridged by blood.

"Been to the dentist?" Jason asked. "Or is that the work of some pugilist?"

"They got theirs."

"I'm surprised anyone would fuck with a Gilbert. Your name should carry weight."

"It carries plenty," Huddles said. "What's improved your pallor so much? You look too pleased to be carried around on those little stumps."

"I was in a beautiful place with a beautiful woman. I only came back because I heard about your troubles. And your troubles are mine, Huddles."

Huddles should have expected something so cynical. Just a trip to see if he was keeping quiet. It made him smile again.

"If I wanted to talk, I would have already," Huddles said. "I've got no designs on turning you over."

"It's not about that," Jason said. "I don't care about myself much anymore."

"What do you mean?"

"You know what I mean. We owe him, Huddles."

Even if the words felt true in his bones, Huddles shook his head. He didn't want to owe anyone else anything. All he wanted was to be abandoned to Tiger or to have one of Ferris' conscripts find him and end the wait. Nothing they could ever do for Terry would cease the hauntings that slipped into his meditations. Huddles knew that for the rest of his life he'd be feeling the slick curls of the boy's phantom hair between his fingers, smelling the scent of that cheap institution-issued shampoo on his palms no matter how much time should fade it away.

Jason moved the phone to his left ear. "I know you're gonna give me permission," he said. "You wouldn't have put me on the list otherwise. We made a mistake. Let me set it right. Afterward, you can tell them everything I did."

Huddles fingered the bruise under his eye and gripped the phone tight.

"You know, everyone I've talked to, they want to carve their slice. Whether it's the one who did this," Huddles touched his eye. "Or my brother. Terry was the only one who wasn't that way inside."

"I know how you felt about Terry," Jason said. "He deserved better than this."

Huddles leaned into the glass until his breath fogged the window.

"We can't really do anything for him now. It would only be something to make yourself feel better."

"It might make you feel better, too," Jason said. "I know you're afraid. The time would be easier without that fear."

"You can't ask me to say it. Not about my brother."

Huddles hung up the phone and went back to his cell. He sat on the end of the bed holding the worn copy of *The Day of the Locust*. They'd allowed him to take it from The Shell since no one else had borrowed it from their library in over a decade. He opened the brittle pages, tried to force Terry and Ferris from his mind's eye. He was alone in the cell for the first time, the others gone on some kind of visitation or mandated activity. Huddles closed his eyes, thought about a world without his brother, the world he now occupied entombed behind concrete barriers and with Terry rotting in the ground. He decided no man had ever been more alone. All that he had left were the words.

Without looking to the page, Huddles began to recite.

"Around quitting time, Todd Hackett heard a great din outside."

CHAPTER TWENTY-FOUR

JASON HAD TIME to think on his drive back from Tiger. He drove past Cherry Tree, around the steep curves of Horse Bend Mountain to a small all-night diner secluded in scrub sycamore and hundred-year oaks where he sat in a booth looking out on the dark road, sipping black coffee brought to him by a tired young waitress with dishwater blonde hair. There were no other patrons. No headlights flashed by going down the hill. Jason stared into the bottom of his mug and considered his options, whether to stay or drive straight through to Charleston and grab a plane back to life with bitter cold prairie winters warmed only by split wood roasting and Sharon's touch. He should know how much sacrifice was enough, but something about Huddles, the idea that he still wouldn't say those betraying words about his brother, made Jason feel like a coward.

The waitress came by with a steaming pot and topped the mug off. She gave him a tired smile, and it seemed the exact kind of look he'd always wished to elicit in women. Something so much more than quiet acknowledgment or politeness. Jason poured heavy with the cream and sugar until the coffee turned to a mud that would taste sweet like desert.

"Anything else?" she asked. Her painted nails picked at the remnants of egg yolk staining her apron.

"Do you know a place open for gas this late?" he asked.

* * *

At the foot of the hill, Jason filled the tank with premium and then filled the five-gallon travel can to its brim. Some spilled on his sleeve and the smell of petrol filled the car until he cracked the window to let it air out. The roads remained untraveled except for his rental. The radio was off. The only sound the sloshing of the can in the back. He turned the car down Cherry Tree and rolled down the main drag. The street looked empty, the few bars and liquor stores closed at such a late hour. None of the girls seemed to be out, but he'd see them if he looked hard enough. The rented Chrysler was a decent automobile. The sight of it would have them hungry to climb into a sedan instead of another beaten pickup. That wasn't what he wanted tonight.

Jason parked in an empty lot across from The Cat's Den and watched it for five minutes. The neon signs advertising beer and women were all extinguished. No one opened the front door and no women walked out reflected in the black windows, but he watched a while longer to be safe. After he was satisfied, Jason climbed out and retrieved the necessary items from the trunk. Three wine bottles and a faded black Tom Petty T-shirt. He leaned against the hood and tore the shirt to strips while the gas can waited between his boots. He used his feet to steady the bottles while he poured with his good arm, then poked long pieces of the cloth down their thin necks and walked across the street. The smell of gas followed him.

Jason stood in the front lot of The Cat's Den with the first bottle and tried to get his Zippo to spark. Fire sprang up after a few weak turns of the wheel. He lit the bottle and hurled it up onto the roof. It was a bad throw with his weak arm. The bottle hit the shingles, refused to bust and rolled off the side, crashing in the back lot and enveloping the pea gravel in fire. Jason lit the next and threw it harder and higher. The bottle sailed in a deep arc, smashed the corner of the building and burst, the fire running wild across the roof and moving lower to lick at the windows. He was watching from the car when the panes shattered from the heat. It was foolish to stay longer, but a part of him knew to wait.

Gilbert came stumbling out, fanning his arms as his back burned bright. He collapsed near the door, clothes smoldering as the bonfire of the building collapsed upon itself behind him, the flame's avarice eating everything until only embers and sparks lifted to the sky. Jason walked over slow as the man groaned, rolled over onto his back and howled as the sizzling flesh touched cool asphalt. Jason removed his grandfather's revolver from his coat and thumbed back the heavy hammer as he approached. Ferris didn't look directly at him, eyes far away somewhere with the pain. Jason stood over the man and waited. Ferris finally turned his head, the burnt skin stretching and the crisp hair still smoking.

"You told me I had to kill something to make it my own," Jason said pointing the gun down at him.

Ferris coughed and looked ready to speak, but no words emitted from his mouth. He let out a roasted breath, a slow hiss as his lungs emptied. Jason waited to see if he would breathe again. When the man didn't, he let the hammer down easy, placed the revolver back into his coat.

He drove away watching for a long time in the rearview. The heat of the fire, the scent of the gas and the coffee had his eyelids peeled back to look at the night. He turned onto the exit for the interstate, crossed the final bridge and began to ascend up the steep hill as he drove away from town, the sight of Lynch shrinking away into a few lights barely tangible.

EPILOGUE

THE DOG RUNS always happened on a Monday, early morning drives that began as soon as Jason parked behind the court house. Uncle Henry waited on the granite steps hunched inside his jacket, arms swallowed by the deep pockets and cheek swollen from Redman. His low brimmed ball caps covered his eyes, but did nothing to defend against the cold October wind that blew the whiskers of his beard, the gray mass moving with a squirrel's tail twitch. They didn't speak on those mornings. Jason simply followed him inside, past the middle-aged preacher's wife who worked security out front. She smiled at Jason, but never at Uncle Henry. Jason assumed his uncle told her that her husband stood behind the pulpit spouting horseshit, but Jason thought his uncle had larger problems than rude disposition that should have kept him from returning to work. Even three days a week running jobs for the county commission kept his uncle from finishing the house. Walking among those ruined boards made Jason remember lying with Sharon and looking up through the hole in the roof. Uncle Henry's drinking wasn't letting up. The brewery scent expelled heavy along with Uncle Henry's huffing as they walked down to the basement to grab the boys.

The county lent out three prisoners. Two brothers named Sharps who were arrested together after burglarizing a trailer in Bradshaw, and Franklin, a boy caught will more pills than the local pharmacy.

The Sharps boys were workers. When they were sent out with orders to collect roadside trash or haul a big load of refuge from the creek, they went straight to working fast and efficient. Both seemed pleased to be outdoors and joked as they did their duty, poked at one another with garbage sticks or stared hard at any woman passing by on the street. Franklin spoke only to bum a daily cigarette. Jason never lent him one.

When Jason and Uncle Henry came into the basement, the boys were standing around in an empty office. Franklin sat perched on an old desk while the brothers leaned against the wall, talking baseball with Trooper Gallihue, who was making a poor case for Mark McGwire as the greatest hitter who ever lived.

"Dog run today," Uncle Henry said.

Franklin rubbed his sunken eyes. "You at least lend me a smoke?" he asked.

THE DOG POUND was ten miles up a mountain road, the path basically deserted aside from the few people who traveled it to reach Bradshaw. It would always be traveled by the same broken Pontiacs, Buicks with bent hinges and two hundred thousand miles on the odometer. No one else wanted to go there. Uncle Henry drove, and Jason sat up front while the inmates piled in the back bench in their orange. Driving made Uncle Henry nervous. During moments alone, he often reminded Jason to keep his eyes on the men, afraid one day they might bash him in the head with a rock and make a run for it. Jason told him if one ever wanted to hit the hills just let him go. His days working security were over.

The windows were rolled up, trapping the smell of absent garbage and dead dogs. The floor mats forever stained from the seeping of thin plastic bags overloaded, the wrapped corpses beginning to thaw on the hour-long trip to Charleston where they would be tossed inside the incinerator. The first time he picked up a batch of dead dogs, Jason was stunned by how many, nearly thirty of various sizes packed out in the cradled arms of thieves. It didn't seem like Lynch could provide so many strays. After The Cat's Den burned, the rest of Cherry Tree withered like a plant without roots. Every bar was abandoned, the few businesses downtown closing shop. Since the arson was never solved, most people lost faith in Sheriff Hood and in the idea of civilization lingering any longer in Lynch. Maybe the dogs were all that was really left.

The pound was a small but serviceable cinder block building in the center of a gravel lot. The sign out front offered no cute picture of a cat or dog, just the words Lynch Animal Clinic in tall font. It was a poor lie. Anyone could see from outside it wasn't the sort of place animals went to heal, just to wait in shit streaked cages until time for the needle. Uncle Henry parked outside the death house and climbed out to release the prisoners.

"No dicking around today, Franklin," Uncle Henry said as he opened the back doors.

On the last run Franklin had drug his feet, carried one mutt and struggled alone with a Saint Bernard for ten minutes while the Sharps brothers hauled all the cats out, tossing their little bagged bodies in the back like they were throwing away wadded paper. Another week, Franklin found an unopened beer in the ditch. Uncle Henry knocked it from his hand, and Franklin cursed the rest of the day.

"I pull my weight," he said, but his voice sounded as if he didn't truly believe it.

The pound smelled of dank fur camouflaged by bleach. The cinder block walls were painted the yellow of stained teeth and the floors were green linoleum discolored by all the animals dribbling piss in the halls. The place always changed the men as they entered. Franklin's shoulders sagged, and the smiling but quiet joking of the brothers silenced. Uncle Henry was the only one who didn't seem damaged. At the front entrance, a woman sat behind the reception desk reading a magazine and fighting stiff hair that looked as if she tried to tame it with repeated squirts of hair spray. She looked up at Uncle Henry, then back to the magazine in front of her.

"Richard's back there waiting on you," she said.

Jason walked down the hall past a room with rows of cages, their confines holding mangy dogs that bit at their matted fur. Two Chihuahuas sat shaking, their long ears flattened to their head and eyes moist. Only the cats seemed at peace, sleeping curled tight in ambivalence to their fate. Across the hall, Jason saw another room with stainless steel tables, cabinets filled with sharps and a drawer he knew was full of black plastic shrouds.

The only way Jason made it down the hall past the whimpers and barks was to try and believe the animals did not understand this room, but perhaps they did. Some would have seen enough enter and not exit, seen the girl at the desk or another staff member carrying a plastic bag towards the industrial freezer. He hoped for their sake they didn't have the same concept of death men did and that they went without mourning the animal that slept next to them, forget their scent so that life continued as best it can in a cage.

Richard, a large balding man with tribal tattoos on his forearms, opened the freezer and chatted with Uncle Henry about Westerns as the men grabbed the bodies. Richard was a disciple of Clint Eastwood and enjoyed arguing that John Wayne and Jimmy Stewart simply couldn't be proper cowboys. Jason tuned them out and stepped into the freezer. It was still strange to look at the massive pile of bags and know the animals inside them would never breathe again even as he watched his own breath mist. The brothers immediately picked up a large sack, carrying it together by opposite ends and speculating on what was inside.

"Labrador," one said.

"Golden Retriever."

Jason went to the pile and picked up three of the smallest bags. The bodies inside were too drawn in on themselves to distinguish a tail or foot from a slim waist. Cats, he thought. Maybe a Pug in the bulkiest one.

It took about thirty minutes to load the majority of the bags, but Franklin slacked behind, dragging a large sack down the three chipped and cracked concrete steps of the pound. He dropped the bag in the dirt, bent to pick it up, and the plastic ripped, spilling the body of a dog out into the dust.

"Goddamn," he said.

There was no odor, but Jason seemed to imagine the fresh rot from looking at the animal. Some indecipherable mix of hound and shepherd, its snout long but the ears floppy and tattered, the left looking as if it had been torn off and reattached several times. The fur was frozen in lumps that sparkled as the early morning sun reflected off the ice. Franklin tried to wrap the dog back up in the plastic but stopped as his hands examined the thick raised scars on the ears, the chewed jowls and riverbed of scars lining the muzzle.

"Roscoe," Jason said. His voice was like a man underwater.

The brothers took the dog and placed it in the back of the truck. The bag was too torn to conceal the animal, so they draped it over its upper body leaving only the stiff tail exposed. Uncle Henry started the van and drove down the hill into the valley with the corpses rattling in the back.

Jason thought of Sharon on these drives, of their late-night phone calls, just voices connected over an endless void of land. Jason stayed up nights talking to her, but he could always hear doubt creeping into her voice, the resolve they'd both built evaporating. He told her he would be back soon. He wanted to love that flat land the way she did, but even driving down Cherry Tree and looking at the burnt ash of The Cat's Den or passing Hendricks' abandoned house, he felt at home. Eventually he would go back west, but he'd leave something of himself when he did.

The tire blew a mile from Bradshaw, and the van slid into a ditch. Uncle Henry sat for a minute feeling the uneven posture of the vehicle, his fingers drumming on the steering wheel before he exhaled.

"Let's see how bad," he said.

Outside, the air had grown cool and in the sky above buzzards circled as if they believed the death cart were a prepared feast. The road was surrounded by trees whose shadows were the only shade and the ground was a hard soil covered by a migrant dust that blew away on each gust. The prisoners climbed out of the back. Franklin was the slowest. When Jason peered in at him, Franklin was stroking the dog's frozen flank.

"Come on," Jason said and he piled out.

Uncle Henry and Jason stood looking at the blown tire. The rim was bent and a long piece of metal stuck out of the rubber.

"Get on the cell," Uncle Henry said. "Get someone out here."

"No signal up here," Jason whispered.

He could see the fear in his uncle, could see he believed the inmates were already plotting an escape. Uncle Henry went to the passenger side and returned with a splintered ax handle kept in the floorboards, his impromptu weapon in case the inmates ever decided to surround him. He poked the stick at the bent rim.

"We're stuck," he said.

The brothers stood spitting in the dirt, both of them looking as if fate shouldn't be tempting them with such an opportunity. They looked like they didn't really want to run but would have been embarrassed not to. Jason tried to remember how much time was left on their sentences, tried to deduce whether it was worth it for them. All he knew for sure was that if one fled, the other would follow.

Jason went back behind the van and found Franklin crouched by the bumper. The back doors were open and he had the dog out in his lap, the dead animal's head on his knee with the bloated tongue lolling out.

"What in the hell?" Jason said.

A sound like a branch cracking came from the other side of the van, and Jason turned to watch as the brothers ran towards the hillside. Uncle Henry was behind them, his hat knocked from his head and his eye already swelling. The ax handle was in his grip, clenched tight as he hit the brush. The sound of twigs breaking underfoot echoed in the stillness.

"Just let them go," Jason shouted after him. "Who gives a shit?" But he was already out of earshot.

Jason looked again to the woods, contemplated chasing after his uncle, but went back to where Franklin held the dog in his arms. Jason watched Franklin's dirty fingers trace the scars and began to remember Terry sniffling and sputtering in B-Unit. The way he collapsed in on himself with worry for the dog, as if the pain of not being able to see it was worse that the walls he lived behind. Jason reached out to pet the cold fur. The ice began to melt, water dripping to be swallowed up by the dirt.

"I'm sorry," Jason said and took the dog from him.

The animal was heavy, but he managed to stumble out across the road to the edge of the woods. He placed the body in a patch of high weeds and began to work his hands into the hard earth. The top layer was stiff from cold, but he managed to dig a hole the size of a fist.

"Bring the tire iron," he yelled.

Franklin came from behind and placed the metal cross in Jason's hand. He used it to soften the soil. The hole was maybe three feet deep when Uncle Henry came back. He smelled of sap and his pants were soiled with mud as he leaned on the ax handle watching Jason dig.

"They outran me," he said.

"Should have just let them go," Jason said.

"What are you doing?" he said.

Uncle Henry knelt down and looked into the small grave. Jason wondered on the permanence of it, on how he'd be able to get through the clay and bury the dog deep enough to keep the coyotes from digging him up. Would they even want Roscoe or leave the body until the bones were all that was left, brittle and easy to break whenever the earth covering his grave washed away during a summer flood and left the white artifacts exposed for strangers to wonder over? It seemed pointless, but some of the old perseverance that had influenced so much of Jason's life arose. He knew he had to keep digging.

"Come on," he said. "Help me get him in the ground."